Mr. Peepers

A SORT OF NOVEL

BY

WALLY COX

With the assistance of William Redfield

19 55

SIMON AND SCHUSTER
New York

ALL RIGHTS RESERVED
INCLUDING THE RIGHT OF REPRODUCTION
IN WHOLE OR IN PART IN ANY FORM
COPYRIGHT, ©, 1955, BY PEEPERS COMPANY AND
W. M. C. ENTERPRISES
PUBLISHED BY SIMON AND SCHUSTER, INC.
ROCKEFELLER CENTER, 630 FIFTH AVENUE
NEW YORK 20, N. Y.

FIRST PRINTING
LIBRARY OF CONGRESS CATALOG CARD NUMBER: 54-9804
MANUFACTURED IN THE UNITED STATES OF AMERICA
BY H. WOLFF BOOK MFG. CO., INC., NEW YORK, N. Y.

Grateful acknowledgment is made to David Swift, Jim Fritzell and Everett Greenbaum, on whose scripts and ideas these chapters are based.

CONTENTS

CHAPTER		PAGE
I	The Return	1
II	Meeting the Remingtons	36
III	A Romantic Student	64
IV	Life among the Meat Packers	91
V	Snowbound	113
VI	The Automotive Age	139
VII	The Thecla Titus	164
VIII	Freedom of the Press	185
IX	Mr. Peepers Speaks	209
X	Mr. Peepers Takes a Vow	235

CHAPTER I

The Return

MR. PEEPERS couldn't sleep. He rolled onto one side and looked at the clock. It read 5:00 A.M. He squeezed his eyes tight and patted several times at his pillow. "I am going to go to sleep now," he murmured.

He was quite wrong. A moment later he rolled onto his back. I can't understand it, he thought. I've never had trouble sleeping before. He wondered if it was because today was his wedding day. After all, he had never been . . .

Suddenly he sat bolt upright. "I'm getting married today!" he cried. He put one hand to his mouth. "Good heavens," he murmured. "I'm not prepared." He jumped out of bed and ran to his closet.

Mr. Peepers

Outside, a rooster was crowing and the first gray streaks of dawn were beginning to show above the horizon. Mr. Peepers looked anxiously through his clothing for the wedding outfit he had rented. "Oh, dear," he said. "It's not here."

He yanked at the cord on the closet light. The light flashed on, blinding him. He shut it off immediately. There were a lot of little spots dancing about in front of his eyes. He thought he saw the swallow-tail coat and quickly tried it on. It turned out to be his blue raglan topcoat. He flung it aside and looked about frantically. Then he relaxed.

His wedding clothes were laid out on a chair in the middle of the room. Indeed, he had placed them there carefully before retiring. Mr. Peepers smiled at his nervousness. The striped trousers, complete with suspenders, were folded neatly on the chair seat. The high silk hat sat squarely on top of them. On the back of the chair his stiff-front shirt and swallow-tail jacket were neatly draped. Mr. Peepers lifted the top hat. Beneath it he had arranged his wing collar, his studs and buttons and the antique pearl cuff links Nancy's father had given him. Mr. Peepers smiled and nodded. I am getting married to Nancy Remington, he thought, the daughter of these lovely cuff links.

He went to his bureau and stared at himself in the mirror. The image of Robinson J. Peepers stared back at him —tousle-haired, pajama-clad, looking a little strained about the mouth. Mr. Peepers wasn't quite satisfied. "I am about to become the husband of Nancy Remington," he announced. "County school nurse." He stared at the image. The image didn't seem satisfied either.

Mr. Peepers took a deep breath and inflated his chest.

The Return

Holding the pose, he appraised himself. "In my youth," he murmured, "I was an athlete of sorts. Rather adept at mumblety-peg. Seven straight tournaments without a scratch."

The image didn't seem impressed. In fact, it seemed to be scowling at him. "I can knit," Mr. Peepers added, "and . . . uh . . . weave baskets."

It was no use. The image was implacable. Indeed, Mr. Peepers did not look sufficiently husbandlike to himself. Somehow he looked too *young*. He wondered if Nancy would be disappointed. A husband, after all, should *look* like a husband. Especially on his wedding day. Mr. Peepers decided to try again. He cleared his throat and squared his shoulders. He tried to think older thoughts. Smiling stiffly, he flexed his biceps. Then he deepened his voice. "How do you feel about the stock market, Ed?" he said. "Frankly, I'm bearish."

The effect was unconvincing. Somehow he seemed even younger. He shook his head and put on his glasses. Then he slumped his shoulders and let his mouth go slack. It made quite a difference. He looked terrible—but older. Both he and the image were satisfied.

The first arc of sun appeared at the horizon, and Mr. Peepers stared at it out of the window. Then a pleasant thought struck him. He remembered his first meeting with Nancy Remington. At the spring Faculty Dance just before he entered the Army. Standing on the balcony and chatting, he had inadvertently placed his hand on top of hers. Instantly he had pulled away and apologized. In fact, he had avoided her for a full hour afterward to prove that his intentions were honorable. Mr. Peepers sighed. An awfully embarrassing moment, as he recalled it. Even now he

Mr. Peepers

wondered if Nancy believed it an accident. He didn't like anyone to think that he did such forward things on purpose.

Mr. Peepers smiled, remembering. They had danced together that night, himself and Nancy. Their first dance. Mr. Peepers had never danced with anyone but his mother before. By the time Nancy persuaded him to try, the orchestra had gone home. They found one record and danced together on the balcony—*The William Tell Overture*. Rather difficult to waltz to, but ever since then Mr. Peepers had thought of it as their song.

Mr. Peepers returned to bed in a mood of great exhilaration. He lay with his hands behind his head, thinking: Today is my wedding day. I'm getting married today. On my wedding day.

It struck him as a wonderful day to get married. He looked at the clock. It read 5:25 A.M. His eyes closed slowly and he smiled. "I'm very fond of Nancy," he murmured. "Very fond. That's why I'm marrying her . . . on my wedding day."

Still, it was unusual the way it had all happened. Just that one Faculty Dance and Nancy seeing him to the train when he left for Fort Digby. At that time, he didn't even know her parents. That was certainly unusual. To like a girl so much and not to meet her parents. Mr. Peepers stirred a little. After all, he was not the sort of person to behave that way. However, it had all worked out so well, and that was certainly a true test of things.

Mr. Peepers shifted and yawned. Then he smiled contentedly. So much had happened. Less than a year since his discharge from the Army and, in that time, Wes and Marge married; two full semesters at school; and now, Nancy. Mr.

The Return

Peepers chuckled quietly, remembering the day of his release. All at once he could see the barracks so clearly: the long rows of neatly made bunks; the freshly scrubbed floors; the duffel bags stacked in rows; and, over his shoulder, the freckled, grinning face of Private First Class Henry Grunthunger.

Mr. Peepers let his head sink deeper into the pillow. . . .

Private First Class Henry Grunthunger leaned over the edge of his bunk and grinned. He was watching a fellow soldier pack his duffel bag. The fellow soldier was a smallish, slender young man who wore horn-rimmed glasses.

"Boy!" Henry said enviously. "Some jokers have all the luck."

Corporal Robinson J. Peepers, Rifle Number 2148769J, looked up at the grinning Henry and smiled. "Yes," he said, "I suppose I am rather fortunate."

Henry nodded emphatically. "I'll say," he said.

Mr. Peepers began to fold a pair of brown tweed trousers and put them into his barracks bag.

"Hey, listen," Henry said. "Where did ya get them civilian pants?"

"Oh, they're mine," Mr. Peepers replied. "It's the suit I wore when I was inducted. They returned it along with my other civilian things this afternoon. Very considerate of them, I thought."

"That's what you think," Henry said, scowling. "For Pete's sake, look at the rear end."

Mr. Peepers turned the trousers over. The initials P.W. were painted on the seat. Mr. Peepers gulped once and tried to conceal his embarrassment. "Well, Henry," he

Mr. Peepers

said, "they probably needed them very badly at the time . . . er . . . the Geneva convention, you know."

Henry nodded skeptically. "Yeah," he said. "Sure."

Mr. Peepers turned to the wall behind his bunk and began to take his pin-up pictures down.

"Hey!" Henry cried, leaning halfway out of his bunk. "Be careful of my Marilyn Monroes."

"Oh, I will, Henry," Mr. Peepers said. Actually he wasn't even looking at them. It always struck him as immodest to observe a young lady in the . . . the way Miss Monroe was dressed. Besides, it wasn't difficult to control himself in her presence when he considered the exciting nature of his own pin-ups. For a moment he stared at the pin-ups proudly. They were color photographs of early crocuses budding through snow on Washington's Birthday. Mr. Peepers had clipped them from the *National Geographic* and had them framed. He now extended them to the reclining Henry.

"Aren't these thrilling?" he said.

Henry gave them a blank look. "Swell," he grunted.

Mr. Peepers smiled, pleased by Henry's enthusiasm. He deposited the photographs carefully in his duffel bag. Then he picked up the brand-new O.D. shirt he had purchased.

"How come ya bought a new shirt?" Henry asked.

"Oh, I like to present a tidy appearance at all times," Mr. Peepers replied. "Besides, it isn't every day one returns home from the Army, you know." He removed a pin from one of the sleeves and dropped it into a near-by G.I. can. It went *tankle*.

Henry leaned down and grinned at him. "Them's mighty fancy-lookin' chevrons," he said.

"That's true," Mr. Peepers said. "They manufacture

The Return

them that way now." He extended the shirt to Henry for feeling purposes. The chevrons were yellow silk, sewed on with large loops of blue thread.

"Boy, Peepers," Henry said, stroking at the chevrons, "I didn't know ya had it in ya."

Mr. Peepers blushed. "Well, I suppose I'd like to impress the folks back home a little," he said. "What with being a corporal and all."

Henry nodded gravely. "Yeah," he said. "You've really come up in the world."

"Yes," Mr. Peepers said modestly, "I suppose that's so." He found another pin, quite suddenly. "Oh, dear," he said, gasping.

"What'sa matter?"

"I stuck myself."

Henry Grunthunger watched the young corporal remove the pin from his thumb and then grinned at him. "So you're gonna teach school again, huh?" he said. "Whaddya teach?"

"General Science."

Henry stared at him for a moment. "You like to do that, huh?"

Mr. Peepers dropped another pin. "Oh, yes," he said. "I can hardly wait to get back. I had a letter just the other day from one of the teachers. He said the new wing had been added to the school and everyone was asking about me." He thought of all his old friends at school and smiled. "My," he said, reminiscing, "I really had a lot of fine chums at the school there."

"Is that right?" Henry said. "Schoolteachers, huh? Well, whaddya know."

Mr. Peepers sensed a bit of prejudice in Henry's tone.

Mr. Peepers

"Oh, yes," he said affably. "You'll never have a better friend than most schoolteachers. There's Mr. Bascomb, the principal; and Harvey Weskit—we call him Wes—a most excellent fellow who teaches history; and there's Mrs. Gurney and Mrs. Mandible and Miss Monitor and . . ."

Then Mr. Peepers thought of Nancy. He didn't know whether to tell Henry about her or not. After all, he was still in the Army and some things were sacred. He looked at Henry for a moment, appraising him.

"What'sa matter?" Henry asked.

"Oh, nothing," Mr. Peepers said. "Er . . . do you have a lady friend?"

Henry shrugged. "I like my mother pretty good."

"No, no," Mr. Peepers said. "I mean someone . . . er . . . nearer your own age. Like a . . . a girl."

Henry looked confused. "I thought you said a lady," he said.

"Well, I . . ." Mr. Peepers began. Then he stopped himself. He didn't want to talk to Henry about Nancy.

Henry, however, seeemed to have other ideas. "Why?" he asked, grinning a little. "You got a regular chick at home?"

Mr. Peepers winced. "Well, no," he said, returning to his shirt. "I wouldn't put it that way exactly."

"Aw, come on," Henry persisted. "You go around with somebody, don'tcha?"

Mr. Peepers smiled, in spite of himself. "Well, on occasion."

"I thought so," Henry said. "Well, what does she do?"

Mr. Peepers felt suddenly apprehensive. "What do you mean what does she do?"

Henry laughed out loud. "I mean for a living."

The Return

"Oh," Mr. Peepers said, blushing a little. "Well, she's a . . . a registered nurse."

Henry looked at him strangely. "Yeah?" he said. "What'sa matter? Are you sick or somethin'?"

"No, no," Mr. Peepers said. "She's a nurse for the county."

"Is that right?" Henry said. "County who?"

Mr. Peepers sighed patiently. "The schools," he said. "She's the county school nurse. For the children."

"Oh!" Henry said emphatically. "I getcha now. Like a baby sitter."

Mr. Peepers decided to let it go at that. "Yes, that's right," he said. "Like a registered baby sitter." He opened the new shirt and started to put his right arm through the sleeve. He couldn't get past the elbow. There was some sort of weblike obstruction. He pushed hard with his hand and a niagara of pins came pouring out of the sleeve.

"Gee whiz!" Henry Grunthunger exclaimed. "Will ya look at that? All them pins in one sleeve."

Mr. Peepers nodded and began picking up pins. "No wonder this shirt was so expensive," he said cheerfully. "They put two dollars' worth of pins in it." He glanced up at Henry, who was not laughing. "That's a little joke," Mr. Peepers said gravely.

Henry merely stared at him.

"A bit of humor makes the long day brighter," Mr. Peepers suggested.

Henry nodded slowly, his face implacable.

Pax vobiscum, Mr. Peepers thought, and returned to his preparations. He finished putting on his shirt and tied his tie. Then he looked in the mirror for a last-minute examination. He had just placed his overseas cap squarely on

Mr. Peepers

his head, which was the way he liked to wear it, when Sergeant Howling appeared at the barracks door howling, "All right, you G.I. goofballs—outside for policin' the area. Let's go, Grunthunger! Snap to it, Peepers!" and then disappeared.

Henry ran out immediately, as did all the others, but ex-Corporal Robinson J. Peepers turned suavely back to the mirror and put a final dimple in his tie. The sergeant, he thought, is in for a rude awakening. I'm a civilian now.

Four hours later he was standing in the Jefferson Junior High Gymnasium, where Mrs. Gurney had prepared a very elaborate home-coming for him. There was a buffet luncheon next to the pulleys and a strawberry punch underneath the punching bag. Mr. Peepers could hardly believe his eyes. He hadn't expected anything so elaborate. A large crowd of students and all of Mr. Peepers' old teacher friends were milling about and talking, while the newly formed school band Wes had written about was winding up a selection. The band was so loud that Mr. Peepers could hardly recognize the melody. It sounded something like "The Old Chartreuse and Blue," which was the school song, but it ended too quickly for Mr. Peepers to tell. Astonished, he set down his duffel bag and gazed for a moment at all the decorations. My, my, he thought, you'd think I were a general instead of a mere corporal.

WELCOME HOME, PRIVATE PEEPERS! said a thick strip of bunting. Mr. Peepers swallowed quickly and stepped behind a potted palm. He certainly didn't want to embarrass anyone by being a corporal. I'll have to find some way of removing my chevrons, he thought. He tried breaking each thread with his fingernail, but it didn't work. Finally he gave a good, stiff yank and the chevrons came off. So did a

The Return

goodly portion of his sleeve. Mr. Peepers sighed. He folded his arms to hide the rip and stepped from behind the palm.

Suddenly Mrs. Gurney caught sight of him. She was standing on the podium in front of the band, waving vigorously. "Oh, Mr. Peepers!" she cried. "Over here! Over here!"

Mr. Peepers was so delighted to see her he started to wave back. Then he remembered his torn sleeve. He ran toward the dais, trying to wave with his shoulders and thinking how wonderful it was that she had gone to so much trouble. There was something awfully endearing about Mrs. Gurney. She was always trying to please.

"Oh, welcome home, you naughty boy!" she cried as Mr. Peepers mounted the podium. "Whatever made you stay away so long?"

Mr. Peepers was about to reply when the band struck up "The Eyes of Texas Are upon You." Mrs. Gurney clasped her hands together. "Oh, how thrilling!" she cried. Then she turned to Mr. Peepers. "Mr. Bowie is from Houston, you know." Mr. Peepers nodded, smiling. Wes had written him about Mr. Bowie. He was the new music teacher. Apparently he was proud of his birthplace. The band played "Eyes of Texas" four times running. In the middle of version three, Mrs. Gurney leaned toward Mr. Peepers. "You arrived too late for 'The Old Chartreuse and Blue.' Oh, it was thrilling! They've just learned it."

Mr. Peepers smiled at her. Chartreuse and blue were the school colors. Mrs. Gurney herself had composed the song some fifteen years before. "Perhaps they can play it again," Mr. Peepers cried above the din.

"No, dear!" Mrs. Gurney caroled. "He won't be back until next week."

Mr. Peepers

Mr. Peepers decided that further conversation would be unwise. The band had swung into an even louder version of "Anchors Aweigh." Mr. Bowie, who had long, white hair, was jumping up and down and swaying from side to side as he conducted. Suddenly he shouted something at Mr. Peepers.

"I beg your pardon?" Mr. Peepers said, leaning forward.

"Ah said," Mr. Bowie repeated, "ah'm sorry we don't know 'Roll On, Old Army Team!' It's a difficult piece!"

"Oh, that's all right," Mr. Peepers said. "I . . . uh . . . was in the Signal Corps, really."

Mr. Bowie nodded enthusiastically. "Tha's right," he said. "It's got a fine tune to it."

Mr. Peepers blushed a little. "I like 'Anchors Aweigh' fine," he shouted.

"Ah was in the Navy!" Mr. Bowie shouted back.

"So was I!" Mr. Peepers cried. "I mean . . . it sounds fine!"

"Yes, tha's right! The stoahmy brine!" Mr. Bowie shouted, and returned to his conducting.

Mr. Peepers was just as glad to have the exchange ended. He glanced happily at all the teachers who were standing below the platform. Wes Weskit was there and all the others, too: Mrs. Mandible, Miss Monitor and good old Charley Meadow, the school janitor. The only ones missing were Nancy Remington and Mr. Bascomb, the principal. Mr. Peepers was disappointed not to see them. For the moment, however, his reception was more than enough. The rest of the teachers were all smiling and wiggling their fingers at him, while he stood alone on the platform waiting for "Anchors Aweigh" to stop. Mrs. Gurney had shouted in his ear, "You speak when they stop playing,

The Return

Mr. Peepers!" and left the platform to attend to the buffet and punch. Mr. Peepers smiled at Wes Weskit and tried to think of what to say.

Suddenly the band swung into a fourth chorus of "Anchors Aweigh." Mr. Peepers looked at Mr. Bowie. The latter seemed rather carried away. He was conducting with a great deal of vigor and his face looked very red and excited. Mr. Peepers watched the long, white hair flying from side to side and wondered if Mr. Bowie ever intended to stop weighing anchors.

Then he saw Mrs. Gurney hurrying back to the platform. She looked a little alarmed. "Band!" she shouted, beginning to gesture wildly at the children. "Look here! Band! Stop playing! Oh, dear. That's enough, Band!" She added several semaphorelike signals with her arms, which were eventually effective. The children stopped playing, one by one, while Mr. Bowie's baton continued to wave. Finally Mr. Bowie turned and looked at Mrs. Gurney. He seemed a little wounded.

"That's enough, Mr. Bowie," Mrs. Gurney said sweetly. She turned to Mr. Peepers. "Speak, dear," she whispered.

Mr. Peepers took half a step forward. All the teachers applauded. For a moment his mind went blank. He couldn't think of anything to say. Then he smiled and cleared his throat.

"I feel like Lucky Lindy," he said. "Thank you all very much."

The teachers applauded again. Wes Weskit whistled. "You tell 'em, sport!" he cried.

"Gosh," Mr. Peepers said. "Uh . . . this is the finest home-coming anybody ever had. And . . . well, it means a great deal to me. I mean, it really does. All the music and

Mr. Peepers

the banner and—" Mr. Peepers paused to get his breath—
"and all the effort you went to for my welcome and . . .
Well, it's very heart-warming. You can't imagine how many
times I sat in my barracks and thought about each and every one of you."

The teachers turned to one another and smiled. Wes
Weskit winked encouragement at him.

"Yes, that's true," Mr. Peepers continued, "and . . .
Well, all I can say is, very sincerely, thank you."

The teachers and students applauded wildly. Mr. Peepers stepped down from the platform to greet them all. Wes
Weskit took hold of his arm with both hands and shook it.
"Great speech, old-timer," he said earnestly. Mr. Peepers
felt embarrassed.

In the distance he saw some of his old students waving
at him: Walter Murdock, Helen Fernley, Elwood Hamper,
the Susskind twins. He wanted to say hello to all of them
individually, but he supposed it would have to wait. Mrs.
Mandible and Miss Monitor were crowding around him,
as was Charley Meadow, and then Mrs. Gurney suddenly
pushed her way through and waved her arms again. "Attention, everybody! Attention!" she cried. "We have an extra surprise for Mr. Peepers!" She giggled happily and
waved a piece of paper. "I've written a welcome-home
poem!"

Miss Monitor applauded. Mrs. Mandible followed suit
and, in the distance, Mr. Peepers saw several students trying to sneak out the doors.

"Yes!" Mrs. Gurney chirped gaily. "It's called . . ." Suddenly her face fell. She began feeling around her eyes and
nose for her glasses. "Oh, dear," she said. "Miss Monitor
. . . er . . . have you seen my glasses?"

The Return

"No, Mrs. Gurney," Miss Monitor said.

"Oh, dear," said Mrs. Gurney. "I can't read without my . . . Where could I have put them?"

She began to look behind and above herself, hoping, Mr. Peepers supposed, to find them dangling somewhere. "Oh, don't worry, Mrs. Gurney," Mr. Peepers began, but Wes Weskit suddenly flung an arm around his shoulders and squeezed tight. It pulled Mr. Peepers a little off balance. Wes did exercises with a rubber expander.

"You crazy, wonderful kid," Wes muttered, "it's *good* to *see* you."

"Oh, dear," Mrs. Gurney said, looking miserable. "I've ruined everything. It's such a lovely poem, too. I wrote it myself."

"Please don't worry, Mrs. Gurney," Mr. Peepers said.

"You'd like it, I'm sure," Mrs. Gurney said.

"I know I would, Mrs. Gurney."

"It's moving."

"I'm sure it is," Mr. Peepers said, hoping to change the subject. "Incidentally, where is Mr. Bascomb?"

"He went to St. Louis for the Teachers' Convention," Wes answered.

"Oh, yes!" Mrs. Gurney said brightly. "I'm glad you mentioned that. Mr. Bascomb told me to be sure to tell you something, dear."

"Oh?" Mr. Peepers said. "What?"

Mrs. Gurney's expression went blank. "Well . . . er . . . I . . . He said it was very important. Now, let me see—what was it?"

The school bell interrupted her, announcing the first class after lunch. "Oh, dear," Mrs. Gurney said. "I'll just have to read the poem to you later."

Mr. Peepers

Mr. Peepers smiled and took her hands. "I'll look forward to it with pleasure and anticipation."

Mrs. Gurney laughed happily. "Oh, Mr. Peepers," she said, "you're so gallant. Er . . . eejaboo!"

Charley Meadow suddenly stuck his ancient, craggy face between them. "What are we gonna do with all this food?" he said. "Nobody's ate anything, Mrs. Gurney."

Mrs. Gurney waved blithely at him. "Cover it with something, dear!" she cried, starting away.

"But they got a gym class in here!" Mr. Meadow shouted.

Apparently Mrs. Gurney didn't hear him. She hurried from the gymnasium singing "Anchors Aweigh."

Mr. Peepers turned to greet all the rest of the teachers. Mr. Bowie extended his hand. "Glad to have you abowhud!" he said.

"Thank you, Mr. Bowie," Mr. Peepers said. "Pleased to make your acquaintance."

"We've missed you, Mr. Peepers," Mrs. Mandible said.

Miss Monitor smiled warmly at him. "You're a Yankee-Doodle boy, Mr. Peepers," she said.

And Mr. Carvel, the new mathematics teacher, shook hands vigorously. "Your shirt is torn," he said.

Before Mr. Peepers had a chance to explain, Charley Meadow nudged him with his shoulder and winked. "You oughta see how I fixed that bad old fuse. I used a Canadian penny. They got less copper in 'em."

Wes Weskit came running back with Mr. Peepers' duffel bag, and Mr. Peepers made his last greetings to all the rest of the teachers. "I'll walk over to the lockers with you," Wes said.

The Return

"Thanks a lot, Wes," Mr. Peepers said. "You're a pal." As he watched the teachers leave for their various classes, he thought how nice it was to be a teacher and to be associated with such friendly people. He could hardly wait to teach a class of his own again. To his way of thinking, there was no finer fun in the world.

"Gee," he said to Wes Weskit as they walked down the hall. "Gee, that was nice of them."

"Sport," Wes said earnestly, "you had it coming, every shred."

Mr. Peepers blushed a little. "Thanks, Wes."

Wes stuck his chin out and nodded seriously. "I *mean* it."

Mr. Peepers nodded. It was remarkable how you could tell when Wes really meant something. They passed a hallway that had canvas spread on the floor and fresh plaster on the walls. "What's this, Wes?" Mr. Peepers asked. "Something new?"

"That's the new wing I wrote you about," Wes said. "Show it to you later." He smiled and shifted the duffel bag to his other shoulder. "Listen, old-timer," he said, "the Army must have agreed with you. You put on some weight, didn't you?"

Mr. Peepers shook his head. "It's my winter underwear," he said. "The suit's a little large."

Wes coughed gently and nodded. "Uh-huh," he said.

"I know it's a little early for winter underwear," Mr. Peepers explained, "being only October. But I don't think anyone will object if I rush the season."

"Well," Wes said casually, "if you don't sit down and cross your legs, no one will ever know the difference."

"That's true," Mr. Peepers said.

Mr. Peepers

They arrived at the teachers' locker room. Wes eased the heavy duffel to the floor. "We saved your old locker for you," he said.

"Oh, that's fine," Mr. Peepers said. He reached up to the top of the locker and got a hammer and yardstick down. "My, the same old locker."

"Hold still a minute, Robby," Wes cautioned.

"What's the matter?"

Wes removed a pin from Mr. Peepers' shirt. "There was a pin in there," he said.

"Oh," Mr. Peepers said. "Well, could you use it to pin my sleeve together, Wes? There's sort of a rip in it."

"Sort of!" Wes exclaimed. "Wow! That's a beauty." He carefully pinned the sleeve together. "How did you get that, for Pete's sake?"

"Oh," Mr. Peepers said, a little embarrassed, "I . . . er . . . had a rough train trip." He reached up and banged the radiator pipe three times with the hammer.

"Well," Wes said, smiling, "seems to me you found a home in the Army. You look like a million bucks."

Mr. Peepers smiled back and jiggled the handle of a locker two down from his own.

"You're a perfect physical specimen," Wes said.

Mr. Peepers went back to his own locker and began to measure it with the yardstick. "I feel fine, too," he said. He took a piece of chalk from his pocket and made a mark on the locker.

"Those Army calisthenics are good for you, eh?" Wes asked.

"Oh, yes," Mr. Peepers said. "They're fine fun." He kicked the locker at the chalk mark and the door flew open.

The Return

"I meant to get that fixed for you while you were gone," Wes said.

Mr. Peepers replaced the yardstick and the hammer. "That's all right, Wes," he said, putting his duffel bag into the locker.

"Say, Robby," Wes said, chuckling a little, "I don't mean to pry, but . . ." He looked up and down the hallway to see if anyone was coming. Satisfied that the coast was clear, he smiled again. "Listen," he whispered, "I'll bet you got some pretty exciting phone numbers while you were away, eh?"

Mr. Peepers smiled inwardly. Suddenly he saw a good opportunity for a joke on Wes. "Oh, I don't know," he said with deliberate casualness.

"Aw, c'mon," Wes pleaded. "Did you?"

Mr. Peepers frowned thoughtfully. "Well, now, let me see. Oh, yes! The fellow in the next bunk to mine gave me a number to call in Elkhart, Indiana."

Wes could hardly contain himself. "Really?" he said. "Well . . . uh . . . did you call?"

Mr. Peepers smiled reminiscently. "Oh, certainly."

Wes practically rubbed his hands together. "Well?" he said eagerly.

"It was his mother. He wanted me to tell her to stop sending homemade cookies."

"Oh, no!" Wes cried.

"Well, they tasted terrible, Wes," Mr. Peepers continued. "Everybody in our barracks said so."

Wes looked suspiciously at him and Mr. Peepers could no longer keep from laughing. "I caught you that time, Wes," he said.

Wes nodded wryly. "You're a sly one, Robby."

Mr. Peepers

All at once Mr. Peepers remembered Nancy. "Say, Wes," he said carefully, "er . . . how's Nancy?"

"Nancy who? Oh—the nurse?"

Mr. Peepers nodded, feeling a little embarrassed. "Yes. Uh . . . she's been around, hasn't she?"

"Oh, sure," Wes said, smiling a little. "Every other day."

"Well . . . uh . . . how is she?"

"What do you mean 'how is she'?"

Mr. Peepers blinked his eyes, puzzled. "Well, I mean . . . uh . . . how is she?"

"I see," Wes said slyly. "You're pretty interested in her, eh?"

"Oh, no, no. It isn't that. It's just . . . uh . . . well, how is she?"

Wes shrugged his shoulders. "She's fine."

Mr. Peepers stared at him for a moment. "You mean . . . er . . . fine?"

Wes nodded. "That's right. Fine."

"Fine, huh?" Mr. Peepers said. "Well, *how* fine?"

Wes made a seesaw motion with his right hand. "Oh, I don't know," he said. "Medium fine."

Mr. Peepers nodded and cleared his throat. "I see. Well . . . uh . . . that's fine."

At that moment Mrs. Gurney, wreathed in smiles, burst into the locker room. "Oh, Mr. Peepers!" she caroled. "There's good news for all. I found my glasses. I can read you my welcome-home poem now."

Mr. Peepers smiled warmly at her. "Oh, that's wonderful, Mrs. Gurney. I was wondering what had happened to you."

Mrs. Gurney waved her lorgnette-type glasses under Mr. Peepers' nose. "They were on my desk where I left them.

The Return

I'm such a silly girl." She giggled and lifted the lorgnette to her eyes. "Now!" she said proudly. Then her expression changed.

"What's the matter?" Mr. Peepers asked.

"I left the poem on the desk. Oh, dear me! I'll be right back." She departed hurriedly, bumping her shoulder against the locker-room door.

Wes Weskit stared after her sympathetically. "Tsk, tsk," he said. "She just isn't related to the physical world."

"Oh, Wes," Mr. Peepers said, with some reproach, "you shouldn't be critical of her."

Wes looked at Mr. Peepers with an intense expression. "I love her," he said, "like my own mother." Then he glanced at his wrist watch and snapped his fingers. "Say, lad, I've got a test to give in three minutes." He took hold of Mr. Peepers' arm and shook it vigorously. "Robby," he said gravely, "you're a grand chap and I *like* you. See you later."

Mr. Peepers watched him pass through the door and smiled. He's a fine fellow, he thought—a really fine fellow. And it's awfully good to be home.

He removed his overseas cap and hung it in his locker. Then he decided to visit the General Science room. Walking down the hallway, humming "The Old Chartreuse and Blue," he thought: The old school looks excellent—just excellent. When he arrived at the door marked SCIENCE I he opened it carefully and peered inside. The room was empty. He shut the door carefully behind him and tiptoed in. He smiled as he saw the familiar blackboard, the little nubs of chalk and all the unoccupied desks. Glancing at one corner of the room, he saw that his geranium plants were still on the dunce stool looking prosperous. He reached up to touch the top leaves and found them damp with droplets of

Mr. Peepers

water. It pleased him to think that someone had been considerate enough to care for them all that time.

He walked to the platform behind his teacher's desk, thinking, I must be awfully rusty, and stood there facing an empty classroom. Gradually the room filled up with young boy and girl faces which he supplied out of his memory. They looked wonderful—so scrubbed and eager. Every one of them seeming so bright and attentive, thirsty for knowledge and self-betterment. Mr. Peepers wanted the students to like studying science. He wanted to make his classes entertaining as well as educational. During his own school days, he had not always enjoyed the teachers and professors. Some of them had been so dry and expressionless. Mr. Peepers did not want the students to feel that way about him. He wanted to live up to his responsibilities as a teacher and a citizen. Moreover, he wanted to make science fun. He sincerely felt that a good teacher combined all the best qualities of actor, orator, counselor and scholar. I'd better do some practicing, he thought. He placed his palms on top of the desk and cleared his throat.

"Good morning, boys and girls," he said aloud. His voice seemed a little rusty. He cleared his throat again. "Er . . . don't let the uniform fool you. I'm not Napoleon." He paused for a moment. Somehow he knew that the students would not be laughing. "The joke there," he explained, "is that Napoleon was known as the 'Little Corporal.'" The children were still not laughing. They were staring at him dumb-faced. Mr. Peepers scratched his head. Then he remembered that he'd torn his chevrons off. "Oh," he said. "Well . . . uh . . . I had a rough trip home. I mean . . . well, anyway, I'm the same Mr. Peepers I used to be and

The Return

I've returned from the Army to resume my old General Science class."

He picked up what he thought was a blackboard pointer and practically fell down. He had the window pole in his hand. "I beg your pardon," he said. "I . . ."

The door to the classroom opened and an old man entered. "Dear me," he said kindly. "What's going on here?"

Mr. Peepers felt a little flustered. "Oh, nothing," he said. "Just testing the windows. I mean . . . uh . . . are you looking for someone?"

"No," the old man said, placing several books on the desk. "I have a science class to teach here in a few minutes."

The old man was very stoop-shouldered and had long, white hair. Mr. Peepers had never seen him before. "In here?" he said.

"Yes," he said. "I'm Mr. Monfrede, the General Science teacher."

Mr. Peepers was stunned. "Here? In this classroom?"

"Yes," Mr. Monfrede said, sitting down at the desk and putting some papers into a drawer. "I see you're in the Army, son."

Mr. Peepers stared at him for a moment. "What?" he said. "Oh, yes. Yes, sir. Are you the . . . General Science teacher here now?"

"Yes," Mr. Monfrede said, smiling, "that's right. Is anything wrong, son? You look a little pale."

"Oh, no . . . no." Mr. Peepers paused a moment. "Uh . . . Mr. Monfrede," he said, "weren't you out in the hall a little while ago when the band was playing and . . . and . . . everybody was there?"

"No," Mr. Monfrede said, sorting test papers, "I missed

Mr. Peepers

it, I'm sorry to say. One of the former teachers was returning from some place, I understand."

Mr. Peepers blinked. "Yes," he said.

"Young fellow by the name of Peepers, I believe," Mr. Monfrede said, smiling. "Odd little name, isn't it? Peepers." Mr. Monfrede laughed. Mr. Peepers laughed along, half-heartedly. "Sorry I missed the celebration," Mr. Monfrede continued. "I was home with my wife. She's bedridden, you see. Been that way for some time."

"Oh," Mr. Peepers said. "I'm sorry to hear that. I hope she'll feel better soon."

"Thank you."

Mr. Peepers stood there for a moment, touching at the desk with his fingers. "Well," he said, smiling bravely, "so you're the . . . uh . . . new General Science teacher?"

Mr. Monfrede looked at Mr. Peepers and rose from the desk. "Did you want to see me about something, son?" he asked.

"No, no," Mr. Peepers said. "No, I came back to . . . ah, to . . . well, that is, I came back here to . . ."

"Hold still a minute, son," Mr Monfrede said. He removed a pin from Mr. Peepers' shirt and dropped it into the wastebasket. "Now, what were you saying?" he asked.

"Oh, nothing," Mr. Peepers said, managing a smile. "Uh . . . I guess I'll just step out and . . . look over the hallway." Mr. Peepers cleared his throat. "Mighty nice little hallway you have there . . . er . . . good-by."

Mr. Monfrede stared at him as he went out the door. "What a peculiar young man," he murmured.

Mr. Peepers found Wes Weskit in the locker room. "Oh, yes," Wes said. "I forgot to tell you. Mr. Monfrede came in when you left."

The Return

"What about my old job?" Mr. Peepers said.

"Gee, I don't know, Robby. Mr. Bascomb must have had *some* plans for you."

"But he's at the Teachers' Convention."

Wes Weskit nodded. "He'll be gone for three weeks."

Mr. Peepers didn't know what to do. "Three weeks," he echoed sadly.

"Listen!" Wes said suddenly. "Why don't you take a bus to Melton and see Superintendent Sidfern at the Board of Education. Maybe *he* knows what Mr. Bascomb's plans were."

Mr. Peepers thought it was a good idea. "I'll get right up there," he said, taking his overseas cap from his locker. Then he remembered the cookies. "Oh, Wes," he said, "if you get hungry, there're some of those homemade cookies that lady in Elkhart gave me. They're in my locker. Help yourself."

Wes looked a little puzzled. "I thought you said they were terrible," he said.

Mr. Peepers nodded. "They are," he said.

Wes took the box from the locker and tried one. "For goodness' sake," he cried, making a frightful face, "they taste like baked cardboard."

"Oh, yes," Mr. Peepers said, "they're extremely unpleasant."

When Mrs. Gurney entered the locker room, Wes offered her the entire box. "Oh, you naughty boy," she said, "you're such a caterer." She bit daintily into one. "Mmmmm," she said, smiling, "they're dreadful."

Up at Melton, Superintendent Sidfern said he had no knowledge of Mr. Bascomb's plans. He offered Mr. Peepers

Mr. Peepers

a cup of water from the Puro cooler. "However, Peepers," he added, "there's certainly no problem. We'll just drop Mr. Monfrede and the job is yours."

Mr. Peepers choked slightly on the water. "Drop him?" he said. "But what will he do?"

Mr. Sidfern began looking through a sheaf of documents. "That isn't the point," he said. "The G.I. Bill states you must get your old job back."

Mr. Peepers started to say something, but halted himself. Mr. Sidfern was one of those impatient-looking executive types whom Mr. Peepers always found difficult to talk to. "But my goodness," he said finally. "Poor Mr. Monfrede—he looks pretty old."

Mr. Sidfern cleared his throat and put his signature to a letter. "He's seventy-two," he said.

Mr. Peepers stared at Mr. Sidfern. It seemed odd to him that the superintendent shouldn't be more concerned about the problem. After all, Mr. Monfrede was a school responsibility. "His wife is sick, too," Mr. Peepers said. "He probably needs the money."

Mr. Sidfern smiled wryly at him. "Well, look, Peepers," he said, "there's no alternative. I'll give Monfrede a few days' notice and you can take over the classroom."

Mr. Peepers stared at the floor for a moment. Then he shook his head. "No," he said, "no . . . don't do that. It just . . . isn't right to put him out of a job for me." He pulled a chair to Mr. Sidfern's desk and sat down. "Mr. Sidfern," he said, "I know you're busy, but isn't there some other spot where you could put me?"

Mr. Sidfern sighed and shoved his work aside. "Well, Peepers," he said, "your attitude is very commendable and I'd like to help you. However . . ." He stopped himself

The Return

and stared narrowly at the science teacher. "Well," he continued, "the only thing I have open is for a football coach at Manual Arts High School. Have you ever *played* football?"

Mr. Peepers shifted uncomfortably. Mr. Sidfern's tone seemed skeptical somehow. He straightened himself and tried to stick his chest out. "Well," he said in a deeper voice, "I went out for the varsity in college."

Mr. Sidfern's eyebrows lifted. "Really?" he said.

"Oh, yes sir," Mr. Peepers said. "But I didn't make the team."

"I see," Mr. Sidfern said. "Why not?"

"Well," Mr. Peepers said, blushing somewhat under Mr. Sidfern's penetrating gaze, "I . . . er . . . I'm left-handed. That is, I'm really right-handed, but they didn't want anyone left-handed."

Mr. Sidfern's jowls began to quiver. "Peepers," he said quietly, "I'm afraid I don't follow you."

Mr. Peepers swallowed and continued. "They accused me of being left-handed. You see, it was merely an excuse. The coach hadn't wanted me from the beginning."

"I see," Mr. Sidfern said.

"It was a clash of personalities."

Mr. Sidfern looked away and tapped on his desk with a pencil. "Peepers," he said, "I hardly think that football is your cup of tea. Now, Mr. Monfrede will have to——"

"I'm quite an athlete for my size," Mr. Peepers said.

"I'm sure you are, but——"

"I played goalie on the basketball team. I was rather adept at field hockey."

"Yes, but——"

Mr. Peepers continued desperately. "I even made the track team," he said. "I was Number One Pole Vaulter.

Mr. Peepers

True, the team was obligated to me, but nevertheless . . ."

"Why were they obligated?" Mr. Sidfern asked, looking puzzled.

Mr. Peepers gulped. "I owned the pole."

Mr. Sidfern shook his head. "Look, Peepers," he said, "with all your accomplishments, I hardly think you're football-coach material. We need someone who has majored in athletics."

Mr. Peepers looked at the floor. It's fruitless, he thought. He doesn't even like me. He probably thinks I'm eccentric.

"I'm sorry, Peepers," Mr. Sidfern said kindly.

Mr. Peepers nodded. "Thank you, anyway, Mr. Sidfern," he said.

On the bus back to Jefferson City, Mr. Peepers wondered what he was going to do. He knew he couldn't put poor old Mr. Monfrede out of a job no matter what the law said. Mr. Sidfern had said to call back in a day or two. Perhaps he would be able to think of something else. Mr. Peepers sighed. He would have to wait and see. *They also serve* . . . he thought. Then he sighed again.

When he arrived at the school the first person he bumped into was Miss Monitor. They were both looking the other way and Mr. Peepers got much the worse of the collision. Miss Monitor was one of those tall, raw-boned types to whom there was a great deal more than met the eye. "Oh, I'm awfully sorry, Miss Monitor," Mr. Peepers said. "I was preoccupied."

"Oh, that's all right," Miss Monitor said with a girlish giggle. "You'll never guess who's looking for you, Mr. Peepers."

"Who?" Mr. Peepers asked.

The Return

Miss Monitor giggled for several seconds. "You'll never guess," she repeated.

Mr. Peepers tried to be patient. "I'll take your word for it, Miss Monitor."

Miss Monitor looked disappointed. "Don't you want to guess?" she asked querulously.

"No," Mr. Peepers said. "I mean . . . the police?"

Miss Monitor put one hand over her mouth and snickered naughtily. "Oh, Mr. Peepers," she said, "you're such an amusing man."

"Thank you, Miss Monitor," Mr. Peepers replied.

"It's that lovely county school nurse—Nancy Remington," Miss Monitor said. "She just arrived from Wrigley High."

Mr. Peepers could hardly contain himself. "Oh, wonderful!" he said. "Where is she?"

"In the dispensary, I imagine," Miss Monitor said coyly.

"Thank you very much, Miss Monitor," Mr. Peepers said, shaking her hand.

"You're welcome, Mr. Peepers," Miss Monitor said. Then she hurried down the hallway and Mr. Peepers heard her murmuring "Romance! Romance!"

On the way to the dispensary, Mr. Peepers thought how wonderful life could become even at the darkest hour. The phenomenon which he called Peepers' Luck (all bad) had seemed in danger of becoming Peepers' Law. Now, however, he felt like the luckiest man in the world.

His heart pounding, he opened the dispensary door. "Nancy!" he called. Then he thought better of such familiarity. "Miss Remington," he said.

Nancy's voice answered him from another room. "I'll be with you in a moment," it said.

Mr. Peepers

Mr. Peepers smiled. He felt almost giddy with anticipation. Taking a comb and mirror from his pocket, he carefully tidied his hair. He removed his glasses and examined his eyes to see if they were clear and bright-looking. Then he replaced his glasses, put the comb and mirror in his back pocket, and sat down happily. He got right up again. A muffled cracking sound told him he had broken the mirror. He removed the three pieces of glass from his pocket and dropped them into a wastebasket. Peepers' Law, he thought.

There was an enormous posture chart hanging in the dispensary. Mr. Peepers stared at it for a moment. The four silhouettes ran from Excellent to Poor. Mr. Peepers thought he could fit the Good position rather handily, but decided to try them all. He had just slumped his shoulders and distended his stomach to fit the Poor position when Nancy Remington appeared in the doorway.

"Robinson!" she said.

Mr. Peepers snapped out of the position and tried to hide his embarrassment by smiling. "Hello, there," he said.

Nancy took hold of both his hands. "Well," she said softly, "welcome home."

"Thank you," Mr. Peepers said. "It's certainly good to be back and it's certainly wonderful to see you again."

"Thank you," Nancy said. "It's wonderful to see you."

"Thank you," Mr. Peepers said, "and . . . it's certainly wonderful to see you."

There was a pause, while they both smiled at each other. "Well," Nancy said, "the Army certainly agreed with you. You look as though you've put on weight."

"No," Mr. Peepers said, "it's just that I've got on my

The Return

winter und——— That is, ah . . . Yes, I have put on a little weight."

Nancy smiled warmly at him. "Either that or you've got on your winter underwear."

Mr. Peepers nodded. "Matter of fact," he said, "I have got on my winter und——— No! I've put on weight all right."

Nancy led him to a chair in front of the posture chart. "Now, sit down and tell me all about the Army," she said. "I want to hear everything."

"Well," Mr. Peepers began, but Nancy interrupted him. "It's so good having you back at the school," she said warmly.

Mr. Peepers smiled at her for a long time. "Well, actually," he said with an attempt at casualness, "I . . . er . . . I'm not going to be here at the school."

Nancy looked astonished. "What do you mean?"

Mr. Peepers sighed and told her about Mr. Monfrede. "He's an awfully nice man," he said.

"Yes," Nancy said, "I've met him."

"Well," Mr. Peepers said, "put the case of an old man like him who really needs the job and then put the case of a young fellow like me. I . . ." Mr. Peepers trailed off into silence.

"Well?" Nancy said softly, looking a little puzzled.

Mr. Peepers stared at his hands. "He's seventy-two," he said, "and . . . and his wife is sick. And he must need the money. And . . ." Mr. Peepers couldn't say any more. He thought fleetingly of how much he would miss Nancy.

"Oh, Robinson, you're giving him your job."

Mr. Peepers gazed pleadingly at her. "Well, it's just———"

Nancy interrupted him. "I understand," she said. She

Mr. Peepers

held both his hands for a silent moment. "Honestly, you're one of the nicest people I've ever known." She reached for his sleeve and removed a pin from it. The torn flap of the sleeve flopped down and dangled.

Mr. Peepers smiled wanly. "My ex-chevrons," he said.

Later, while he was packing in the locker room, Wes Weskit came in. Mr. Peepers' overnight bag was already full. There was a pile of books placed next to it, held together by an Army cloth belt.

"Hey, sport," Wes said, "what is all this?"

"Just my things, Wes."

"Oh," Wes said. "Well, did you get everything fixed with Mr. Sidfern?"

Mr. Peepers decided not to burden Wes with his troubles. In some ways, he was even sorry to have told Nancy. "Oh yes, fine," he said. "As a matter of fact, I won't be around here any more."

"What are you talking about?" Wes said.

"I . . . er . . . got a better job."

Wes stood with his mouth open. "You're kidding," he said.

"Oh, no," Mr. Peepers said. "No . . . er . . . you see, there's this job. They need me very badly. I'll . . . uh . . . be teaching football."

Wes Weskit could hardly speak. "Football?" he said.

At that moment Mrs. Gurney came hurtling into the locker room, waving a piece of paper. "Whoo-hoo, Mr. Peepers!" she cried. "I've been looking all over for you. I have my glasses *and* the poem now. Are you ready?"

"But, Mrs. Gurney——"

"Quiet, everybody! Quiet!" Mrs. Gurney said. She turned

The Return

to Wes Weskit, who was still looking stunned. "Shhhh!" she said sternly.

"But, Mrs. Gurney," Mr. Peepers said, "there's something you don't——"

Mrs. Gurney ignored him. " 'The Return of Mister Peepers,' " she said proudly, "in two stanzas by Bernice M. Gurney." She coughed and lifted one finger. "Lo!" she shouted. "The one who left us has returned; To us who love him dearly; Swing wide the portals of embrace; And we mean that so sincerely." Mrs. Gurney stopped for a moment and giggled. "I should admit I used this first stanza once before. When my little nephew returned from Boy Scout camp one summer. Of course, that was many years ago. He's in the State Department now." Mrs. Gurney giggled and lifted her finger again.

"Mrs. Gurney," Mr. Peepers said, "before you go on——"

"Lo!" Mrs. Gurney shouted. "Welcome back to these old classrooms; Filled with memories of your parting——"

"That's what I was trying to say," Mr. Peepers said. "I'm taking a job someplace else."

Mrs. Gurney was beaming. "Your shining face and fertile mind make our jobs that much . . . What? Job? You're taking a job someplace else?"

"Yes," Mr. Peepers said, "I've . . . uh . . . had a better offer. I'm going to another school."

Nancy appeared suddenly in the locker room with Mr. Peepers' geranium plant. Mr. Peepers hoped she wouldn't tell Wes and Mrs. Gurney the truth just yet. "Bu-but, Mr. Peepers," Mrs. Gurney protested, "we . . . we thought you liked us all here."

"Oh, I do, Mrs. Gurney," Mr. Peepers said. "I do, believe me, but . . . Well, you've got to keep, ah, moving for-

Mr. Peepers

ward and . . . well, I guess I'd better say good-by." He picked up the overnight bag and his books. Then he turned back, trying not to look as dejected as he felt. "Oh, Mrs. Gurney," he said, "will you say good-by to Mr. Bascomb for me when he comes back from the convention?"

"Oh, yes," Mrs. Gurney said sadly. "Dear me, he *did* want me to tell you something. Now what was it?"

Mr. Peepers glanced at Wes and Nancy. "Well . . . good-by, everybody," he said.

"Oh, Mr. Peepers," Mrs. Gurney said, brushing a tear away, "do you mind if I finish the poem?"

Mr. Peepers smiled gratefully at her. "Oh, excuse me, Mrs. Gurney," he said, "that was awfully thoughtless of me. Of course. Please finish it."

"All right," Mrs. Gurney said, her lip beginning to tremble. "Oh, dear . . . Lo! Hearts are lighter, smiles are brighter; Your return's dispelled the gloom; And now, for you, our great surprise—your brand-new science room." Mrs. Gurney strangled slightly. "Oh, heavens," she cried, "the science room! That's what Mr. Bascomb wanted me to tell you." Mrs. Gurney began to quiver with delight. "Come with me, Mr. Peepers," she cried, leading him by the hand through the brand-new hallway into a room that had SCIENCE II engraved on the door. Mrs. Gurney waved at it proudly. "The new wing was finished while you were gone. This is your new science room!"

Mr. Peepers stared wide-eyed at all the brand-new fixtures and spankingly varnished desks. "Oh, my goodness," he said, "is this really for me?"

"Yes, yes!" Mrs. Gurney chirped gaily. "Mr. Monfrede will teach Science I in your old room and you'll have the advanced class in here."

The Return

Wes Weskit tapped him on the shoulder. "Look at this," he said. There was a name plate sitting on the desk. In polished bronze letters it said: MR. ROBINSON J. PEEPERS, B.S.

Mr. Peepers grinned from ear to ear. "Oh, this is beautiful!" he said. "This is the sort of room you can really learn something in."

Mrs. Gurney stared at him anxiously. "You mean, you'll stay, Mr. Peepers?" she said.

Mr. Peepers nodded vigorously. "I certainly will, Mrs. Gurney."

She leaned close to him and kissed him lightly on the cheek. "Welcome home, my dear," she whispered. She took a pin from his shirt and dropped it into the brand-new wastebasket. It went *Bong!*

The following morning, Mr. Peepers was standing behind his new desk, addressing the students. "Good morning, boys and girls," he said. "I'm Mr. Peepers. I'm an old friend to some of you, but for those of you who are new here, I'll show you how to spell my name." He reached for the name plate, but it wasn't there. Then he remembered that he had taken it home to stare at. "Well," he said, "uh . . . I'll write it on the blackboard for you."

He reached up to write the first letter and felt something sticking him. He felt under his arm and picked it out. "Ah," he said, "it's a pin. Well, that's a good omen. You know the old adage. Find a pin and pick it up; means your day is full of luck. Very appropriate. Because I feel indeed lucky to be back with all of you again."

He meant it, too.

CHAPTER
11

Meeting the Remingtons

ALL THE TIME he was in the Army, Mr. Peepers had written to Nancy Remington once a month. Writing more often had seemed too aggressive somehow. Although Nancy invariably replied to his letters, Mr. Peepers always thought, Better a little too little than a little too much, which was a favorite saying of his Grandmother's.

One morning Mr. Peepers woke up smiling and turned off his alarm. For a moment he lay still in bed with his hands behind his head. He had been dreaming of Nancy. Together they had been looking through a thrilling copy of Pavlov's researches. Mr. Peepers sighed happily. Nancy certainly knew a great deal about the human body. Com-

Meeting the Remingtons

bined with what he knew about plant life and the elements they made an unbeatable amalgam. Mr. Peepers thought how nice it would be to wake up in the morning and see Nancy near by, looking over someone's health chart, while he proceeded to air his views on, say, the mating habits of the polyp. Mr. Peepers sighed again. Breakfast with Nancy could be a veritable seminar.

Mr. Peepers looked at the alarm clock. It read 8:15 A.M. The time for dreaming had ended. He bathed quickly and got dressed. Since he was still, as he put it, a single bachelor, he always ate breakfast at the corner drugstore. He had the same order every morning: a glass of prune juice and two scrambled eggs. Sometimes, on payday, he lost control of himself a little and purchased a side order of piggy sausages. Outside of that he never varied. But he enjoyed perusing the menu anyway. He thought the Economy Specials particularly commendable. There was a Businessman's Luncheon of salad, coffee and dessert for only forty cents. Sometimes he ordered it at lunchtime. The people at the drugstore didn't seem to know that he wasn't a businessman.

Mr. Peepers looked at his wrist watch. It was twenty minutes to nine. His good friend Harvey Weskit ordinarily arrived by eight-thirty. Mr. Peepers decided to order. He was about to ask for sausages and eggs when Wes arrived, looking more than a little peaked.

"Good morning, Wes," Mr. Peepers said.

Wes Weskit said, "Good morning," in a croaking, exhausted voice. He did not remove his hat or topcoat. "Sorry I'm late," he said.

"That's okay," Mr. Peepers said.

Howard Fulgit, the redheaded counter boy, leaned over

Mr. Peepers

the cream-colored counter. "Ready to order, chaps?" he said pleasantly. Howard had one of those sardonic senses of humor.

Wes Weskit looked miserable. "Take your hair away, Howard," he said.

"I'll have my payday special," Mr. Peepers said, smiling.

Howard stared at him. "Going a little crazy, aren't ya? No sausages until Thursday."

Wes Weskit groaned. "Sausages," he murmured. "Let me have coffee and a toasted English muffin." As Howard Fulgit walked away Wes tried to catch a fly with one hand. He failed. He turned to Mr. Peepers and stared at him gloomily. "Well, Robby . . ." he said.

"Excuse me, Wes," Mr. Peepers said. "Howard!" he called. "I think I'll splurge a little. Let me have a bowl of porridge."

"Porridge?" Wes Weskit said. "Easy, boy. You've got a class to teach today."

Mr. Peepers chuckled. "Honestly, Wes," he said, "you've got the darnedest sense of humor."

Wes closed his eyes and pressed two forefingers against the lids.

"You still sleepy, Wes?" Mr. Peepers asked.

Wes nodded sadly. "Went to a real tired party last night."

Mr. Peepers examined him for a moment. Wes needs a home life, he thought.

Howard Fulgit placed a white bowl of gray oatmeal on the cream-colored counter. "Here's your coffee," he said to Wes Weskit. "Drink it while it's cold." He walked away, sniggering to himself.

"Hand me the sugar, Robby," Wes said. He breathed

Meeting the Remingtons

deeply three times and rolled his eyes clockwise. Then he rolled them counterclockwise. He looked at Mr. Peepers and smiled, seeming somewhat recovered. "Yep," he said, "it was a tired old party, all right, but I did meet a pretty interesting character."

Mr. Peepers had begun spooning oatmeal into his mouth. It affected his diction adversely. "It seems you're always meeting inresting peeble," he said.

Wes grinned and leaned closer. "She was sitting at the piano in a lavender dress with no shoulders," he whispered. "She looked at me with that exquisite face and there I was, staring into those dreamy, half-lidded, soft blue eyes . . ."

Mr. Peepers stopped eating and looked at Wes's face. His spoon was arrested in mid-air and his mouth was open.

". . . and that tiny carmine-colored mouth," Wes continued, "no more than half an inch away." He stopped for a moment and stared at Mr. Peepers. "Steady, Rob. Your porridge is dripping."

Mr. Peepers gulped and laid his spoon down. "Then what happened?" he asked.

Wes took a ravenous bite of his muffin. "Weh, shuh," he said, "she'sh fum Georgia." He swallowed the interfering lump and continued. "Her father's very wealthy—big, Southern family. Anyway, there I was, just hypnotized by those big old blue eyes, and she looked right at me and smiled and said in one of those milky, Southern voices, 'Hehlow thayuh, *yew-w-w-w-w.*'"

Mr. Peepers nodded. "A Southern girl, eh?"

Wes looked over his shoulder to see if anyone was listening. "Southern?" he whispered stealthily. "Robby . . . if you ever want to get magnolia blossoms wholesale, *she* is the Northern distributor!"

Mr. Peepers

Mr. Peepers stared at him. "Really?" he said. "Is her father in the magnolia business?"

Wes Weskit coughed. "Eat your porridge, sport," he said.

Mr. Peepers returned to his oatmeal. He found it difficult to understand Wes at times. What earthly use would *he* ever have for magnolia blossoms?

"Seen Nancy lately?" Wes asked.

"Yes," Mr. Peepers said, smiling, "we had a date last night. My, it was an exciting evening."

"What'd you do?" Wes asked. "Go to a movie?"

Mr. Peepers shook his head.

"Dancing?"

Mr. Peepers' mouth was full of oatmeal. He indicated "no."

"Bowling?"

"Uh-uh," Mr. Peepers said.

"Well, what did you do?"

Mr. Peepers finished his oatmeal. "Well," he said, "we couldn't go to her house because her parents were out and I've never met them."

"Check," Wes said.

"And we couldn't go to my rooming house, of course, because . . . uh . . . well, Mrs. Busby frowns on that sort of thing."

"Perfectly understandable," Wes said.

"Yes," Mr. Peepers said, "so we came back to the science room after dinner."

Wes's eyes opened wide. "Well, good for you, Robby. What happened?"

Mr. Peepers smiled happily. "Oh, it was fine. I showed her my butterfly collection."

Meeting the Remingtons

Wes Weskit choked on his coffee. "We better get over to school," he said.

Mr. Peepers nodded. He left fifty-five cents on the counter. That included a nickel for Howard. He knew that he was not obliged to tip at the counter, but he did not like to think of himself as stingy.

On the way out he stopped at the gum-ball machine. He always liked to purchase a gum ball for use during recess. He placed a penny in the slot and heard a creaking sound. He bent down and examined the aperture. It was empty.

"Oh, Howard," he said cheerfully, "something is wrong with the machine. I put a penny in . . ."

Howard shrugged his shoulders. "All you have to do is hit it." He whacked the machine lustily. The glass ball shattered and fifty-odd gum balls poured onto the counter.

Mr. Peepers stared at them, smiling. He picked a purple one. "Thank you, Howard," he said.

A few minutes later, as he was entering his classroom, Mr. Peepers was surprised to see Nancy Remington leaning over his desk and writing something. He attracted her attention by clearing his throat.

"Oh, good morning, Robinson," Nancy said. "I was just leaving a note for you."

"Really?" Mr. Peepers said.

Nancy looked a little flustered. "I . . . uh . . . I'm awfully sorry," she said, "but I can't keep our date for the movies tonight. A friend of mine is coming through town. He'll be here only one night."

Mr. Peepers suddenly felt apprehensive. "He?" he said.

"Freddie Willis," Nancy said apologetically. "I knew him when I was in training at St. Luke's Hospital."

Mr. Peepers

"Oh," Mr. Peepers said. "Well . . . er . . . I hope he's recovered."

"He wasn't a patient," Nancy said. "He was an ambulance driver."

"Oh," Mr. Peepers said. "Well, I hope he's recovered. I mean—can we make it some other night?"

"Listen—better yet," Nancy said, "why don't you come over tonight too? We're just going to sit around the house."

"Oh, I don't think so," Mr. Peepers said.

"And it'd give you a chance to meet Mother and Dad," Nancy said. "I've wanted them to meet you and this would be such a good opportunity."

Mr. Peepers smiled. "I'd love to come, if it's all right. I won't be in the way?"

"Don't be silly," Nancy said. "And besides, you'll enjoy meeting Freddie. He's a lot of fun."

Mr. Peepers wondered if Nancy ever said that about him. "Can I bring anything with me?" he asked. "Some ice cream perhaps?"

Nancy smiled. "Just bring your own charming self," she said. "Mother and Dad'll just love to meet you. See you tonight around eight."

"Thank you, Nancy," Mr. Peepers said.

"Good-by, Robinson."

Mr. Peepers sighed when she left. He wondered if Nancy was stringing him along, as the saying went. Nancy was so warm and openhearted. He wondered if he did not seem awfully dry and uninteresting to her. He was more than a little apprehensive about meeting her parents too. Somehow people never seemed to be impressed by him at first acquaintance. It was as if they thought him an odd creature, separated from the normal run of things. He was not

Meeting the Remingtons

sophisticated. He was not "peppy." Not only that, he had never been introduced to a girl's parents before. At least not since birthday parties during his youth. He wasn't sure he knew exactly how to behave.

He went to the closet and put his topcoat on a hanger. He looked in the mirror on the back of the door and combed his hair slowly. Then he smiled at himself. Be debonair, he thought. He wondered if the smooth manners of one of the motion-picture stars could perhaps be duplicated for an occasion.

"Good evening, Nancy," he murmured. He was thinking of Ronald Colman. It seemed to make his voice a bit more musical. "Oh, I'm fine, thank you," he continued. "And this is your father, I presume?" He reached into the closet and shook hands with his topcoat. "How do you do, Mr. Remington? It's nice to meet you." He looked a bit to the left, as though Nancy's mother were there too. "Why, Nancy!" he said expansively. "You didn't tell me you had a sister! . . . What's that? . . . Your mother? . . . Well, I can hardly believe that such an attractive, youthful woman could be the mother of old Nancy—I mean, young Nancy." He laughed heartily. "Oh, no, Mrs. Remington," he said. "I *don't* say that to every woman I meet. I mean it very sincerely."

He laughed again, boomingly, and saw Wes Weskit standing beside him with his arms folded. Mr. Peepers was very embarrassed. Mrs. Gurney was there, too. "Er . . . how long have you been here?" Mr. Peepers asked.

"Actually," Wes said, "we were just passing by. Isn't that right, Mrs. Gurney?"

Mrs. Gurney did not hear him. She was looking in the closet to see who was there. "Hmmmm?" she said.

Mr. Peepers

"I said we were just casually passing by."

Mrs. Gurney turned away from the closet and beamed at Mr. Peepers. "Yes!" she said happily. "We heard everything."

Wes Weskit winced and shook his head. "Actually, sport," he said gravely, "we're here because we think you need us. The cat's out of the bag about tonight. I think Nancy's treating you pretty shabbily. Don't you, Mrs. Gurney?"

Mrs. Gurney looked stern. "Repre*hen*sibly!" she said.

The firmness of Mrs. Gurney's tone interrupted Wes Weskit. "Hm," he said. "Good word."

Mrs. Gurney smiled. "I only use it when I'm furious," she said. She assumed a frown. "Repre*hen*sibly!" she repeated. "Having another man over when you had a date with her. Fuff!"

"Oh, Mrs. Gurney," Mr. Peepers said, "he's an old friend of hers, that's all."

"Oh, I know," Wes said acidly. "He's just passing through. Well then, what are you worrying about?"

Mr. Peepers looked surprised. "Do I seem worried?" he asked.

Wes nodded.

"I'm not worried," Mr. Peepers said.

"You sound worried."

Mr. Peepers stared at him. "I am worried," he said.

"I thought so."

Mr. Peepers shrugged. "I'm always lost in the competitive race for smart things to say. Especially when someone else is around. In a word, one might simply say I'm not 'peppy.' I lack dash. Perhaps I'd better not go tonight."

Meeting the Remingtons

Mrs. Gurney was shocked. "Ohhhh! I'm surprised at you, Mr. Peepers. Nobody likes a quitter."

Wes Weskit hit his palm with his fist. "She's right, Robby!" he said. "Now look here, Mrs. Gurney . . . I think we should brighten up his repertoire, give him a little something to fall back on tonight when the chips are down and the starting gun has sounded. Now, let's see . . . what's peppy?"

They thought for a moment. Mrs. Gurney mumbled to herself incoherently. "Well," she said finally, "a funny story is always good."

Wes nodded. "Know any funny stories, Robby?"

Mr. Peepers blushed. "I'm afraid I don't," he said.

Wes closed his eyes. "Hmmmmm," he said.

"Of course," Mr. Peepers said, chuckling, "there *was* a favorite joke of mine. I used it in my college thesis. It's an excellent joke, but I don't think anyone would get it."

"Why not?" Wes queried.

"It's in Latin."

Wes deliberated for a moment. "Is it the real you?" he asked earnestly.

Mr. Peepers didn't hear him. He was smiling, remembering the joke. "It's one of those fine cracks Cicero got off in front of the Senate."

Wes cleared his throat. "Nope," he said. "It isn't the type we're looking for." There was a pause while he thought. "Hey!" he cried happily. "Here's a funny one. It's about this fellow who goes into a delicatessen—" Wes chuckled for a moment. "It's very funny," he apologized. "He goes to the girl behind the counter and says—" Wes stopped altogether and chuckled for several seconds. "He says, 'I'd

[45]

Mr. Peepers

like a pound of potato salad, miss,' and then she says . . ."

Wes halted himself suddenly. He looked at Mrs. Gurney and paused. "You'd better not tell that one, Robby," he said. "It's a mixed crowd."

Mrs. Gurney beamed at Wes for no apparent reason. "I know something good for living rooms," she said gaily. "It's an attention getter."

"What's that?" Mr. Peepers asked.

"Bird imitations. I'll show you a very simple one." She cupped her hands. She duplicated the call of the Woodbank whippoorwill loudly and with astonishing accuracy.

Mr. Peepers was amazed. "Oh, that's excellent!" he exulted. "The male Woodbank."

Mrs. Gurney simpered happily. "The female differs slightly," she said. She cupped her hands again and proceeded to do the female. It was totally indistinguishable from the male.

"Swell," Wes Weskit said. "And listen, Robby. Do you know any good card tricks?"

Mr. Peepers shook his head.

"Where's that deck of cards you play solitaire with, sport?"

Mr. Peepers opened a desk drawer. "Here they are."

Wes shuffled them expertly. "The hand is quicker than the eye!" he announced. "Calahoony DeMassetina! Take a card, young man. Any card. It makes no difference to Professor Silkenthumb."

Mr. Peepers stared at him. He took a card from the deck and opened his mouth.

"Don't tell me!" Wes cautioned. "Keep the secret locked behind your lips. The ancient formulas of Zoroaster Zilch

Meeting the Remingtons

will reveal all." Wes slapped the deck confidently on the desk. "What was your card, sport?" he asked.

"The five of diamonds," Mr. Peepers replied.

Wes smiled broadly. His head quivered with triumph. He pulled the five of diamonds from his breast pocket. "Secrets of Allah," he said.

Mr. Peepers and Mrs. Gurney applauded. "Capital!" Mrs. Gurney said. "Simply capital. . . ."

"Never fails," Wes said. "I'll show you how it's done." He put the five of diamonds in Mr. Peepers' breast pocket.

Mr. Peepers shook his head. "Wait, Wes, don't——"

"No—leave it in there, Robby," Wes said. "That's how it's done. Now——"

Mr. Peepers interrupted. "No, now really, Mrs. Gurney and Wes, I appreciate this very much, but it's not the . . . uh . . . the real me. I can't do card tricks and tell funny stories and make bird calls. It's not my personality."

Wes Weskit shrugged. "Well, it's up to you, sport."

"But you should go tonight, anyway," Mrs. Gurney said.

"Absolutely," Wes concurred.

"All right, I'll go," Mr. Peepers said, "but no card tricks or anything. I'll just have to stand or fall on my own personalized feet. If they don't like me—" Mr. Peepers paused and coughed.

"Well . . . ?" Wes said.

"Well," Mr. Peepers continued firmly, "they just won't like me."

Punctually at eight o'clock, Mr. Peepers was standing on the Remingtons' front porch muttering to himself. He felt very nervous. He knew it was foolish, but he did not want to ring the bell. Meeting a girl's parents was like going on

Mr. Peepers

trial. He wondered if Freddie Willis was already there. He had never met Freddie Willis, but he didn't have to. The name was enough. Mr. Peepers squared his shoulders and readied his finger. He touched at the tiny, white button and jumped back when it bonged. He had expected a buzz.

"Why, Nancy," he murmured quietly, waiting for someone to answer, "you didn't tell me you had a sister. . . . What's that? . . . Your mother? Well, I can hardly believe . . ."

The door opened suddenly and Nancy stood there, smiling at him. "Hello, Robinson," she said. "Come in."

Mr. Peepers cleared his throat. "Good evening, Nancy," he said. "My, don't you look nice in your civvies. I mean, you're out of uniform. You look very pretty."

"Thank you, Robinson," Nancy said. "Here, let me take your coat."

A pleasant-faced woman came into the hallway, and Nancy said: "This is Mr. Peepers, Mother."

"How do you do, Mr. Peepers," Mrs. Remington said.

Mr. Peepers turned around quickly. "Oh!" he said, startled. "How do you do? I mean, my, Nancy, you didn't tell me you had a mother. I mean . . . uh . . . how do you do?"

"Come in. Make yourself at home, Mr. Peepers," Mrs. Remington said.

Mr. Peepers smiled. "My!" he said. "You certainly have a lovely home here." They walked into the parlor. There was a rug frame standing near the wall. "Oh, you're making a hooked rug, I see."

Mrs. Remington nodded. "Yes," she said.

Nancy smiled at her mother. "She's been working on it for almost six months, now."

Meeting the Remingtons

"Very nearly," Mrs. Remington said. "Are you interested in hooked rugs, Mr. Peepers?"

"My mother used to make them," Mr. Peepers said. "When I was in the Army, she sent me one for the floor beside my bunk."

"Mrs. Remington smiled warmly. "How nice! All the comforts of home."

"It was very attractive," Mr. Peepers said eagerly. "It was sort of ivy green with a yellow design in the middle. It was quite intricate the way Mother worked out the design. From one angle it looked like a pine tree, but when you turned it around, it spelled out, 'HELLO, CAMP KILMER!'"

Mrs. Remington nodded slowly. "That was certainly thoughtful of your mother," she said. "Come in, Mr. Peepers."

There was a tiny, middle-aged man seated on the living-room sofa. He stood up as they entered. Mr. Peepers was surprised to see that he had a mustache.

"Dad, this is Mr. Peepers," Nancy said.

They exchanged how-do-you-do's, and Mrs. Remington said: "Will you excuse me? I'm getting a little snack prepared in the kitchen."

"I'll give you a hand, Mother," Nancy said. "Freddie should be here any minute." She smiled at her father and Mr. Peepers. "Now, you two sit down and get to know each other. I'll be back in a minute."

Mr. Peepers was glad that Freddie Willis hadn't arrived. He waited for Mr. Remington to sit down. "Welllll," Mr. Remington said expansively, easing himself against the back of the sofa. "Oh, sit down, son. Sit down." Mr. Peepers smiled and sat down beside him.

Mr. Peepers

"Wellll," Mr. Remington said, smiling broadly, "so you're a friend of Nancy's, eh?"

Mr. Peepers smiled back. "Yes," he said. He stared at Mr. Remington, expecting him to say something further. Mr. Remington didn't say anything. He just kept smiling. "Yes . . ." Mr. Peepers said tentatively, "we sort of know each other."

Mr. Remington nodded several times. "That's fine," he said, "fine."

They stared at each other for several seconds. Mr. Peepers' cheeks began to hurt a little from smiling. Mr. Remington kept nodding. "Wellll," he said, finally, "that's fine."

Mr. Peepers looked at the coffee table which was placed in front of the sofa. "That's a very handsome table you have there, Mr. Remington," he said.

Mr. Remington brightened considerably. "Yes," he said, touching it, "that's made out of fruitwood."

"Ohhh," Mr. Peepers said, "fruitwood, eh?" He ran one finger over the top of the table.

Mr. Remington nodded proudly. "Picked that up in New York City."

Mr. Peepers was very impressed. "Ohhh," he said. He stared at the table for quite a long while. He hoped that Mr. Remington would say something more. Mr. Remington didn't say anything. Mr. Peepers waited for several seconds. Then he coughed. He tried to think of something more to say about the table, but nothing occurred to him. He stared at Mr. Remington and coughed again.

Mr. Remington smiled at Mr. Peepers. Mr. Peepers smiled back. Then Mr. Remington coughed. "Welll," he said, "Nancy tells me you're in the teaching game."

Meeting the Remingtons

Mr. Peepers nodded vigorously. "Oh, yes. I teach General Science at Jefferson Junior High."

"Oh, yes," Mr. Remington said. "Yes, that's fine."

"Yes," Mr. Peepers said. "Er . . . are you interested in science, Mr. Remington?"

"Oh, no," Mr. Remington said. "No, no . . . no, sir. I . . . er . . . never went in for that much."

Mr. Peepers tried to keep his expression cheerful. "Well . . . er . . . that's the way . . . things are . . . sometimes."

"No," Mr. Remington continued, "I never . . . er . . . liked it. Nope."

There was an uncomfortable pause.

"Well, sir!" Mr. Remington said brightly. "Uh . . . say, I'll tell you—a funny thing happened at the country club today. We were coming in on the eighteenth hole and—ha! ha!—by gosh, this was funny—Ed Herli was on in two about twenty feet from the cup, see—" Mr. Remington interrupted himself and laughed heartily. Mr. Peepers smiled, anticipating the joke. ". . . and Joe Renny and I had Ed and Carl Linn one down. Well, sir—Ed Herli was so nervous when he took his putter out—" Mr. Remington began to laugh again and Mr. Peepers laughed with him. "Oh, boy," Mr. Remington said. "Do you know Ed Herli?"

"No," Mr. Peepers said eagerly. He could hardly wait to laugh at the punch line.

"Oh," Mr. Remington said. "Well, you wouldn't appreciate the story then."

Mr. Peepers was very disappointed. He didn't know what to do with his smile. He looked at the coffee table again and ran his finger over the top. "Uh . . . fruitwood, eh?" he said.

Mr. Peepers

"Yes, sirree," Mr. Remington replied. "I got that in New York City."

Mr. Peepers nodded. He couldn't think of anything more to say. Then suddenly a thought occurred to him. "Well," he began, "that certainly is a nice hooked rug your wife is making there."

Mr. Remington's expression faded to neutral. "Yes," he said halfheartedly, "she makes a . . . nice hooked rug."

"Indeed she does," Mr. Peepers said. "Yes, indeed. She . . . uh . . . makes a *nice* hooked rug."

Mr. Remington sighed and shook his head. "My wife is making that rug for my den." He looked over his shoulder to see if anyone was within hearing distance. Then he leaned toward Mr. Peepers. "Listen," he whispered, "how would you feel about a hooked rug in your den?"

"I don't have a den."

"Oh."

"I just have a rented room."

"Oh, I see," Mr. Remington said. "Well, I guess you wouldn't know what I mean then."

Mr. Peepers wondered if his father's old den would do. He had spent a great deal of time in his father's den as a child. He looked carefully at Mr. Remington. The subject seemed to be cold. Mr. Peepers returned his attention to the coffee table and ran his finger over the edges. "So this is . . . fruitwood, eh?"

Mr. Remington merely stared at him.

At that moment Mrs. Remington and Nancy returned with a trayful of cookies and ginger ale. "Well now," Nancy said, smiling. "Did you two have a nice little chat?"

"Yes!" Mr. Remington said. "Yes, sir."

"Yes, indeed," Mr. Peepers said.

Meeting the Remingtons

"Well, Mr. Peepers," Mrs. Remington said, "Nancy tells us you teach the science class at school."

"Oh, yes," Mr. Peepers said. "I'm in the teaching . . . er . . . game. General Science Two . . . advanced."

"That's fascinating," Mrs. Remington said.

The doorbell went *bong-bong*.

"That must be Freddie," Nancy said, as she went to the door.

"Are you an only child, Mr. Peepers?" Mrs. Remington asked.

"Yes," Mr. Peepers said, in his confusion. "I mean . . . no. I have an older sister."

"Is she married?" Mrs. Remington said.

"Er . . . no," Mr. Peepers said, trying to think of something entertaining to say. "I . . . er . . . Oh, I have a cousin who's married, though. She married a fellow from right around here and they moved to Setuba, Ohio. He has a combination gas station and restaurant there."

Mr. Remington seemed interested. "Oh?" he said.

"Yes, it's one of those places," Mr. Peepers continued, "where you can eat and get gasoline at the same time. Or, if you're not hungry, you can just get gasoline."

"I see," Mrs. Remington said.

"Of course," Mr. Peepers added, "if you're not hungry *and* you don't need gas, you can . . . er . . . well, you could just drive right on by."

Mr. Remington nodded. "Yes," he said. "Well, I always say——"

"Dad," Nancy said, "this is Freddie Willis."

A tall, good-looking young man stepped forward confidently and extended his hand. "Mr. Remington," he said, smiling, "it's good to meet you."

Mr. Peepers

Mr. Remington stood up and shook hands with him. "How do you do?"

"Superbly, thanks," the young man said. He looked at Mrs. Remington and cocked his head. Then he looked at Nancy. "Why, Nancy," he said loudly, "you didn't tell me you had a sister."

Nancy smiled. "Oh, Freddie, this is my mother."

The young man looked astonished. "What's that? Your mother? Well, I can hardly believe that such an attractive, youthful-looking woman could be the mother of Nancy."

Mr. Peepers felt very chagrined. He wondered how people got to be as glib and confident as Freddie Willis.

"Freddie," Nancy said, "this is Robinson Peepers. He teaches science at our school."

Freddie Willis's expression tightened slightly. "Hello, there," he said. He shook hands with Mr. Peepers curtly. Then he beamed at the Remingtons and cast several knowing glances around the room. "Well," he said, "isn't this a lovely place you have here? Yes, indeed. If you have to live in a small town, this is the way I'd like to live. Yes, indeed."

"Well, Mr. Willis," Mrs. Remington said, "Nancy tells us you're on your way to San Francisco."

"Yes," Freddie said warmly. "San Francisco is my home. I love the swirling fog and the towering metropolitan air of my town. Every time I come home from a trip, I stand right down there on Market Street and look up at those buildings and say: 'Hello there, San Francisco!'"

Freddie Willis held one hand in the air. He sounded very much like a radio announcer. "Beautiful!" he whispered. Then he lowered his arm and smiled at the Remingtons.

Meeting the Remingtons

Mr. Remington cleared his throat. "Yes," he said, "San Francisco's a nice place."

"That's where I met Freddie," Nancy said to Mr. Peepers. "He was at the hospital where I took my nurse's training. Do you still do those bird calls, Freddie?"

Freddie laughed heartily. "Well, I haven't done them in a long time, but let's try the jackdaw." Freddie Willis cupped his hands and cawed energetically. Mr. and Mrs. Remington applauded and Nancy complimented him on the verisimilitude of the sound. Freddie winked at her. "I think I can do a little better than that," he said. "Do you remember?" He cawed again.

Mr. Peepers reached for a cooky and sat there munching it, while Freddie Willis essayed several other birds. He thought it was a remarkable demonstration. Except that the jackdaw didn't sound like that. Nor did any of the others. Mr. Peepers sighed. He ate another cooky. He supposed that there was something admirable about Freddie Willis. He was spirited and funny. At least Nancy was laughing and applauding, and the Remingtons certainly seemed diverted. Mr. Peepers wondered if Wes and Mrs. Gurney hadn't been right after all. Perhaps he *was* a little too dry for popular consumption. Perhaps he should try to be a little more peppy and dashing instead of merely boring people with his company. He wondered if Freddie Willis were really so ebullient by nature. Somehow Freddie's face looked strained and anxious at times, as though he thrived on applause and laughter and couldn't live happily without them. But then, as Mr. Peepers himself had said so many times, we always think that people are feeling what we would be feeling if we were doing what they are doing. Mr.

Mr. Peepers

Peepers tried to go over the thought again. He had lost track of it somewhere in the middle. It was while Freddie Willis was doing his masterpiece (the pied-billed grebe) that Nancy whispered: "What are you thinking, Robinson?" and Mr. Peepers murmured: *"Podilymbus podiceps."*

"What?" Nancy asked.

"Oh, I'm sorry, Nancy," Mr. Peepers whispered, trying not to distract Freddie, who was honking fiercely. "That's just an academic name for a grebe. I was just thinking what people feel when they are thinking what other people feel."

"What?" Nancy asked.

Mr. Peepers smiled. "It doesn't matter."

"Isn't Freddie funny?" Nancy asked.

"He's amazing," Mr. Peepers said.

Nancy smiled at him. "You're awfully nice," she said.

Later in the evening Freddie Willis announced that he had some marvelously entertaining card tricks to show them. "I picked this first one up in little old Las Vegas," he said. He was shuffling the cards like a professional. He leaned toward Mr. Remington and nudged him with his elbow. "Big gambling town, you know," he said. "Pick a card. Any card." Mr. Remington did so, and Freddie slapped the deck on the table. "What was your card, my good sir?" he asked, grinning.

"The five of diamonds," Mr. Remington said.

Freddie lifted one finger. "Hahahaha," he said, "and where do you think that very card is?"

Mr. Remington grunted. "I'm sure I don't know."

Mr. Peepers felt a sudden thrill. Remembering Wes Weskit's demonstration of the same trick, he reached into his breast pocket and pulled out Wes's five of diamonds.

Meeting the Remingtons

"Well, sir," Freddie was saying, reaching into his own pocket, "it's right here in my——"

Mr. Peepers waved the card so that Nancy could see it. "Why, look at that, everybody," Nancy cried. "It was in Robinson's pocket!"

Mrs. Remington applauded delightedly. "My gracious—how in the world did you do that, Mr. Willis?" she asked.

Freddie Willis stared strangely at Mr. Peepers. Mr. Peepers was still holding the card in the air, grinning. "Hmmmmm?" Freddie said. "Oh . . . er . . . nothing—it's just a trick." He laughed uncomfortably and removed the card from Mr. Peepers' fingers, inspecting it closely. "Hahaha." He laughed mechanically. "Uh . . . just a trick." He pocketed the card and clapped his hands together. "Well," he said, "now, here's another one. You take the deck, Nancy. Pick any card and don't show it to me."

As Nancy examined the deck, Freddie turned away. He sneaked furtive looks at the two fives of diamonds, comparing them. They seemed identical. Then he stared at Mr. Peepers again. Mr. Peepers was still smiling.

"All right, Freddie," Nancy said.

Freddie Willis took the deck from her and shook off his confusion. "Now," he said loudly, "the object of this trick is for me to pick your card without your knowing how I do it."

Mr. Peepers excused himself and went into the kitchen. Standing there alone, toying with an egg beater, he could still hear Freddie's relentless voice droning on and on. He felt more than a little depressed. Despite his good fortune with the card trick, he was the evening's prize wallflower. Lucky at cards, he thought, unlucky at love. Well—perhaps

Mr. Peepers

that's the way of the world. He put the egg beater down and scratched at his head. It wasn't that he ever expected to get on with all the Freddie Willises in the world. Long ago he had given up on that. But the Remingtons and Nancy were something else again. They were nice people. They were Nancy's parents and the Remingtons' daughter. Yet it was Freddie Willis who entertained them; it was Freddie Willis they laughed at and listened to. And Mr. Peepers wondered why it was that he was left out and lonely. Perhaps, he thought, I just don't give enough. He squared his shoulders and returned to the living room.

By that time Freddie Willis was in the midst of telling humorous stories. ". . . and I know how long it takes a good joke to get way back here to the little old Midwest," he was saying, "so here's one right fresh out of that good old metropolis by the Golden Gate. I think you'll get a chuckle out of it. It's about this fellow who goes into a delicatessen and he says to the girl behind the counter: I'd like a pound of potato salad, miss . . ."

Mr. Peepers strangled slightly on his eleventh cooky and began to clear his throat. Freddie stopped speaking and stared at him. "What's the matter, chum?" he asked. Mr. Peepers did his best to signal him not to tell that one in mixed company. Freddie Willis laughed out loud at him. "Oh, for Pete's sake," he said, "it isn't *that* joke, chum. You've been going to too many stag parties." Then he turned back to Nancy and Mrs. Remington, saying: "So the girl says, I'm sorry but we're all out of potato salad, and the fellow says . . ."

This time it was Mr. Remington who left the room. He seemed to be muttering to himself. Mr. Peepers wondered if there were something wrong.

Meeting the Remingtons

After Freddie Willis had finished telling another five stories, he suddenly looked at his watch. "Well," he said loudly, "I have to catch the early-bird plane tomorrow A.M. I'd better be toddling along."

Everyone stood up to bid him good-by. "I'd better go, too," Mr. Peepers said. "It's past my bedtime."

"I'll get your coat, Robinson," Nancy said.

Mr. Peepers followed her into the hallway, while Freddie Willis made his farewells to the Remingtons. "It was a very enjoyable evening," Mr. Peepers said to Nancy. "Thank you for inviting me."

Before Nancy could say anything, Freddie burst into the hallway singing "California . . . here I come." "Well," he chirped, "next stop . . . San Francisco!"

"I'll get your coat, Freddie," Nancy said. She went to the closet, leaving Mr. Peepers and Freddie alone.

Freddie looked around furtively. Then he leaned close to Mr. Peepers. "Listen," he whispered, removing Mr. Peepers' five of diamonds from his pocket, "about this card —where the heck did you——"

Nancy interrupted him with his coat. Freddie hemmed and hawed and winked at Mr. Peepers. "Well, sir!" he cried loudly, "on to the Golden Gate, eh what?" He began singing again, even louder than before: "San Fran-cis-co-o-o . . . Here is your wand'rin' bo-y-y——"

"Excuse me," Mr. Peepers said, interrupting him deliberately. "I'll say good night to your parents, Nancy."

"Of course, Robinson," Nancy said.

Mr. Peepers made a dejected way back to the parlor. "Thank you for a most enjoyable evening, Mr. and Mrs. Remington," he said.

"A pleasure," Mr. Remington said.

Mr. Peepers

"You must come again," Mrs. Remington said.

"Thank you," Mr. Peepers said. He wished that he could think of something notable to say, but as usual nothing occurred to him. "Well . . . er . . . good night." When he got back to the door, he saw that Freddie Willis had no intention of being the first to leave.

"Ta-ta, old man," Freddie said. "If you're ever out Golden Gate way, give me a toot on the horn."

"The horn?" Mr. Peepers said.

Freddie smiled tolerantly. "The telephone."

"Oh," Mr. Peepers said. "Yes, of course."

"Thanks for coming over, Robinson," Nancy said.

"Oh, that's . . . all right," Mr. Peepers said, wondering how long Freddie would be staying. "Well . . . er . . . good night."

He closed the door behind him. Sighing once and taking a good, deep breath, he scuffed his way down the front walk. It takes practice, he thought. I'll just have to keep visiting people until I find out how to behave.

He had just rounded the front gate when he felt something tugging at his shoe. He leaned down and unhooked what seemed to be a strand of wool. A piece of chewing gum was stuck to the end of it. Behind him, the wool strand extended all the way back to the Remingtons' front door. Mr. Peepers began winding the yarn over his hand and made his way gradually back to the porch. By the time he rang the bell he had a ball of wool the size of a grapefruit coiled around his fist. He was extremely puzzled by it all. Nancy opened the door and he showed her the ball. "Something seems to have followed me out," he said.

Mr. and Mrs. Remington were standing in the hallway.

Meeting the Remingtons

Mrs. Remington looked at the ball and shuddered. There was a long woolen strand hanging between the ball and the rug frame. "My hooked rug!" Mrs. Remington cried.

Mr. Peepers gasped. He too saw the connection. For a moment no one spoke. Then: "By George," Freddie Willis said, "there's hardly anything left of it!"

Mr. Peepers could have died. He tried lamely to extricate his fist from the ball of wool. "Oh, my goodness, I—Oh, look what I've done," he said. "Oh, I'm so sorry, Mrs. Remington."

"I don't think that will put the rug together again," Freddie Willis murmured.

"No," Mr. Peepers said. "No . . . it won't."

Freddie Willis shook his head. "Well," he said, shrugging, "I hate to leave on a note of tragedy, but . . . good night, everybody."

Everyone bade him good night in a whisper.

"Rather clumsy, old man," Freddie whispered, as he closed the door behind him.

Mr. Peepers looked at Mrs. Remington. She had her hands clasped tightly together and she was biting her lip. "Oh, Mrs. Remington," he said pitifully, "what can I say? I just . . . don't know what to say."

Mrs. Remington walked over to the rug frame. "Now, now," she said. "It's not that big a tragedy."

Nancy touched at Mr. Peepers' shoulder. "Please . . . don't worry about it, Robinson."

"But . . . all that time and effort," Mr. Peepers said. "I'm terribly sorry, Mrs. Remington and . . . Well, I knew I shouldn't have . . . come over here tonight."

Mrs. Remington didn't say anything. She and Nancy were

Mr. Peepers

disconsolately staring at the rug frame. Mr. Peepers tried to replace his hat on his head with his left hand and turned to go.

"Now, just a minute," Mr. Remington said, taking hold of Mr. Peepers' arm. "Listen," he whispered, "I never liked that doggone hooked rug anyway. Who wants a thing like that in his den? I've been trying to unravel that rug for two months."

Mrs. Remington turned back and re-entered the hallway. "What's that you're saying, dear?" she asked.

Mr. Remington winced and turned scarlet. "Oh, nothing, dear—nothing. But I was just telling Mr. Peepers it isn't really such a tragedy—is it?"

Mrs. Remington smiled and took Mr. Peepers' arm. "Oh, of course not," she said warmly. "The truth is, I don't think Harry liked that design anyway. Did you, dear?"

Mr. Remington took a good, deep breath. "I'll be honest," he said. "I didn't."

"All right then," Mrs. Remington said. "I'll start all over and hook another one."

Mr. Remington's smile faded perceptibly. "Well . . . anyway, now that that big bore and his corny jokes and bird whistles has left, why don't we all sit down and have some bacon and eggs, huh?"

Mrs. Remington and Nancy concurred. "That's a wonderful idea," Mrs. Remington said. "I haven't drawn a relaxed breath all night."

Mr. Peepers was amazed. Could it be true? Hadn't they been as delighted with Freddie Willis as they'd seemed? "Me, too?" he whispered to Nancy.

Nancy smiled at him, puzzled. "Well, most certainly you!" she said.

Meeting the Remingtons

Mr. Peepers could have jumped up in the air. "Well, now," he said. "Well, hasn't this turned into a most pleasurable and delightful evening."

Mr. Remington winked at him. "You'd better get that wool off your hand, son."

Mr. Peepers and Nancy laughed. Nancy helped him to extricate his fist.

Later, as the four of them sat around the kitchen eating everything Mrs. Remington could force upon them, Mr. Peepers stole glances at Nancy and her parents. He sighed happily. He had met the enemy. And they were friends.

CHAPTER III

A Romantic Student

BUT THERE WAS THE SCHOOL, too, and the various problems that arose with the students. Mr. Peepers was hardly a man to sidestep knotty problems. As a Sea Scout, during his youth, he had been known to spend hours untangling a single strand of rigging. Yet, at times he questioned his ability to handle the students' problems properly. For instance, there was the case of Helen Fernley.

". . . and to acquaint yourselves still further with the amoeba," Mr. Peepers was saying, "I suggest you read Chapter Twenty-Seven of your *Cells in Action* text tonight, entitled 'Everything Begins with the Amoeba,' keeping in mind what we have learned today about how the amoeba

A Romantic Student

perpetuates itself." A paper airplane floated onto Mr. Peepers' desk. Mr. Peepers paused. The students did not seem to be paying undivided attention. "The nucleus," he continued, "or heart of the amoeba dividing itself, each part going its separate way."

Elwood Hamper interrupted Mr. Peepers to ask a foolish question.

"No, Elwood," Mr. Peepers replied, "I hardly think they wave good-by." He decided not to make an issue of the students' unruliness. It was nearly three o'clock and he supposed they were anxious to get home. "Has everyone completed his or her drawing?" he asked.

The students howled "Yes!" in remarkable unison.

"Excellent," Mr. Peepers said. "Now, who would like to volunteer to collect the papers?" Helen Fernley and Leonard Gorf raised their hands as usual, like grinning automatons. "Oh, come now," Mr. Peepers said, "let's see some new hands in the classroom. Carl—would you do it, please?"

Carl Dagny glowered at Mr. Peepers and began to wiggle in his seat. Mr. Peepers sighed. Carl was perhaps the largest boy in school, scaling close to a hundred and fifty pounds. Mr. Peepers felt outweighed. "Very well then. Leonard," he said, "would you do it, please?"

The school bell bonged loudly. "That will be all now, class," Mr. Peepers said, as the students began closing their books and jabbering at each other. "Please try to leave quietly," Mr. Peepers added. "The classroom is never a place for idle conversation."

A moment later Leonard Gorf appeared at Mr. Peepers' desk with the class drawings. "Thank you, Leonard," Mr. Peepers said. Leonard clicked his heels together smartly and saluted. He had spent his early school years at the Crossed

Mr. Peepers

Rifles Academy. "That really isn't necessary, Leonard," Mr. Peepers said. Leonard saluted again, did a crisp about-face and left the classroom. Mr. Peepers sighed, staring after him. He thought of having a talk with Leonard's parents. There was a rumor about that the Gorf family did close-order drill before supper. If true, Mr. Peepers felt they were running a good thing into the ground.

He also thought that something would have to be done about Walter Murdock. The continual flow of paper airplanes was getting very much out of hand. Not only that, Walter had failed to answer any questions on the first-semester astronomy test. Instead he had drawn a large cartoon of a teacher hanging from a scaffold. Mr. Peepers wondered fleetingly whom he'd had in mind. Wes Weskit, he supposed. Wes *had* confessed to being stern with Walter in history class.

Mr. Peepers crumpled several of the paper airplanes and dropped them into the wastebasket. The one remaining had Walter's signature on it. It read: Walter Murdock's Poison Plane! BEWARE! beneath a carefully drawn skull and crossbones. Mr. Peepers stared at it for a moment. Then he nudged it into the basket with his elbow. He noticed that Helen Fernley and Mary Ellen Gleeb were still in the classroom, standing by the door.

"Well, aren't you going to walk home with me?" Mary Ellen was whispering. "You said you'd help me with my *Movie Mirror* cutouts."

"No, Mary," Helen answered fiercely. "I have to stay and talk to Mr. Peepers about my project."

"Gee whiz," Mary Ellen said. "You got awfully interested in science all of a sudden. How come?"

Helen sighed deeply and glanced at Mr. Peepers. "Oh,

A Romantic Student

I've been just crazy about it ever since I saw Gregory Peck in 'The Passionate Chemist.' "

Mary Ellen shook her head. "Well, all right," she said. "I'll see you later."

Mr. Peepers heard the door close and Helen's footsteps approaching. Then Helen's voice said: "I'm here, Mr. Peepers." The voice sounded unusually deep for a young girl. Mr. Peepers wondered if poor Helen had a cold. He looked up from his drawings and smiled. "Well, Helen," he said, "you're here indeed."

"I was wondering," Helen said strangely, "if you'd look at my science project again."

She seemed to have something in her eye. At least, her eyelids were fluttering in a most peculiar way. Mr. Peepers decided to ignore it. "Why, I'd be delighted to help you," he said. "A teacher always has time to help a willing student." He was genuinely pleased. Despite Helen's unusual physical habits, such as pasting her A-student gold star on her forehead to look like Jean Simmons in "The Egyptianess," Mr. Peepers found her an exemplary scholar, so uncomplicated and hard-working. He thought what a pleasure it would be to teach a roomful of Helen Fernleys. "It's always encouraging," he said to Helen, on the way to the lab corner, " to see a youngster so much interested in the scientific nature of things."

Helen Fernley could have fainted with delight. She thought that Mr. Peepers was the most exciting man alive. Still waters run deep, she had said to Mary Ellen, and Mr. Peepers was the stillest man she knew. She held her breath as Mr. Peepers examined her work.

Mr. Peepers was delighted with Helen's project. He had asked her to construct a radio by hand. Oddly enough, it

Mr. Peepers

was an almost exact replica of Marconi's final model. Mr. Peepers wondered if Helen had been sneaking looks at the school library copy of *Sound Is Everywhere*. "Well, it's certainly coming along," he said approvingly. "Let's see here: variable condenser, vacuum tube, grid condenser and grid leak, your air core transformer, your single pole throw switch—what's this object in here that looks like a banana?"

"A banana," Helen said. "I put it there to hide it from Georgie Hogart." Helen removed the banana. "*You* may have it, if you like," she said devotedly.

"Thank you," Mr. Peepers said, chuckling. "For a moment I thought perhaps you'd made a rare scientific discovery—a banana with electronic properties."

Helen Fernley opened her eyes wide. She hoped Mr. Peepers thought she was beautiful.

"That was a little joke," Mr. Peepers said. "I always feel an occasional humor point, if well placed, can help inscribe a scientific point indelibly on the enduring tablets of the memory." Mr. Peepers laughed again. He didn't seem to be getting through to Helen. "Well," he said seriously, "*sic semper comedis.*"

"Mr. Peepers," Helen said quietly, "could I walk you home this afternoon?"

Mr. Peepers didn't hear her, having returned to the radio. He was amazed at how successfully Helen had managed to make tuning coils out of hairpins. "You certainly have an inventive mind, Helen," he said.

"If I walked you home," Helen continued, "I'd carry your books."

Mr. Peepers glanced at her. He wasn't at all sure that he had heard her correctly. "I beg your pardon?"

Helen's face was transformed. She felt like Tyrone Power

A Romantic Student

in "The Song of Bernard." "I'm asking if I might walk you home, Mr. Peepers."

"Good heavens!" Mr. Peepers said. Suddenly Helen's intentions were clear to him. "I mean . . . well, that's very thoughtful. But I . . . well, Helen, I have numerous chores that must be attended to: papers to file . . . blackboards to clean . . . a banana to eat. I mean . . . another time, perhaps."

Helen smiled beatifically. "Okay," she said. She did not feel disappointed. She was glad to step aside for Mr. Peepers' devotion to science. He was one of the vanguards of progress. On her way out of the classroom, she thought of Barbara Stanwyck in "Bad for His Work." Then she paused at the doorway. "Mr. Peepers," she said, "how old are you?"

Mr. Peepers was stunned. "How old?" he said. "Well, I'm . . . uh . . . twenty-six . . . going on twenty-seven." He hoped that his rapid approach to thirty would impress upon Helen that he was out of the question.

"Gosh," Helen said, "only twelve years' difference in our ages." She wafted slowly from the classroom. She wondered if she resembled Audrey Hepburn in "The Wafter."

Mr. Peepers brought one hand to his mouth. Helen Fernley? His best student? He had never dreamed. Suddenly Helen's unnatural voice and fluttering eyelids were clear to him. She was hopelessly, desperately, passionately in love . . . with him? "Oh, dear," Mr. Peepers murmured, shaking his head. He had never been confronted with such a situation before. What was he to do? The fixed stare of devotion in Helen's eyes had alarmed him considerably. He remembered a sickly tadpole he had owned as a child. The mealtime look of supplication blended with Helen's devoted one in his mind. Mr. Peepers shuddered. Such looks

Mr. Peepers

had always made him uncomfortable. He leaned back against the lab table, trying to think. His elbow pushed at the radio switch. Music blared suddenly at his ears with drum-splitting volume. It was "The Star-Spangled Banner." Mr. Peepers snapped to attention and saluted. Leonard Gorf is here! he thought, in a panic. Then he got control of himself and began to wrestle with the radio.

That evening, at Harvey Weskit's apartment, Mr. Peepers asked Wes for advice. He remembered how knowledgeable Wes was in feminine matters. He hoped that Wes might resolve the dilemma painlessly, with a few well-chosen words.

". . . and when Helen Fernley asked me to walk home," Mr. Peepers said, "I was completely taken aback."

"Don't worry about it, sport," Wes Weskit said. "Lots of kids get crushes on their teachers. It's part of growing up. I'll never forget my first crush on a teacher. Miss Ludlow in 4B."

"How did you get over it?"

"Well, one day she ordered me to stay after class," Wes said, "and then she didn't show up."

"Unrequited, huh?" Mr. Peepers said.

Wes nodded. "Crushed."

Mr. Peepers shook his head. "But I couldn't do that, Wes. We have psychology these days." He was genuinely worried. His whole classroom seemed to be erupting in problems: how to discipline Walter Murdock; how to undiscipline Leonard Gorf; and now Helen. "I just wish I knew what to say to her," he said.

"Oh, come on," Wes said, "don't worry about it, kiddo." He was busily trimming his fingernails with a pair of

A Romantic Student

manicuring scissors. "Perfect ovals," he said proudly, showing his hands to Mr. Peepers. "A professional manicurist showed me how to do them. Laura La Trimmée her name was. She was a pretty sharp girl."

"Really?" Mr. Peepers said.

Wes coughed and put the scissors away. "Hand me the after-shave lotion like a good egg, would you, Robby?"

Mr. Peepers stared at the row of bottles. "Which one, Wes?" he asked. "Old Hunting Dog? Old Outfit? Or Old Rocking Chair?"

Wes ran a careful palm over his freshly shaven face. "This is a pretty special date tonight. Better hand me the bottle without a label."

Mr. Peepers picked up the bottle and smiled. It was always good sport being in on Wes's ablutions. "What's the name of this lotion, Wes?" he asked.

Wes Weskit turned and stared at him. "That lotion," he said proudly, "is so effective they don't dare *give* it a name."

"How do you ask for it?"

"By number," Wes said. "And you have to have an appointment." He took the bottle and unscrewed the top. "Take a whiff."

Mr. Peepers smiled, sniffed and began coughing violently.

Wes nodded. "It's dynamite," he said.

Mr. Peepers grinned at him. "It makes my eyes water," he said.

Wes Weskit began to apply the lotion sparingly. "The stuff's like opium. Once you start it, you can never stop."

Mr. Peepers laughed. "Oh, Wes, honestly, you just like to make sport of me."

Wes laughed. "You're a pretty sharp apple, Robby."

Mr. Peepers

"My Dad always used Lilac Water," Mr. Peepers said happily. "Of course . . . not in the summer. It attracted mosquitoes."

Wes sighed. "You've gotta be careful," he said.

Mr. Peepers observed Wes's preparations for a moment. It seemed to him that they were particularly elaborate. "This young lady you're going out with tonight," he said. "She must be pretty special. How did you meet her?"

"She's the friend of a friend of a friend of my brother."

Mr. Peepers nodded. "It's nice when you can keep it in the family."

"City girl," Wes continued. "Chicago. Blonde, blue eyes, and loaded with charm. Yes, sir, Rob—this just might be the one for old Wes."

"My goodness," Mr. Peepers said. "I've never seen you this serious before. Are you . . . er . . . contemplating matrimony?"

"Well," Wes said, grinning, "it isn't the farthest thing from my mind."

Mr. Peepers was delighted. "What's the young lady's name?"

"Marge Bellows." Wes took a fresh shirt from his dresser. "We hit it off right from the start." He showed the shirt to Mr. Peepers. "Like this, Rob?" he asked.

It was a pale-blue Oxford with thin black stripes. Mr. Peepers tried to look impressed, but Helen Fernley kept popping rudely into his mind. "Seriously, Wes," he said, "did *you* ever have a student get a crush on you?"

Wes Weskit grunted. "Ten, twelve, twenty times a semester," he said.

"Oh, dear," Mr. Peepers said. "Well, what did you do about it?"

A Romantic Student

Wes finished inserting his cuff links and braced himself against the bureau with one hand. Then he turned to Mr. Peepers and gripped his shoulder for a moment. "Rob," he said seriously, "you've got to realize that you're an ideal to these youngsters and you have to—" He made a circling motion with his right hand— ". . . and then the child will—" He repeated the circling motion.

Mr. Peepers thought for a moment. "But what," he said, "if the child doesn't . . . uh—" He made the same circling motion with his right hand.

Wes Weskit winked at him. "Right!" he said proudly.

Mr. Peepers smiled. "Thanks, Wes," he said.

The following morning, as Mrs. Gurney was summing up her weekly Shakespearean lecture, Helen Fernley was composing a note which she intended to leave for Mr. Peepers. "My dear Mr. Peepers . . ." she began. Then she stopped writing and chewed on the end of her pencil. There were so many things she wanted to say and so few ways to say them. She felt like Marlon Brando in "The Writing Fool."

"So keep in mind," Mrs. Gurney was saying, "in the study of Shakespeare, children, that there are those who believe the immortal bard was not really the author of all those marvelous plays that have come down under his name, but that Sir Francis Bacon . . . uh . . . Oh, George—will you pick up all the themes before the bell rings, please . . ."

George Gatsby stood up and began collecting the themes from every desk. Helen Fernley was chewing her eraser and staring at the ceiling. George Gatsby picked up her letter to Mr. Peepers. By the time Helen noticed, it was too late to stop him. "George!" she whispered fiercely. "George!"

Mr. Peepers

Mrs. Gurney tapped for silence with a pencil. "Louder, please," she said severely. "I mean . . . er . . . quiet! Yes, quiet."

Mrs. Gurney cleared her throat. "We must pay attention . . . uh . . . undividedly and indubitably. Now, as I was saying, Sir Francis Bacon, who was a very good writer indeed, but hardly a Shakespeare, is sometimes mentioned as the author of Shakespeare's plays. Ridiculous, of course; but we must be fair. So I suggest that tonight you read Bacon's essays 'On Love' and 'On Truth.' Read and compare, read and compare; be tolerant . . . open-minded. But, of course, anyone who thinks Bacon is responsible for Shakespeare's plays . . . er . . . Well, you make up your minds for yourselves. I certainly don't wish to influence you in any way."

The school bell bonged. Mrs. Gurney jumped. "Oh, my goodness!" she cried. "Well—time does fly by, doesn't it?" She smiled at the students. "That will be all, my dears."

George Gatsby appeared at her desk with the themes. "Thank you, George," she said. Then she saw Leonard Gorf standing rigidly at attention before her. "Oh, dear me," she said, always confused by Leonard's behavior. "Er . . . carry on, Leonard." Leonard, satisfied, did a crisp about-face and left.

Then Helen Fernley, who had waited until the classroom was empty, came forward and spoke to her. "Mrs. Gurney," she said softly, "when George picked up——"

"Now, now Helen," Mrs. Gurney said, "on your way to your next class. I have many things to do."

"But I've——"

"You only have a few minutes, dear," Mrs. Gurney said. "Hurry, now."

A Romantic Student

Helen turned, dejected, to go. She felt like Mario Lanza in "The Lost Theme."

Mrs. Gurney began perusing the papers. The first was Leonard Gorf's. "My rifle is a good rifle . . ." it began. Mrs. Gurney put it aside and coughed. "I'll read it later, dear," she murmured. "Bless you." She picked up the next one. "My dear Mr. Peepers . . ." she read. "Mmm," she said, "very novel title for a theme." She lifted her lorgnette and read aloud. "I'm thrilled to know that you don't think twelve years is too big a difference in our ages . . . bu . . . bu . . . too big a . . . Oh, my!"

Mrs. Gurney hurried to the water cooler. She took a long drink. She would have to have a talk with Mr. Peepers.

She found him in the science room, bent over a microscope. Mr. Peepers heard the door open and waved for silence. "Please don't slam the door or you'll disturb the polyps."

Mrs. Gurney jumped. "Polyps?" she said. She had visions of little men with ray guns. "Where are they?"

"Here," Mr. Peepers said, "under the microscope."

Mrs. Gurney felt relieved. "That's cozy."

Mr. Peepers removed his eye from the microscope and rubbed it vigorously. "Take a look," he said, smiling. "They're little invertebrates with tentacles at one end and a means of attachment to some foreign body at the other end."

"Foreign?" Mrs. Gurney said, "Bu . . . bu . . . Oh, well . . ." She quelled her dismay and bent down to look. "Ohhhh," she said, smiling, "how charming! Make a lovely pattern for a doily!" She straightened and beamed at Mr. Peepers. "Lovely," she said, reassuringly.

"Did you wish to see me about something, Mrs. Gurney?"

Mr. Peepers

Mrs. Gurney couldn't remember. "Oh, yes," she said suddenly, "I almost forgot." She waved Helen Fernley's theme. "Read this, Mr. Peepers. It's Helen Fernley's."

Mr. Peepers read it and bit his lip. "Oh, dear," he said.

"That's what *I* said," Mrs. Gurney concurred. "Oh, dear."

Mr. Peepers shook his head. "This situation has become quite serious."

"I should say," Mrs. Gurney said. "That's why I said, 'Oh, dear.' What are you going to do about this, Mr. Peepers?"

"I haven't any idea. Nothing like this has ever happened to me before. It's a very delicate subject."

Mrs. Gurney agreed absolutely. "Oh my, yes, very delicate . . . very delicate. It must be handled with children's gloves. Young girls are quite sensitive, you know, quite sensitive."

Mr. Peepers wasn't listening. "Above all," he murmured, "I mustn't hurt Helen's feelings."

"Oh, no," Mrs. Gurney said. "Mustn't do that. You see, it's a very delicate subject, very delicate."

Mr. Peepers looked at Mrs. Gurney. "Perhaps if I spoke to Helen's parents," he said.

Mrs. Gurney clasped her hands. "Now, there's a capital idea," she said. "Capital! Speak to Helen's parents."

"Do you know them, Mrs. Gurney?"

"Quite well," Mrs. Gurney said. "Oh, quite well. Mrs. Fernley's very nice."

Mr. Peepers felt that Mrs. Fernley was only half the problem. "And Mr. Fernley?"

Mrs. Gurney's expression flattened. "A trifle eccentric,"

A Romantic Student

she said. "Invents things, you know. Yes. Quite inventive. Frightening, really. I do think you should speak to them."

Mr. Peepers smiled at her. "I'll do it this evening."

"Capital," Mrs. Gurney said. "Well, I must be off." She took a last look through the microscope. "Lovely," she whispered. She beamed at Mr. Peepers. "I must remember that pattern." Humming to herself, she left the classroom.

When the door closed, Mr. Peepers picked up Helen's note and perused it carefully. The words "not too big a difference in our ages" made him shiver. He wondered what he could possibly say to Helen's parents. A sincere approach, he thought—warm, gentle. Perhaps a practice session would prove of some assistance. Mr. Peepers cleared his throat. He smiled sweetly. "Mrs. Fernley," he said, "and Mr. Fernley . . . I have something very important to tell you. It's about your daughter Helen. I think you'd better . . . sit down." Mr. Peepers leaned against his desk and sighed. "Believe me, this is going to hurt me more than it will you. But there comes a time in the affairs of men—" Mr. Peepers saw that one of his hands was making aimless circles in the air. Dissatisfied, he shook his head. The approach was too soft. He would have to seize the bull more assertively. He stood up straight and squared his houlders. "Mrs. Fernley!" he said loudly. "Sam! . . . I suppose your daughter Helen has told you about . . . us. Maybe you'd better stand up."

Mr. Peepers stopped again. He chewed at his lip for a moment. A businesslike approach wouldn't do either. He wondered if he should assume some sort of character for the occasion. He removed his glasses and jammed his hands into his pockets. "Ethel!" he cried, "and you, too, Sam!

Mr. Peepers

You'd better sit down. Now, get this—I'm a science teacher, all right, but I'm tougher than I look . . . I'm too tough for Helen——"

Nancy Remington coughed politely.

Mr. Peepers replaced his glasses. "Nancy!"

"Hello, Robinson," Nancy said, looking tentatively about the room. "I thought I heard you talking to someone."

Mr. Peepers blushed. "I was talking to Mr. and Mrs. Fernley."

"Oh?" Nancy said. "Where are they?"

"Home," Mr. Peepers said. "I mean . . ."

"Robinson," Nancy said, touching at his forehead, "are you feeling all right? You look rather upset."

"No, I'm fine," Mr. Peepers said. "I feel dandy. It's only that—well, I . . . I just discovered that a certain young lady is in love with me."

Nancy's face got a little red. "Oh?"

Mr. Peepers made a futile gesture. "A thing like this has never happened to me before."

Nancy stared at him strangely for a moment. "It was bound to happen sooner or later, Robinson," she said. "After all, you do have a world of charm."

"Oh, no!" Mr. Peepers said. "I mean—you've got this all wrong. We're only fourteen. That is—the young lady is fourteen years old. Helen Fernley. She's one of my students."

Nancy's expression seemed to get brighter. "Oh, of course. I know Helen Fernley—but Robinson, this happens all the time with teachers. Why are you taking it so seriously?"

Mr. Peepers smiled ruefully. "I'm an amateur."

A Romantic Student

"I'm sure it'll work out," Nancy said, taking his hand. "Are you going to talk to her about it?"

"I don't dare," Mr. Peepers said. "I have to see her parents first. Tonight."

Nancy nodded. She had intended to ask Mr. Peepers to her house that evening. Under the circumstances, she thought it best not to mention it. "It will work out, don't worry."

"Did you want to see me about something?" Mr. Peepers asked.

Nancy smiled again. "Just to say hello."

"Hello," Mr. Peepers said.

Nancy laughed and opened the door. "Good luck tonight."

"Thank you, Nancy."

Mr. Peepers sighed as the door closed. Nancy certainly was wonderful. He thought how nice it would be to get a note from Nancy like Helen Fernley's but he knew it was impossible. After all, he and Nancy were the same age.

He arrived at the Fernley home at eight-thirty sharp. Steeling himself, he pushed at the doorbell. As the door swung open a sign dropped down from a niche in the jamb reading: WELCOME. Mr. Peepers jumped back from it. The sign disappeared. A second sign dropped down reading: ENTER. It also disappeared. Mr. Peepers obeyed cautiously and removed his hat. The door slammed shut quickly. He had to leap out of the way. There was no one in the vestibule. It was also rather dark. Mr. Peepers stood there for a moment fingering his hat. He couldn't hear anyone coming. "Yoo-hoo!" he called.

Mr. Peepers

The silence continued. Mr. Peepers opened the nearest door. A coat hanger sprang out at him, with two signs dangling at the front. Your hat, said one. Your coat, said the other. Mr. Peepers delivered his coat and ear muffs. The hanger sprang back into the closet. Mr. Peepers closed the closet door.

"Yoo-hoo!" he called again.

He heard a pop and a swishing sound, like a phonograph record. Suddenly a voice boomed at him: I'm in the basement, make yourself at home. . . . I'm in the basement, make yourself at home. . . .

After his initial surprise, Mr. Peepers traced the voice to a small loud-speaker. It was mounted on the wall. Turn this off if you've heard it already. . . . I'm in the basement, make yourself at home. . . . Turn this off if——

Mr. Peepers pushed the switch on the loud-speaker. Stealing nervous, backward glances at it, he entered the living room. He wondered what further evidences of electronic progress Mr. Fernley had devised. Somewhat afraid to get close to anything, Mr. Peepers stood in the center of the floor for a moment. Then he saw an easy chair with a lamp and an end table next to it. He sat down in the chair and the lamp lit up. Startled, Mr. Peepers jumped up from the chair. The lamp went out. He smiled and sat down again. The lamp went on. He tested it several times by raising and lowering himself. Then he quickened his tempo. The lamp flashed on and off like a semaphore. This is rather fun, Mr. Peepers thought, good for signaling the neighbors in an emergency.

At that moment Mr. Fernley entered the living room. He was wiping his hands with a rag and he had his sleeves

A Romantic Student

rolled up. "Oh, hello there," he said. He was a tall, slender man with a very intense demeanor. "Glad to see you made yourself at home." He flung a monkey wrench on the divan and extended his hand.

"I'm Robinson J. Peepers," Mr. Peepers said, standing up. "Helen's science teacher."

"How do you do?" Mr. Fernley said.

When they separated hands Mr. Peepers noticed that his own was covered with blue grease.

"Sorry," Mr. Fernley said. "Been fixin' the Missis' can opener. Here—use this rag."

Mr. Peepers wiped his hands on the rag. It had some sort of reddish paint on it. Mr. Peepers returned the rag. His hand looked like an American flag. "Thank you," he said. He pointed to the closet. "That's a very ingenious idea you have there."

"One of my many inventions," Mr. Fernley said. "Got a million of 'em. Sit down."

"So I've noticed," Mr. Peepers said. He sat down. He got up instantly. He had landed on the monkey wrench.

"Excuse me," Mr. Fernley said, throwing the monkey wrench on a chair. "Of course," he continued, "some of my inventions still have some bugs in them." He pulled Mr. Peepers' arm away from the wall. "Careful of those exposed wires," he said, adding, "By the way, I can't guarantee you'll get your own coat back."

Mr. Peepers raised his eyebrows. "Oh? But there's a test tube full of young polyps in the left-hand pocket."

Mr. Fernley nodded. "Don't worry about it. Everything seems to turn up in the laundry chute sooner or later. I don't know why."

Mr. Peepers

Helen and Mrs. Fernley entered the parlor. "Mr. Peepers!" Helen said excitedly. "Golly, it was nice of you to come over. This is my mom."

"How do you do, Mrs. Fernley," Mr. Peepers said. He began to shake hands but remembered the grease and changed his mind.

Mrs. Fernley looked puzzled. "Hello, Mr. Peepers," she said softly.

Mr. Fernley slapped Mr. Peepers on the back. "Helen tells us you're just about the smartest teacher at school, Peepers."

"Daddy . . ." Helen said.

"Yes, sir," Mr. Fernley continued. "Smart as a whip, she says."

"Daddy, please . . ." Helen said.

Mr. Fernley stared at his daughter. "Well?" he said. "You're always saying it, aren't you?" He nudged Mr. Peepers clubbily. "Talks on about you like you were her beau or something." He looked at Helen again and his expression flattened. "Yes, sir," he said grimly, "talks on and on and on and on and——"

Mr. Peepers thought it advisable to interrupt. "Er . . . as a matter of fact, that's what I——"

"Sit down, son," Mr. Fernley said. "Yessirreee, Bob," he said, laughing, "Helen thinks you're the bee's knees!"

Mr. Peepers reddened slightly. "Well, I think Helen's an extremely bright girl herself." He wished that Helen were out of the room, so that he could speak candidly. "A very bright girl," he added, lamely.

"Well, you don't have to tell me, son," Mr. Fernley boasted. "I taught her everything she knows."

Mrs. Fernley shifted a little in her chair. "I wish you'd

A Romantic Student

let me teach her how to dance," she said, with some emphasis.

Mr. Fernley grimaced. "Oh, there you go, Agnes, always wanting Helen to waste her time."

Mr. Peepers sensed that the nub of the situation was at hand. "It might not be a bad idea," he said carefully. "She'd be better acquainted with boys her own age." Despite Helen's haunting presence, Mr. Peepers felt it advisable at least to hint at the problem in some way. "That leads me——" he began, but Mr. Fernley interrupted.

"Peepers," he said sternly, "let's keep this in the realm of pure science. Helen's a quick one in the mind. I'd like to see her *mind* advanced. Now, you take me—twenty-seven years in the cement business and I hate it."

Mrs. Fernley shook her head ruefully. "The cement business has been awfully good to us, Sam Fernley."

"But one of these days," Mr. Fernley continued, "an invention of mine is really going to pay off. Got an outfit in Los Angeles interested in one of my ideas right now."

Mr. Peepers nodded. The situation looked hopeless. Helen was grinning at him like a predatory animal. Not only that, Mr. Fernley's preoccupation with his hobby seemed insurmountable. Mr. Peepers decided to blow with the prevailing breeze. "What sort of invention is that, Mr. Fernley?"

Mr. Fernley smiled proudly. "You're sitting on it right now," he said. "It's my Tabedco—combination couch, bed and table—should revolutionize the entire household industry. I figure they can make the thing for, ohhh, say a hundred and seventy-five dollars easily."

"Sounds very reasonable," Mr. Peepers said.

At that moment Helen Fernley, who had been sitting on

Mr. Peepers

the floor, became so occupied with keeping Mr. Peepers in her line of vision that when her father crossed in front of him she lost her equilibrium and fell to the side.

"Helen," Mr. Fernley said, frowning, "what are you doing?"

"Nothing, Papa," Helen said, righting herself. "Mr. Peepers, how tall are you?"

"What's that?" Mr. Fernley said. "What kind of a question is that?"

"Behave yourself, dear," Mrs. Fernley said to Helen.

Mr. Fernley shrugged and began pacing again. "Never say die is my motto, Peepers. If one invention doesn't sell, hit 'em with another one."

Mrs. Fernley interrupted. "Like your invention for the kitchen, I suppose. The last time I went in there I was almost electrocuted."

"Now, Ethel," Mr. Fernley said, "it was your own fault. Hanging on the wall, as big as life, was a sign that said 'High Voltage.'"

"You know very well the lights were off, Sam Fernley," Mrs. Fernley countered.

Mr. Peepers decided to give it one more try. It seemed an opportune time. "I hate to talk and run," he said, "but I have some papers to correct at home, and I'd like very much to discuss something——"

"Oh, Peepers, no," Mr. Fernley said. "You can't go before you see the Tabedco in action. Only take a second. Stand up, please."

Mr. Peepers complied.

"Simplest thing in the world to operate, Peepers," Mr. Fernley said, pulling levers at the sides of the couch. "Watch it . . . the Fernley Tabedco . . . turns every house

A Romantic Student

into a hotel, one room into a paradise." Mr. Fernley pushed a button and the couch became a long, fully made bed. "Lie on it, Peepers," Mr. Fernley commanded.

Mr. Peepers obeyed reluctantly, feeling rather like a ventriloquist's dummy.

"Bounce on it!" Mr. Fernley said. "She'll hold up."

Mr. Peepers saw the upside-down faces of Mrs. Fernley and Helen staring at him. Helen looked as though she were crying. Then he remembered her disquieting grin. He decided that he preferred seeing her upside down.

"Go on!" Mr. Fernley said. "Make a circus out of it!"

Mr. Peepers bounced sheepishly. He wondered if Mr. Fernley did this to all his guests.

"Ever feel anything so comfortable in your life?" Mr. Fernley said gleefully. "Of course you haven't. Can't you just see the commercial on television?"

"I don't have a set," Mr. Peepers said, as he stopped bouncing.

"Now, if you'll just get up again, Peepers," Mr. Fernley said, "I'll show you the coop de grass."

Mr. Peepers rose and straightened his clothing. Sam Fernley hummed happily, pulling levers and pressing buttons. The Tabedco began to move in what looked like several directions. Things closed and opened and overlapped each other. In a matter of seconds the bed had become a dining table, complete with place mats and silver.

"There we go!" Mr. Fernley said. "What do you think of that?"

Mr. Peepers was flabbergasted. "That's remarkable!"

"Correct," Mr. Fernley said.

Mr. Peepers bent over the table to see how it worked. "How do you get this silver to stay on here?" he asked.

[85]

Mr. Peepers

"It's glued on," Mr. Fernley said. "Not very practical, I know, but I think I can work it with removable clamps. Yessirreee, I knew you'd like her. Wait a minute. I'll show you the candelabra I'm going to put in there." Mr. Fernley hurried to a closet and began tugging at something on one of the shelves.

"Help!" Mr. Peepers cried. He had pushed one of the buttons. The bottom of the Tabedco had moved up and clamped his hand between two unfriendly pieces of metal. "I'm stuck!" he cried. "All I did was push a button. . . ."

Mr. Fernley stared at him for a moment. "Er . . . that's one of them bugs I've got to work out," he said. "Excuse me. I'll go get my tool box."

Mrs. Fernley left the room with him, leaving Mr. Peepers alone with Helen. The amorous young lady immediately came closer and widened her eyes. "Mr. Peepers," she whispered to the helpless science teacher, "how tall *are* you?"

Fortunately, Mr. Fernley was able to free Mr. Peepers shortly thereafter with the aid of a monkey wrench and a crowbar. He apologized profusely, but Mr. Peepers demurred and told him he thought the Tabedco a very unusual contrivance.

He bade the Fernleys good-by as cheerfully as possible, trying to keep from rubbing his wrist in their presence.

The love light in Helen's eyes very nearly blinded him as he departed. On his way down the Fernleys' front walk, Mr. Peepers shook his head. He thought it was a shame that Mr. Fernley didn't allow Helen to be a normal young girl like her schoolmates. Mr. Peepers knew now why Helen had such a crush on him. Mr. Fernley had taught her contempt for the ordinary adolescent activities. Her mind was

A Romantic Student

crammed to the bursting point with science and mental prowess. Aside from her interest in the movies, her father had done a good job of making her grown up before her time.

As Mr. Peepers retired for the evening, secure in the uneventful normalness of his single-function bed, he wondered if parents would ever learn to leave their children alone as his own parents had him. Perhaps Helen could be encouraged to go to one of Mrs. Mandible's after-school dancing classes. As he was falling asleep, he thought of telephoning Mr. Fernley and suggesting it.

The following day, in the cloakroom, Helen Fernley ran breathlessly to Mary Ellen Gleeb. "Mary Ellen!" she whispered. "Oh, guess what?"

"Golly, you're all excited," Mary Ellen said.

"Guess!" said Helen, jumping up and down.

"You're going to marry Mr. Peepers," Mary Ellen said.

"No!" Helen said. "Daddy got a letter from Los Angeles this morning. A company out there is going to manufacture his rotating typewriter. Isn't that exciting?"

"Gosh!" Mary Ellen said.

"And we're going to live out there," Helen said. "Imagine! Only a couple of miles from Hollywood!"

"Gee, how dreamy!" Mary Ellen said. "Montgomery Clift!"

"And Stewart Granger!"

"And Jerry Lewis!" Mary Ellen said. "Gee, you're lucky. . . . When are you leaving?"

"Daddy's leaving right away," Helen said, "and Mommy and I will go in about a week."

"Have you told the teachers yet?"

Mr. Peepers

Helen Fernley gasped. Suddenly she realized what was happening. Since her father's proud announcement of the news at breakfast, she had not thought of anything else. Now Mr. Peepers stood before her, long-faced and wounded, reminding her of all her pledges and responsibilities. She felt like Susan Hayward in "The Betrayer."

"Oh, my gosh," she said softly. "How'll I break this to Mr. Peepers? You know how we feel about each other."

"Yeah . . . golly. He'll be heartbroken."

In a flash, Helen remembered that life was life, after all, and romance fleeting, as Bette Davis had so often said. "Well," she said, "he'll have to find out sometime. See you later, Mary."

She thought she would go to see Mr. Peepers in his science room. She was sure he'd understand. After all, a girl had to take advantage of her opportunities.

In the science room, Mr. Peepers was talking to Nancy Remington. ". . . and then her father got to talking about his inventions," he was saying, "and I didn't get a word in."

"That's a shame, Robinson," Nancy said. "Perhaps you can call him later today."

"I'm going to," Mr. Peepers said. "I've already talked to Miss Monitor about having Helen join the girls' basketball team."

"Good idea," Nancy said.

The door opened suddenly. Helen Fernley stopped short. "Oh, I'm sorry . . ." she said.

"No, come in, dear," Nancy said. "I was just leaving. See you later, Robinson."

Mr. Peepers smiled at her gratefully. "Good-by, Nancy," he said.

As the door closed, Helen took a step toward him. She

A Romantic Student

clasped her hands at her breast. "Oh, Mr. Peepers!" she said dramatically.

Mr. Peepers was instantly on the defensive. He backed up and bumped into his desk. "Er . . . Helen," he said, "did you want to see me about something?"

"Oh, yes, Mr. Peepers," Helen said tearfully. "Something very important."

Mr. Peepers made an effort to seem calm. "Oh?"

Helen Fernley sighed deeply. She looked at him with compassion. "Mr. Peepers," she whispered, "you'd better sit down."

Mr. Peepers was startled. It seemed to him that he had heard those words before. He complied with Helen's request.

"This is going to hurt me worse than it hurts you," Helen began. "Oh, Mr. Peepers, dear—our family is moving to Los Angeles in a week, and I . . . I won't be seeing you any more and I . . ." She brought one hand to her face and thought of Joan Crawford in "The Sufferer." "Oh, Mr. Peepers," she added loudly, "don't you understand? I'm no good! These are crazy times we live in. I'm a mixed-up kid. And this whole wonderful crazy romantic world is all upside down!"

Sobbing bitterly, she ran from the classroom.

Mr. Peepers stared after her for a long, long time. It seemed to him as though she'd left a trail of smoke. He took a handkerchief from his pocket and wiped his forehead with it. He wondered if Helen wasn't younger than he'd thought, after all. Perhaps he had exaggerated the situation. Mr. Peepers smiled. He felt very lucky. A wiser authority than he had handled the problem with dexterity and discretion. Peepers' Law would have to be revised.

Mr. Peepers

Later that afternoon he had a minor contretemps with Mrs. Gurney. She insisted on examining his polyps through the microscope. She kept it up for five minutes, drawing scribble after scribble on a piece of paper.

"Mrs. Gurney," he said quietly, "I have to have those polyps diagnosed for this afternoon's science period."

"I'll be through in a moment," Mrs. Gurney said, smiling. "Lovely. Lovely!"

Mr. Peepers was really impatient. "What are you doing?" he asked.

Mrs. Gurney giggled. "I'm copying this doily pattern, of course. If only they'd hold still . . ."

Mr. Peepers looked at his watch. He thought of insisting, but decided against it. After all, there could be worse problems. Walter Murdock had not thrown a paper airplane for two mornings in a row. And Leonard Gorf had said "Hello" at lunchtime without adding "Sir." If Mrs. Gurney's cheerful silliness was all Mr. Peepers had to put up with, he would be a very happy man.

"Well," he said cheerfully, "the bitter with the sweet."

"What did you say?" Mrs. Gurney murmured.

"Nothing, Mrs. Gurney," Mr. Peepers said, smiling. "You take all the time you want."

CHAPTER IV

Life among the Meat Packers

It wasn't long after Wes Weskit began going out with Marge Bellows that they became engaged. Mr. Peepers was amazed and delighted. It seemed to him that Wes Weskit should indeed settle down.

"Congratulations!" he said happily to Wes when he heard the news.

"Yep," Wes said, grinning, "it's ball-and-chain time."

But Marge had to return to Chicago to "prepare my parents," as she put it. Soon after, Wes received a letter asking him to come on and meet them. He told Mr. Peepers about it. "I've got to help mend the fences," he said. He took a week's leave of absence from the school. Before

Mr. Peepers

he left, he asked Mr. Peepers to visit Chicago over the week end. "Marge's brother is giving a stag party for me," he said, nudging Mr. Peepers and winking. "Bring your best stag."

"I don't know any, Wes," Mr. Peepers said, smiling. But he agreed to make the trip.

That week end he made his good-bys to Nancy at the station and boarded the train feeling light of heart. Mr. Peepers liked to travel. He felt it broadened a person.

Toward the end of the trip, however, he began to get a little bored. He had read two copies of *Botany in Color* and one of the *National Geographic*. The time had come, it seemed to him, for a little socializing with his fellow passengers.

There was a rather corpulent gentleman seated next to him, looking out of the window. Mr. Peepers saw no harm in striking up a friendly conversation. His Grandmother had always said: Give of yourself to others and they will give of themselves to you, if they have anything to give. Mr. Peepers had a great deal of respect for his Grandmother.

He smiled carefully at the man. The man wasn't looking at him, but Mr. Peepers smiled anyway. He felt that people could *feel* a nice smile.

"I'm going to Chicago!" he said suddenly.

The man turned his face slowly. He stared at Mr. Peepers. A moment later he returned his gaze to the window.

Mr. Peepers nodded. "Illinois," he said.

The man ignored him.

Mr. Peepers decided to persevere. "One of my colleagues at the school where I teach is getting married."

The man shifted in his seat and coughed.

Life among the Meat Packers

"His name is Harvey Weskit," Mr. Peepers said, "though we all call him Wes. His friends in Chicago are giving him a pre-wedding stag party."

There was no response from the corpulent man.

"That's why I'm going to Chicago," Mr. Peepers said. Then he paused for a moment. "Illinois," he added.

The man showed no sign of unbending. Mr. Peepers twiddled his thumbs for a moment. Then he began to sing softly: "Chicago, Chicago, that rollicking town . . ." He glanced at the man. The man's eyes were closed. Mr. Peepers sighed. Perhaps, he thought, the poor fellow has nothing to give. Still, he wished he could inveigle him into a word or two. Mr. Peepers glanced at him again. He smiled doubly hard.

"Want to play animal, vegetable or mineral?" he asked.

The man's eyes opened. He looked at Mr. Peepers. He lifted his left arm to reveal that he was handcuffed to the window seat.

Mr. Peepers stifled a gasp and kept his peace for the remainder of the journey.

It was a long cab ride from the railroad station to the Bellows address. Mr. Peepers was delighted with the opportunity to observe Chicago first hand. Certainly is a big city, he thought. In fact, the largest in the Midwest and the second largest in the country. Mr. Peepers smiled. While a mere slip of a schoolboy, he had made a Commencement speech entitled, "Chicago—the Second Largest City, or Hog Butcher for the Nation." He still remembered it with pleasure. The applause had lasted for nearly half a minute.

The taxi pulled to a halt in front of what looked to Mr. Peepers like a mansion. After gaping silently for a mo-

Mr. Peepers

ment, he paid the driver and added a ten-cent tip. The cabbie scowled at him and drove away muttering. Mr. Peepers was confused. It seemed to him that ten cents was very generous. Old Harry Stubbs, who drove the cab in Jefferson City, never accepted any tips at all. Perhaps the custom in large cities is a bit different, he thought. I shall have to ask Wes about that.

Making his way through the tall iron gates and up the carefully tended gravel path, Mr. Peepers felt a little uncomfortable. The Bellows seemed to have an uncommon amount of acreage. There were cottonwood and northern spruce trees flanking the path, and a mixture of arborvitae and elm trees concealing the house. Mr. Peepers felt dwarfed by all the largeness.

Hanging on the front door was an enormous brass knocker with a Christmas wreath around it. The wreath was prolific with large holly berries. Mr. Peepers arranged himself nervously and lifted the knocker. He banged it so hard that a few of the holly berries fell off. The berries made remarkably audible sounds as they struck the ground. Mr. Peepers was startled. He wondered if the berries were stale. He bent down to pick them up, thinking, I can jam them back on. . . .

It was while he was in that compromising position that a butler in livery opened the door. Mr. Peepers straightened up quickly and smiled. He handed the berries to the butler. "I believe these belong to you," he said. "They're the berries . . . I mean . . ."

The butler nodded. "Whom did you wish to see?" he asked coolly.

"My name's Robinson Peepers. I'm a friend of Mr. Weskit's."

Life among the Meat Packers

The butler smiled. "Oh, yes," he said warmly, "we've been expecting you. Please come in."

He took Mr. Peepers' hat and coat. Tit for tat, Mr. Peepers took it upon himself to close the door. By accident he slammed it rather hard. His ears were rewarded by what sounded like a volley of muffled rifle shots. Apparently the berries. Mr. Peepers opened the door to reveal a skeleton wreath. The berries were scattered all over the ground. He gulped and glanced at the butler. "An inferior grade of berry, perhaps," he murmured.

The butler nodded and carried Mr. Peepers' ear muffs to the closet.

At that moment, a young man came thundering down the stairs. He rounded the newel post rapidly and pulled up short. He was a large, lantern-jawed youth wearing a camel's-hair coat and a Tyrolean hat. A sprig of edelweiss stood jauntily in the band. He glanced at Mr. Peepers and spoke to the butler. His voice was a cocksure, round-voweled bleat.

"If I get any calls," he said, "I'll be at the Gridiron Club."

"Yes, Mr. Bellows." The butler nodded. "This is Mr. Peppers, sir. He's——"

"Peepers," Mr. Peepers said.

"Yes," the butler said. "He's a friend of Mr. Weskit's."

"How are ya?" the young man said loudly. "I'm Marge's brother, Rock Bellows. Put 'er there."

The bone-crushing grip made Mr. Peepers wince. It took him some effort to suppress an outcry.

Rock Bellows grinned. He popped a piece of chewing gum into his mouth. "What was that monicker again?" he asked.

Mr. Peepers

"Monicker?" Mr. Peepers asked.

"Handle," Rock said.

Mr. Peepers paused. "Handle?"

Rock Bellows frowned. "Your name!" he said sharply.

"Oh!" Mr. Peepers said. "Er . . . Peepers." He decided to spell it. "P-double E-P-E-R-S."

Rock Bellows stopped chewing. His enormous jaw hung loose for a moment. "Peepers?" he repeated. "Haw!" Then he began to snort and snigger. "Come on," he said. "What's your *real* name?"

"Peepers," Mr. Peepers said, deciding to conceal his umbrage. "I suppose it is a bit strange," he added, "to those who haven't heard it before."

"Yeah," Rock said, chewing again. "My name's Rock."

Mr. Peepers chuckled. "Rock?" he repeated. "Well, that's rather a humorous . . ."

Rock Bellows cracked his knuckles together. His expression hardened. Suddenly he looked to Mr. Peepers like a motion-picture gangster. Mr. Peepers stopped smiling.

"Uh . . . where's Wes?" he asked lightly.

The butler interceded. "I believe he's in the Green Room, sir. You may wait for him in the library."

Rock Bellows pointed to a large mahogany door. "It's right in there," he said. He looked Mr. Peepers up and down and snorted. "Well," he added, "see ya at the stag party tonight . . . Peepers!" He opened the door and began to laugh. Mr. Peepers could hear him laughing all the way down the path.

"This way, sir," the butler said. He ushered Mr. Peepers into the library and left him alone.

The walls were lined with books. Placed here and there were deep leather chairs such as Mr. Peepers had seen in

Life among the Meat Packers

dentists' offices, and a few ornate lampstands. There was also a three-step ladder on rollers hinged to the bookshelves. Mr. Peepers mounted it happily. He soon discovered a shelfful of volumes entitled *Entomology in Action* by Rodney Tick. Mr. Peepers smiled. They were beautiful books, all identically bound in leather. He selected one volume from the middle, subtitled, *From the Measuring Worm to the Tsetse Fly,* and decided to peruse it for unusual tidbits. It took quite an output of ergs. The books were jammed together very tightly. Mr. Peepers tilted the volume, pushing and pulling, until, finally, it tugged free. He was so eager to scan the pages that he didn't notice the hole between the volumes closing up.

He dismounted the ladder and sat down happily. He had heard a great deal about the late Professor Tick. His daughter, Arethma Tick, was now chief botanist for the University of Chicago. Mr. Peepers had often been entertained by her lectures. Especially the one concerning monocotyledons and the maidenhair tree. Miss Tick's comical premise that angiosperms and gymnosperms were like hostile lovers, vying with each other eternally, but secretly infatuated, had afforded Mr. Peepers a full afternoon of enjoyment. He leafed through the pages eagerly. He was soon disappointed. The book had no photographs and very few illustrations. Not only that, the prose was very dry and pretentious. Mr. Peepers saw that it had been published at the turn of the century. What is the use of a book without pictures? he thought. He closed the volume and remounted the ladder.

When he saw that there was no space left his mouth fell open. He tried to pull two of the books apart. They wouldn't budge. Good Heavens, he thought. Then he

Mr. Peepers

spotted a ruler on a near-by desk. He inserted the ruler between the two volumes, pressing to and fro. The books refused to co-operate. Mr. Peepers began to perspire. Suppose someone comes in, he thought. He pushed a little harder. The ruler snapped in half. Mr. Peepers trembled. "Oh, my!" he murmured. He tried to wedge one finger between the books. He scratched and scraped with the finger until the broken piece of ruler scudded free. Mr. Peepers smiled. Thank heavens, he thought.

Then he wondered what to do with the book. He shrugged, placed it on top of the others and dismounted the ladder. While he was descending, the book fell down behind the shelf. Mr. Peepers heard the sound and looked up. Seeing the book gone, he scratched his head. It seemed to him that the book must have fallen back into its original slot. But how? he wondered. For a moment he stared at the bookshelf. Then he shrugged his shoulders. His Grandmother had always said: If you can't figure something out, let it come back and figure you. She called it the Yankee version of Mahomet and the Mountain. Mr. Peepers decided to follow her advice.

He whistled softly, perusing the shelves. High up on the right there was an enormous volume, two feet high and a foot thick. Mr. Peepers grinned. He enjoyed large books. He adjusted the ladder and made his way to the top. Securing the volume was difficult. It was slightly beyond his reach. Mr. Peepers stood on tiptoe and pushed at the bottom of it with his fingers. The book tumbled loose and catapulted into his arms. Mr. Peepers sank to an unwilling squat. Suddenly he heard the cheerful voice of Wes Weskit.

"Robby!" it shouted. "You old son of a gun!"

Life among the Meat Packers

Mr. Peepers tried to wiggle a greeting. "Hello, Wes," he said, smiling.

"Sport," Wes said proudly, "meet the little woman."

He had put his arm around a bright-faced, blue-eyed, blonde girl who had entered the library with him. She was, of course, Marge Bellows.

"How do you do, Miss Bellows," Mr. Peepers said. He was a trifle out of breath.

"Finally," Marge said gaily, "after hearing so much about you, I meet the great Robinson Peepers."

She extended her hand.

Mr. Peepers' heart sank. He tried to shift the huge book into his left hand. Upon succeeding, he veered dangerously to one side. Wes Weskit reached for the book. "I'll take that," he said. He assisted Mr. Peepers down from the ladder. Mr. Peepers' legs were trembling somewhat. Even simple descent was a task.

On reaching the floor, he smiled at Marge Bellows and shook hands. "Wow!" Wes Weskit said, plopping the huge book on a chair.

Mr. Peepers blushed. "Oh, I'm sorry, Wes. I was rather intrigued by the size of that particular volume."

"Oh, that," Marge said. "It's been in our family for years. It's a composite edition of all dictionaries."

"My!" Mr. Peepers said. "We could use something like that at our school." He stole a sidelong glance at the entomology shelf. Despite his Grandmother, he felt uncomfortably baffled.

"Anything wrong, sport?" Wes said.

"No, no," Mr. Peepers said, "it's just . . . er . . . Lovely home you have here."

"Thank you," Marge said.

"Have a nice trip, amigo?"

"Oh, yes," Mr. Peepers said, "wonderful. We were three and a half minutes late out of Indianapolis. However, the engineer made up the lost time. I believe there was a downgrade as we approached Cicero."

"Swell," Wes said. "Look, Robby—I gotta get some wedding invitations mailed, and I want to check on the stag party, too. So you kids'll excuse me for an hour or so. Okay?"

"You run along, dear," Marge said, smiling. "I'm sure Robby and I can find a lot to talk about."

Wes Weskit's expression changed. Something in Marge's tone seemed to have made him uneasy. Mr. Peepers wondered if Wes anticipated some sort of discussion concerning his romantic past.

"On second thought," Wes said brightly, "maybe I'll stick around for a while."

"That won't be necessary, dear," Marge said warmly. "I know you have things to do."

Wes cleared his throat. "Right!" he said. "See you later." He kissed Marge on the cheek. Once her back was turned, he made frantic signals to Mr. Peepers.

"Is something wrong, Wes?" Mr. Peepers asked.

Marge turned around. Wes smiled broadly. "No, no, nothing. Well . . . see you later!"

As Marge turned back, Mr. Peepers was looking at the entomology shelf again. There must be *some* explanation, he thought.

"Looking for something special?" Marge asked.

"Hm? Oh, no, no," Mr. Peepers said, still staring at the

Life among the Meat Packers

shelf. "Probably a case of humidity's expanding or contracting the books."

"I beg your pardon?" Marge said.

"Nothing," Peepers said, "just talking to myself. What date have you set for your wedding, you and Wes?"

"March fifteenth," Marge said.

Mr. Peepers smiled. "I'd better remember that. I'm to be the best man."

"I know," Marge said. "Wes thinks a great deal of you."

"I think a great deal of him, too," Mr. Peepers said. "We've had some wonderful times together." Mr. Peepers laughed. "My goodness, I'll never forget the time the four of us went out—Nancy Remington and myself and Wes and this terribly pretty . . ." Mr. Peepers caught himself. "Pretty good driver," he said.

Marge Bellows nodded. "I'm sure you had some wonderful times."

"Yes," Mr. Peepers continued. "He's a keen fellow. And very popular, too. He's got a little black book that's just chock-full of . . ." Mr. Peepers nearly strangled. He had done it again. "I suppose you read a lot, too," he said.

Marge smiled. "I sort of felt that Wes was a popular boy the first time we met."

"Oh?" Mr. Peepers said.

"He was with three girls at the time," Marge said. "You see, I knew one of the girls, so I walked over to them and—" Marge made a circling motion with her right hand—"you know," she said.

Mr. Peepers was astonished. "Where did you learn that?" he asked, making the circling motion.

Marge laughed. "Oh, he's told me many things about you

Mr. Peepers

and the school and Jefferson City. He says it's a wonderful town."

"It is," Mr. Peepers said. "Especially this time of year. Snow and everything. You've never seen anything like it. The evergreens are coated with snow and frost, and at night the light from the stars turns them into beautifully decorated Christmas trees . . ." Mr. Peepers paused and blushed. "It's just lovely," he said. For a moment he thought of Jefferson City, and how pretty things were. "Ever eat an icicle?"

Marge giggled. "No, I never have."

Mr. Peepers sucked breath through his teeth. "Oh, it really hurts your molars and bicuspids. Cold!" Mr. Peepers laughed. "First time I ever ate one we were all on a sleigh ride. That crazy Wes."

"What'd he do?"

"He made me eat the icicle," Mr. Peepers said. "He double-dared me. . . . We were acting like a bunch of kids."

"Sounds like loads of fun," Marge said.

"Certainly was. But you'll be in on all that fun as soon as you and Wes get married and come back home."

Marge Bellows was surprised. "Oh . . . didn't Wes tell you?"

"What?"

"Well," Marge said, "after we're married he won't be living in Jefferson City any more."

Mr. Peepers nearly gasped. "He won't?"

Marge shook her head. "We talked it over and . . . Well —my father has offered him a job here with his meat-packing firm."

"Oh," Mr. Peepers said, nodding slowly. He could hardly

Life among the Meat Packers

believe his ears. Wes? he thought. A meat packer? "My," he said, "this is quite a surprise. But, of course—if he *wants* to live in Chicago instead of Jefferson City . . ."

Marge leaned forward and touched his shoulder. "Maybe we'd better get tidied up for tea," she said.

Mr. Peepers nodded.

"Shall we go?" Marge said, rising.

"Yes, yes—of course," Mr. Peepers said. "I'll be right along."

But he lagged behind slightly. Watching Marge leave the room, he ran his finger sadly across one of the bookshelves. A meat-packing firm, he thought. He wondered if he would ever be able to eat packed meat again.

After a quiet supper with Marge, Wes and Mr. Peepers left for the stag party. It was being held at a night club called Randy's Rendezvous. The two friends were a little late arriving. By the time they got to the table, Rock Bellows already had a cigar in his mouth and a drink in his hand. He greeted them loudly, and Wes introduced Mr. Peepers to a quartet of burly men who were grouped around the table smoking cigars and drinking.

"That's Frank Hacker, Robby," Wes said, "ex-All-American fullback from Colgate and that's Buck Loomis, All-American guard from Northwestern; and Stanley Stanislavski, All-American end from Purdue; and Dave Howard from Illinois, All-State."

Dave Howard looked friendly. He was the only one who smiled. "Nice to know you, Peepers," he said. "Glad you could make it."

They shook hands. "Thank you, Mr. Howard," Mr. Peepers said.

Mr. Peepers

"And, of course," Wes Weskit said, "you've already met Rock—all-time All-American."

Mr Peepers tried to look pleasant. "Yes, we've met."

Wes grinned. "Well, that's everybody, sport. Now, sit down and enjoy yourself."

Wes sat down at the head of the table. Mr. Peepers was forced into the end chair, right next to Rock.

"Something to drink?" a table waiter said.

"Oh, no thank you," Mr. Peepers said. "I never imbibe."

"C'mon!" Rock bellowed, "gotta have *one*. Bring the little man a Scotch."

"No, thank you, really," Mr. Peepers said. "I don't——"

"It's your buddy's stag party," Rock said. "It can't hurt ya."

"Well," Mr. Peepers said, "I suppose one little one."

"What'll it be?" the waiter said.

Mr. Peepers paused. "Do you have some cooking sherry?"

Rock Bellows' lower lip collapsed. "Cooking sherry?" he hooted. "Haw!" He began to guffaw loudly.

Dave Howard leaned across the table. "Come on, Rock," he whispered, "cut it out."

Rock Bellows ignored him. "Live a little!" he said to Peepers. "You're acting like a guy who's come to town to spend the egg money!"

While Rock was laughing at his own joke, Mr. Peepers observed the dilation of his pupils. It seemed to him that Rock had already overindulged in alcohol. He mused, with some satisfaction, on the severe Vitamin B deficiency that Rock Bellows would experience the following morning.

Rock's laughter faded gradually to snorting and sniggering. He pulled a large cigar from his pocket.

Life among the Meat Packers

"Have a stogy, Poopers!" he shouted.

"I beg your pardon?"

"A cigar!"

Mr. Peepers shook his head. "I don't smoke," he said softly.

"Aw, come on," Rock said. "Good for what ails you."

Mr. Peepers saw that there was no sense resisting. "Well," he said, giggling slightly, "may as well go whole hog." He placed the cigar carefully in the center of his mouth.

"That's the ticket!" Rock shouted, making quite a show of lighting the cigar.

Mr. Peepers smiled and puffed carefully. Once the cigar was lit, he began to cough. The smoke had affected his sinuses adversely.

Rock Bellows slapped him on the back. "Great, huh?"

"Oh, yes . . . wonnaful," Mr. Peepers said. He had some difficulty enunciating past the cigar, but no one seemed to mind. Wes Weskit smiled at him approvingly. Mr. Peepers smiled back. It wasn't often that a small-town person got to live in the midst of such glitter. Despite Mr. Peepers' basic convictions, he was really beginning to enjoy it.

Suddenly, the lights in the night club dimmed down. A nasal voice on the public-address system loudly announced the beginning of the show. A large spotlight illuminated the center of the floor, and a group of partially clad young ladies hurried out and began dancing.

Rock Bellows leaned back in his chair and grinned. Mr. Peepers stared at him for a moment. Rock was chewing his cigar vigorously, shifting it back and forth from one side of his mouth to the other. Mr. Peepers tried to emulate him.

Mr. Peepers

He rolled the cigar on his tongue slowly. Then he did it faster. The cigar fell out and landed ash-down in his hands. Mr. Peepers suppressed an outcry. But he tried it again. This time the cigar fell onto the floor. Mr. Peepers shrugged. He looked at Rock to see if he were watching. Then he stamped the cigar out.

Wes Weskit leaned over to him. "Having a good time, sport?"

Mr. Peepers smiled. "Oh, yes," he said, "very nice."

Rock Bellows turned to look at them. "Hey!" he said. "Where's your cigar, Peepers?"

"Hm?" Mr. Peepers said. "Oh, I . . . ah . . . finished it."

"Have another one!" Rock shouted.

"No thanks—really," Mr. Peepers said.

"Aw, come on," Rock said. "Why not?"

"Well," Mr. Peepers said, "I'm . . . ah . . . er . . . I'm in training."

Rock Bellows lifted his eyebrows. "No kiddin'?" he said. "Well—good for you, fella," he added, putting the cigar away. Then he leaned forward and grinned. "So—you're gonna be best man at the wedding, huh?"

"Yes," Mr. Peepers said. "You see—I'm Wes's best friend."

"Hmph!" Rock said. "Weskit!" He looked at Wes, who was enjoying the floor show. Then he leaned closer to Mr. Peepers and whispered: "Just can't figure my sister marrying a guy who never played football. Can't figure it."

"Well," Mr. Peepers said softly, "Wes makes up in intelligence for what he might lack in physical prowess."

Rock Bellows stared at him. "I don't care much for guys

Life among the Meat Packers

who never played football," he said. He cracked his knuckles brutally. The sound made Mr. Peepers chilly.

"I've played a little *touch* football," he said. Rock's face was impassive. "Two handed," Mr. Peepers added.

"Guys what never played football," Rock said, "I don't dig."

Mr. Peepers nodded. "I also played a little volley ball."

"Football players are different," Rock said. "They got guts."

"On occasion, I dabbled in table tennis," Mr. Peepers said.

"But I'll make a man out of Weskit yet," Rock said. "Wait'll I get him down at the meat plant. I'm gonna be his boss down there." He cracked his knuckles, both hands at a time.

"How nice," Mr. Peepers said brightly. He thought of cautioning Rock about arthritis of the knuckles, but decided against it. Rock winked at him, iron-jawed, and returned to the show.

Mr. Peepers sat frowning for a moment. He didn't think he liked Rock Bellows very well. And he was more than disappointed about Wes Weskit's decision to give up teaching and Jefferson City. He was genuinely concerned.

He glanced covertly at Rock Bellows to see if he were fully absorbed in the entertainment. He was indeed absorbed. He was, in fact, transfixed. Mr. Peepers made careful finger signals at Wes Weskit.

"Say, Wes . . ." he whispered.

Wes leaned closer to him. "What is it, sport?" he said.

"About your coming here to live . . . er . . . are you really giving up teaching?"

Mr. Peepers

"Well, I——" Wes began, but a burst of fanfare interrupted. "Talk to you later, sport," Wes said. "I don't want to miss this act."

A very provocative-looking girl stepped into a blue spotlight. She had long blonde hair and a deep, sultry voice. Mr. Peepers found her lack of sufficient clothing a little embarrassing. Not only that, she was singing in French. He gathered, however, that it was a classical piece of one sort or another. A loud voice on the public-address system had announced her as: "Francine! . . . Singing 'Symphony.'"

Rock Bellows glanced at Mr. Peepers. "Murder, eh, Peeper?" he said. He nudged Mr. Peepers clubbily with his elbow. Mr. Peepers doubled over.

"She's very nice!" he gasped.

"Very nice?" Rock said. "She's dynamite!"

"Well, I think I'd enjoy it more," Mr. Peepers whispered, "if I understood French. The language requirement for a bachelor of science degree is technical German."

"Are you kiddin'?" Rock said. "Who needs words!"

Francine left the center of the floor and began a round of the tables. She toyed expertly with neckties and balding heads, pirouetted sexily and rolled her stomach.

Rock Bellows nudged Mr. Peepers. "Wow!" he said.

Mr. Peepers tried to smile. "She's awfully well co-ordinated," he said.

Francine arrived at their table, still singing and undulating. She drew her silky handkerchief past the noses of the football players. They all grunted and moaned. Then she found Mr. Peepers. She wrapped the handkerchief around his head, so that he looked like Little Red Riding Hood. She sat on his lap and sang softly in his ear. She mussed his

Life among the Meat Packers

hair and made a great show of playing ticktacktoe on his necktie. She took a sip of his cooking sherry and almost gagged. Mr. Peepers was very embarrassed. As she left, Rock Bellows guffawed loudly. Mr. Peepers knocked over his sherry. It spilled all over his sleeve.

"Excuse me," he said, standing up. "I'd better get cleaned up."

"Yeah!" Rock said loudly. "You musta set your sleeve on fire with that cooking sherry."

Mr. Peepers blushed. As he turned to go, he bumped into a pillar. Everyone at the table howled except Dave Howard and Wes. Mr. Peepers said, "Excuse me," and made his way to the men's room.

"Hey, Weskit!" Rock bellowed. "Where'd ya ever find this guy Peepers? He's a real character!"

"Come on, Rock," Dave said, "lay off him."

Wes Weskit tried to seem casual. "Peepers is a very bright fella, Rock," he said. "Got a lot on the ball."

"Him?" Rock snorted. "He's a real jerk. The minute I saw him I knew he'd come to town to spend the egg money."

Stanley Stanislavski laughed goonily. "Egg money," he repeated slowly.

"He happens to be a very good friend of mine, Rock," Wes said, bristling. "Now let's forget it and watch the show."

"Who needs a show," Rock said, "when you've got Peepers around?"

"Rock," Wes said, "I'm asking you as a friend, and as a future brother-in-law, to please cut it out. Robby's very sensitive and I——"

Mr. Peepers

Rock interrupted, waving his hand. "Aw, who cares," he said. "Let's face it. He's strictly hayseed."

Mr. Peepers stood behind the pillar, hiding. He had heard Wes's defense of him and Rock Bellows' final remark. After a moment of silence, he emerged from behind the pillar and started to sit down.

"Hold it a second, Rob," Wes said. He took hold of Mr. Peepers' arm and led him away from the table. "Listen," he whispered, "I know you were planning to stay and see the rest of the show . . . but . . . ah . . . Well, something came up. So let's go."

"But it's early, Wes . . ."

"Come on, sport," Wes said.

As they were getting their coats from the hat-check girl, a bewildered Mr. Peepers reopened the issue. "But we didn't say good-by to Rock and the fellows," he said.

"To heck with them," Wes said. "I hope they all get fried in cooking sherry."

They took a cab to the Bellows residence. Much to Mr. Peepers' surprise, Wes said curtly: "Wait for me here," and entered the house alone. Two minutes later he emerged and ordered the driver to the railroad station. His expression was very set and determined. Mr. Peepers was afraid to talk to him. They boarded an idle train, and Wes deliberately chose an almost empty car. He flopped into the seat furiously and jammed his hands into his pockets. Mr. Peepers stole occasional peeks at him. He was very concerned. He hoped Wes wasn't making any sacrifices on his account. Finally, he could hold his peace no longer.

"Wes," he said, "I'm sorry, but, well, I don't understand. I thought we were going to catch the midnight train—" Mr Peepers pointed to his watch—"It's only ten-twenty-six."

Life among the Meat Packers

"This train leaves at ten-thirty," Wes said grimly.

"But, Wes . . ."

"Let's not discuss it. . . . Okay, amigo?"

"But you didn't even say good-by to Marge."

Wes Weskit chafed. "I left her a note."

Mr. Peepers shook his head. He couldn't believe that Wes had gotten offended over something as trivial as Rock's remarks. "Wes," he said, hesitantly.

"Hmmmmmm?"

"There's something you're not telling me. What is it? Are you angry at me?"

Wes Weskit looked at Mr. Peepers. "Uh-uh," he murmured.

"Did I drink too much cooking sherry?"

Wes laughed. "No, of course not, Robby." He put his arm around Peepers. "It's just that . . . Well, sport, I guess Chicago just isn't for me. I've had it."

Mr. Peepers was elated. "You mean you aren't going to live here? You're going to continue teaching at Jefferson City?"

Wes nodded. "For the rest of my life, I hope."

"But what about Marge?" Mr. Peepers said. "She's planning . . ."

"Yeah, I know," Wes said. Suddenly he sat up straight. "Look, sport—maybe I'd better catch the later train. I'd like to see her and explain my note. I'll see you at school Monday."

He hurried down the aisle before Mr. Peepers had a chance to say good-by. On the way to the platform, he bumped bodily into Marge. She was carrying the big dictionary from the library.

"Marge! Baby!" Wes cried.

Mr. Peepers

"Oh, Wes!" Marge said. "Dave Howard told me what happened at the stag party. Rock insulting Robby and all —I was furious. . . ."

Wes threw his arms around her. "Aw, let's forget it, honey," he said. "Come on—I'll get you off this train."

"No," Marge said proudly, "I'm going with you— Where's Robby?"

"But Marge . . ." Wes said.

Marge strode assertively down the aisle. "Robby . . . ?" she said.

"Why, Marge," Mr. Peepers said. "What are . . . ?"

"I've brought you a book," she said.

Wes's face appeared over Marge's shoulder. He was smiling broadly. "She claims she's going with us."

"Oh! That's wonderful!" Mr. Peepers said.

"You did such a good job of describing Jefferson City," Marge said, "I'm coming down for the holidays."

"And you and Wes," Mr. Peepers said, "are really going to live there after you marry?"

"Right," Wes said.

"Check, sport!" Marge said.

"Wow!" Mr. Peepers said.

Wes Weskit put his arm around Marge, and they all settled down. The conductor went through the train shouting BOAARD! and the train chugged slowly out of the station.

Later, when Marge and Wes fell asleep head to head, Robinson Peepers pulled the shade down on the window. He didn't want the moonlight to awaken his friends.

CHAPTER V

Snowbound

ON NANCY REMINGTON'S BIRTHDAY, which fell on a Friday, Mr. Peepers went to Charley's Palace of Tonsor for a haircut. His heart was light. He loved celebrations. Especially birthdays. Especially Nancy's. Moreover, the whole thing had worked out very conveniently. Mr. Peepers got his hair cut on alternate Fridays at lunchtime, no matter what.

Wes Weskit accompanied him "for laughs," as he put it. "Also to skip lunch," he said. "I'm on a diet."

Mr. Peepers frowned. He did not approve of meal-skipping. He regarded regular replenishment of the glucose in the blood stream as essential. Getting a haircut instead of lunch was unfortunately a bimonthly necessity, but Mr.

Mr. Peepers

Peepers always fortified himself with B-complex capsules beforehand. Sometimes he also took along a pocketful of sugar cubes to combat stomach growl. He offered a cube to Wes now before entering the barbershop.

Wes shook his head. "Uh-uh," he said. "Marge says I'm too fat for a wedding."

"You shouldn't starve yourself," Mr. Peepers said.

Wes sighed. "It's the only way."

Charley's Palace of Tonsor was a two-chair barbershop with one barber. The barber was named Charley. He was a dandy fellow. At least Mr. Peepers thought so. He had one of those backwoods cracker-barrel senses of humor which Mr. Peepers always found so affable. One time, Mr. Peepers had laughed so heartily at one of Charley's jokes that Charley had accidentally stabbed Mr. Peepers' neck with the scissors. After that, Mr. Peepers controlled his risibilities. It wasn't too difficult really. Charley's jokes got a little monotonous after a while. Indeed, Wes Weskit often complained that there hadn't been a new one in months.

While Mr. Peepers got his hair cut, Wes sat quietly reading a magazine called *Girls! Girls!*. Mr. Peepers was peering carefully at his own image in the mirror. He had to watch Charley's actions like a hawk. Charley was not a very dependable barber. In fact, he was not the original Charley. The shop had been founded by another Charley: an eccentric little man who hated people and hair. Whenever the original Charley saw Mr. Peepers entering the shop, he used to scowl and say: "When are you going to go bald?" Mr. Peepers had always found it very entertaining. In fact, the whole town had come to believe that the original Charley was only spoofing; that he really liked being a barber. But, sure enough, one day he sold the barbershop and ran

Snowbound

away with a medicine show. It turned out he'd just been waiting for a buyer named Charley all along. He had a sense of the rightness of things that way. The present Charley bought the shop and had been telling old jokes and mutilating innocent heads ever since. Mr. Peepers called him Charles the Second. Wes Weskit called him Henry the Eighth.

When Charley picked up a pair of hand clippers, Mr. Peepers was instantly tense. Charley had a tendency to inscribe half-moons over the ears. Mr. Peepers felt they made him look like a convict.

"Not too high in the back, Charley," he whispered.

"Gotcha," Charley said, poising the clippers for action.

"Trash!" Wes Weskit said suddenly. "Pure, unadulterated trash!" He tossed *Girls! Girls!* aside and picked up a magazine called *Boys! Boys!*.

"Why do you read them, Wes?" Mr. Peepers asked.

Wes shrugged. "I don't need a haircut," he said.

"You better take your specs off, Mr. Peepers," Charley said.

"Oh, yes, Charley," Mr. Peepers said. "Excuse me."

"Do an extra nice job, Charley," Wes Weskit said. "The sport has a pretty heavy date tonight."

Mr. Peepers blushed. "Aww, come on, Wes . . ."

Charley chuckled. "Goin' steppin', eh?"

Mr. Peepers nodded happily. "Yes. It's Nancy Remington's birthday, and we're going dinner dancing. She's the school nurse."

Charley held Mr. Peepers' head and looked in the mirror. "How's that over the ears?" he asked.

"Splendid," Mr. Peepers said.

Charley chortled and snickered. "Goin' steppin', eh?"

Mr. Peepers

"Uh-huh," Mr. Peepers said. "The four of us are going to the South Seas House of Italy restaurant in Midville."

"Oh, yeah," Charley said, nodding. "That's where they got that doggone spaghetti and poi."

"Don't tell Nancy," Mr. Peepers cautioned. "It's a surprise party. She knows I'm taking her out, but she doesn't know that Wes and his girl Marge are going to be there."

Wes glanced out of the window. "Looks like snow," he said. Then he looked at his watch. "See if you can speed it up, will ya, Chaz? We have to be back at school pretty quick."

Charley nodded and grinned. "High altitudes bother ya, Mr. Peepers?" he asked slyly.

Mr. Peepers was puzzled. "Why, no. Why?"

There was a fierce glint in Charley's eyes. "I'm gonna pump up the chair!" he cried, laughing immoderately.

Wes Weskit folded a magazine called *Pulchra-Parade*. "Trash!" he shouted. "Pure, unadul——" He gave up and tossed it aside. Looking again at his watch, he got up restlessly and went to the plate-glass window. The weatherman had predicted snow. There was even some town talk about a blizzard. Wes stared through the window for a moment. A tiny snowflake flew against it, right at his nose. Wes grinned.

"Here she comes!" he said gaily.

Mr. Peepers smiled happily. "Snow?" he asked.

Wes nodded. A few translucent flakes were flying haphazardly in the air. "Uh-huh," he said. "Kind of light, though."

Charley grunted. "Light now mebbe, but I'd say we're in for a good one." Charley loved to talk about the weather.

Snowbound

Wes strolled to beside the barber chair. "What time are you going to pick up Nancy, sport?"

"We're leaving right from school. She's going to wear her best dress today instead of her uniform."

"Nice," Wes said.

"Yep," Charley said, "light now mebbe . . ."

"It's blue," Mr. Peepers said, "and around the neck there's a big ruffly part that looks like a curtain."

Wes nodded gravely. "Nan has excellent taste."

"Yep," Charley sighed, "light now mebbe . . . but I'd say we're in for a good one."

"Oh, Rob," Wes said, "before I forget, here are the keys to my coupé. I borrowed Fred Wilson's car."

Mr. Peepers smiled gratefully. He thought it was awfully nice of Wes to keep lending him his car. Even if it was a 1935 Airflow. "Thanks an awful lot, Wes," he said, taking the keys. "Does it have gas in it?"

Wes thought for a moment. "It's a little light now maybe," he said.

Charley was right in there. "But I'd say we're in for a good one!" he said. He brushed the stray hair strands from Mr. Peepers' neck. Then he secured a bottle of Dandy Dressing. He squirted several drops onto Mr. Peepers' head and began massaging vigorously. Mr. Peepers always enjoyed the massage. It made him feel like a person of some importance. He smiled and closed his eyes, while Charley blithely expatiated on the weather. "Hope she don't snow as hard as she did in forty-six," he said. "There was a doozy for ya. Came down like fury. Couldn't move from the house. Couldn't get the car started for two hours."

Charley stopped massaging and removed a comb from his

Mr. Peepers

breast pocket. Still chattering, he began to part Mr. Peepers' hair in the middle. Mr. Peepers opened his eyes quickly. He saw that Charley was going to give him another one of those slicked-down, old-fashioned hair combs.

"Charley . . ." he said quietly.

Charley ignored him. "Not for two hours," he said. "Y'know, I had to prime that car. Was drivin' a twenty-eight Reo then. Good car, too."

Mr. Peepers protested several times, but Charley was too voluble and energetic to be stopped. Mr. Peepers gave up. He supposed he would just have to recomb his hair after he left the shop. That meant stopping in a doorway somewhere and having Wes stand in front of him to hide the sight from passers-by. Charley finished the coiffure and stepped back proudly. Mr. Peepers' hair was black and flat against his head. The part in the middle looked like a highway.

"Well—there y'are!" Charley said happily. "If I hadn'ta known you since you was a tot, I'da mistook ya for Rudolph Valentino."

Mr. Peepers got up from the chair and stood before Wes Weskit with no expression on his face. He pointed to his hair comb.

Wes Weskit nodded. "Great," he said. "Does he keep a shaving mug with your name on it?"

Mr. Peepers stared wanly into the mirror. "He does it every time," he murmured.

The two friends put on their coats and mufflers. After Mr. Peepers had paid Charley, they stared out of the window at the snow. The flakes were getting thicker and whiter. Some of them were beginning to cling together on the ground.

Snowbound

"Still snowing," Wes murmured. "Not too bad though."

Mr. Peepers nodded. "Little light now maybe, but I'd say we're in for a good one."

Wes Weskit stared at him. "Put your hat on, sport."

They made a rapid way through the gathering storm. Mr. Peepers had to get back to his classroom early. He had made a post-lunch appointment with Elwood Hamper to give him a reprimand. Mr. Peepers disliked reprimands, but Elwood was really getting out of hand. The previous week, for three days in a row, the boy had painted Sara Everett's pigtails with guava jelly. Mr. Peepers had kept him after school and made him write "Guava jelly is not a hair tonic" on the blackboard one hundred times. He had also telephoned the boy's parents, asking them to curtail Elwood's supply of jams, jellies and peanut butter. The parents agreed to co-operate but asked Mr. Peepers to handle Elwood unaided otherwise because, as they put it, "We give up." The damages to Sara Everett's hair-do ceased by the end of the week, but Elwood had other resources. On several occasions he managed to produce distracting sounds during Mr. Peepers' classes.

Now, as Elwood stood shamefaced with his hands behind his back, Mr. Peepers stared sternly at him. Despite the boy's doe-eyed, cowering attitude, he decided to be firm. Elwood's latest offenses were downright insubordinate.

"Elwood," he said, "I've told you time and again, the noises you make from the back of the room are very disturbing."

"I'm sorry, Mr. Peepers," Elwood whispered.

"Now, how would you like it," Mr. Peepers said patiently, "if I sat in back while you were lecturing and did this?" Mr. Peepers formed an "O" with his mouth and

Mr. Peepers

struck himself repeatedly on the top of the head with his knuckles. Primitive music resulted. Elwood Hamper lowered his eyes.

Mr. Peepers stopped knocking. The demonstration was painful to both head and fingers. Mr. Peepers wondered if Elwood had a more impervious skull than normal. "Now, Elwood," he said carefully, "not only may that damage your cerebrum, it may very well cause a swelling in your knuckles. In order to avoid unsightly fingers for yourself and a nervous breakdown for me, discontinue the process. Is that clear?"

Elwood looked terrified. "No, sir."

Mr. Peepers sighed. "Nobody likes a boy with swollen knuckles. Please stop making the noises."

Elwood's lip was beginning to quiver. "I promise I won't do it again."

"See that you don't. Now, take your seat."

Mr. Peepers went to his desk. The rest of the children had been slowly drifting into class. Most of them were seated and buzzing secretly about one thing or another by the time Mr. Peepers finished straightening his papers. He picked up a ruler and tapped for order.

"Take your seats, everyone," he said, "Lunch period is over. Back to the business of developing our minds."

He heard Elwood Hamper conking his head resonantly.

"Elwood!" he said, astounded.

Elwood lowered his eyes in shame.

"Good!" Mr. Peepers said. "Now, to continue . . ."

Genevieve Garner thrust her hand in the air.

"Yes, Genevieve?" Mr. Peepers said.

"May I get my coat from the cloakroom, Mr. Peepers?" she asked.

Snowbound

"Yes, certainly," Mr. Peepers said. Genevieve's teeth were chattering a little as she left the room. Mr. Peepers began to notice little puffs of vapor popping from his own mouth as he spoke. "Dear me," he said, "it certainly is chilly, isn't it?" Mr. Peepers blew on his hands. "Is anyone else chilly?"

The entire class raised their hands.

"Hm," Mr. Peepers said, "perhaps I'd better run down to the furnace room. It shouldn't be this cold. Leonard, you may be monitor. Now, everyone be quiet, please. Remember—there are other classes going on in the building."

Down below in the furnace room, the assistant janitor, Mr. Mumsey, was grunting and sniffling in front of the furnace. Poor old Charley Meadow, the regular janitor, was home in bed with sciatica. Mr. Mumsey opened the door to the furnace and closed it again. Then he stepped back from the furnace with his hands on his hips.

"Durn furnace," he murmured. "Durn thing. Durn!"

He hauled off and took a good kick at it. Then he cried out in pain and jumped around holding onto the injured foot. When the pain had abated, he picked up a stick and began to beat the furnace with it. "Durn furnace!" he said sternly. "Doggone. Durn!"

Mr. Peepers watched the demonstration tactfully. He was a little afraid to speak—Mr. Mumsey seemed very upset. Then all at once a terrific pounding echoed through the steampipes. It sounded as though all the teachers had picked the exact same time to protest.

"Awright!" Mr. Mumsey shouted at the pipes. "Awright! I'm doin' the best I can." He looked at the furnace and fell to muttering again. "Durn people ain't got no patience," he said. "Durn furnace."

Mr. Peepers

Mr. Peepers cleared his throat. "What seems to be the trouble, Mr. Mumsey?"

Mr. Mumsey turned to him slowly. His eyes were very angry looking. He put his nose practically against Mr. Peepers' nose and breathed heavily. After several seconds of silence, he spoke.

"Furnace is broke," he said.

Mr. Peepers smiled. "Well," he said, "do you suppose the low temperature has caused an increase in the viscosity of the fuel? That's Bernoulli's Principle of Fluids, you know . . . might just make the needle valve inoperative."

Mr. Mumsey stared at Mr. Peepers for a good long while. A few of the muscles in his face were jumping and twitching. He seemed to be contemplating hitting Mr. Peepers with his stick. Then he turned away and delivered another good hard kick at the furnace.

"Durn furnace!" he said.

"Do you think you can get it fixed?" Mr. Peepers asked.

Mr. Mumsey exhaled. "Doin' the best I can."

"Can I give you a hand?"

Mr. Mumsey began to laugh. He turned to look at Mr. Peepers again. Mr. Peepers found being face to face with the harried old fellow a little disturbing.

"Mrs. Gurney wanted to give me a hand," Mr. Mumsey said tensely. "Mr. Weskit wanted to give me a hand. Miss Remington and Mr. Nelson wanted to give me a hand. And now *you* want to give me a hand. . . ."

Mr. Peepers smiled. His Grandmother had always told him to handle excitable people in whispers. "Well?" he said softly.

Mr. Mumsey breathed fiercely into Mr. Peepers' face. Then he began to shout.

Snowbound

"Durn furnace!" he bellowed, brandishing his stick.

Mr. Peepers left immediately. On the way back to the classroom he stopped off at the cloak rack and got his coat and muffler. He hoped the children had done the same. It was bitter cold in the hallways. When Mr. Peepers opened the classroom door he saw that the children were all gathered by the radiator. Some of them were banging on it with rulers, and they were all bundled up in overcoats, ear muffs and mittens.

"Don't bang the radiator, children, please," he said. "Mr. Mumsey is doing his best to fix the furnace. Be patient."

He looked out the window and saw swirling snow flying every which way. Mr. Peepers blew on his hands and jumped up and down.

Mrs. Gurney entered, wearing a heavy coat. "Oh, dear, oh, dear, oh, dear," she said. "It's getting colder and colder. I just wish you could feel my hands."

"Did you wish to see me about something, Mrs. Gurney?" Mr. Peepers asked.

"Hm?" Mrs. Gurney replied. "Well, I . . . er . . . see me? Oh, yes! Yes, Mr. Peepers . . . I stopped by to tell you the storm has grown worse. We've decided to send the children home."

A howl of approval came from the children. A few of them began dancing and stomping.

"Here, here!" Mr. Peepers cried. "Let's conduct ourselves like young ladies and gentlemen."

The noise subsided quickly. Mr. Peepers kept staring at the children to ensure quiet. Suddenly there was the sound of Elwood Hamper's head being vigorously conked.

"That will do, Elwood!" Mr. Peepers said. He looked at Mrs. Gurney. "Is the bus here, Mrs. Gurney?"

Mr. Peepers

Mrs. Gurney nodded. "Mr. Weskit went to call the bus service. It will be here shortly."

Nancy Remington, smiling, entered the classroom. She had her coat on, too. "Anyone in this room with sniffles? I brought some cold tablets up from the dispensary."

Mr. Peepers was delighted to see her. It was almost worth the storm to get a surprise hello from Nancy. "No one's complaining," he said. "Seems we're all healthy."

Wes Weskit came in shaking his head. "Plenty trouble," he said, "plenty trouble. The telephones won't work. According to the radio downstairs, all transportation is at a standstill. We've got a real blizzard on our hands."

"I just wish you could feel my hands," Mrs. Gurney said.

"Do you think we'll have to spend the night here?" Nancy asked.

"Very possibly," Wes said. He looked out of the window. "That storm isn't going to let up without a struggle."

Mr. Peepers rubbed his hands together. "Well, we'd best get things organized. One for all and all for one."

Mrs. Gurney raised one arm proudly. "Stout fellows stand together in all kinds of weather. Curfew will not ring tonight! I mean, as we Campfire Girls used to say . . . er . . . Now, what was it . . . ?" Mrs. Gurney paused to think.

"I just wish you could feel my hands?" Mr. Peepers suggested.

Mrs. Gurney laughed. "Bless you," she said. "Now, look here—I have an electric heater in my room. So why don't we make our headquarters there for the duration . . . er . . . the nonce."

Mr. Peepers and Wes agreed heartily.

"I'll get some blankets from the dispensary," Nancy said.

Snowbound

"Stout fellow!" Mrs. Gurney cried. She and Nancy left together.

Mr. Peepers called to the children. "May I have your attention, please," he said. The children stopped murmuring and stood still. To Mr. Peepers they looked like so many wan Teddy bears. "We have reached a crisis in man's battle against the elements," he said gently. "There is no cause for alarm. However, we may be forced to spend the night here at school."

To his surprise the students roared approval.

"The cafeteria has some hot soup, Mr. Peepers," Wes whispered.

"Thank you, Mr. Weskit," Mr. Peepers said quietly. He raised his voice for the children. "The cafeteria has some hot soup left, class—so we shan't suffer for lack of nourishment. Now, in such a crisis as this, co-operation is the keynote."

"In other words," Wes said, "no fooling around."

Elwood conked his head.

"That applies to you, Elwood," Wes said.

Mr. Peepers looked at Wes. "I see you two have met," he said.

Wes nodded. "The most talented head in school."

Mr. Peepers returned to the students. "Now," he said clearly, "let us proceed to Mrs. Gurney's room—3A—in alphabetical order, and——"

The children howled happily. They stampeded from the room with not a semblance of order, alphabetical or otherwise.

Mr. Peepers smiled weakly at Wes. "Excitement of the blizzard and all." He felt that some excuse should be offered for the lack of discipline.

Mr. Peepers

Wes nodded grimly. "It takes an iron hand," he said. Suddenly his expression changed. "Say, listen! The blizzard sort of wrecks your surprise party for Nancy, doesn't it?"

Mr. Peepers sighed. "Yes, it's a disappointment all around. I left Nancy's present at home, and René, the headwaiter at the South Seas House of Italy, not only made a birthday cake with kumquats and spumoni, he said he was going to serve the spaghetti with a coconut and pineapple sauce."

Wes Weskit nodded. "Disgusting," he said.

By nightfall, after an improvised supper, the children were all wrapped in their coats and what blankets the school infirmary afforded, while Nancy, Wes, Mrs. Gurney and Mr. Peepers sat bundled up in a corner of the room. Some of the children were playing games, like "paper, scissors and rock." Others (led by a tight-lipped Walter Murdock) were furiously involved in a mumblety-peg contest.

Mr. Peepers smiled and whispered to Nancy, "Are you warm enough, Nancy?"

"I'm fine," Nancy said. "How about you?"

"Dandy," Mr. Peepers said. He was, too. He was delighted that the children appeared so calm and contented. It seemed to him a sort of tribute to the teachers' patience and skill. At that moment Marilee Dagny began to cry.

"Who's that?" Mrs. Gurney asked. "What? Here. Who? . . . er . . . Marilee?" Mrs. Gurney hurried to where Marilee was huddled. The child's face was buried in her hands. "What's the matter, dear?" Mrs. Gurney asked softly.

Snowbound

Marilee lifted her face. She looked like a forlorn angel. "I wanna go home!" she bawled.

Her brother Carl was seated next to her. He was a large boy who always looked as though he needed a shave. He was also captain of the football team. To everyone's dismay, he, too, began to cry. "I'm hungry!" he wailed. Soon the entire classroom had taken up the cry, with one complaint or another.

"Look here, Carl," Mr. Peepers said gently, "a lower intake of calories is sometimes beneficial to the body chemistry. . . ."

Carl Dagny glowered at him. Mr. Peepers cleared his throat and left the boy alone.

"Oh, dear," Mrs. Gurney murmured, "the poor darlings —they're all so tired and uncomfortable."

"Isn't there some way we can keep them entertained?" Nancy asked. "It won't be long before they'll fall asleep." She looked at Mr. Peepers. "Robinson?"

Mr. Peepers reddened. "Well," he said, "I suppose with a little coaxing I could tell a story."

"Bravo!" Mrs. Gurney said. She applauded vigorously. Suddenly her expression changed. "I just wish you could feel my hands," she murmured. Then she continued. "Children!" she said gaily. "Your attention, please. Mr. Peepers is going to tell you a story."

The children oohed and aahed and scurried to where Mr. Peepers was standing.

"Well," Mr. Peepers said, "if you'll all gather around the electric campfire here . . ." He grinned at the children, hoping they would giggle and repeat his remark. No one made a sound. They were all staring at him. Mr. Peepers

Mr. Peepers

coughed. "A little closer, children," he said. The students obeyed. Mr. Peepers stood with his hands folded. Suddenly a disturbing thought occurred to him. He looked at Wes Weskit. "Wes," he whispered, "I don't know any stories."

Wes whispered back. "Make one up. You write articles for *Petal and Stem,* don't you?"

Mr. Peepers sighed. "I'll try." He cleared his throat. "Well, folks . . . I mean . . . Well, children, this is the tale of two geologists. Let us call them, purely for purposes of identification, Homer and Max. Any similarity to actual persons living or dead is purely coincidental." Mr. Peepers paused and looked around the group. Each face looked eager, transfixed. "One day," Mr. Peepers continued, "Max said to Homer: 'Homer, let's take the mule to a sedimentary rock formation I know about,' and Homer said: 'Fine.' Then Max said: 'I think we can find some starfish fossils there,' and Homer said: 'You'll never find starfish fossils in limestone.' . . ." Mr. Peepers stared at the children. "Well, he had him there, didn't he?" he said. The children concurred. "Anyway," Mr. Peepers continued, "they saddled up their mule and——"

"What was the mule's name?" cried Sidney Lee.

"Hmm?" Mr. Peepers said. "Oh! Ah . . . er . . . King of the Plains! He was rather an attractive mule—dappled gray. Any similarity to actual mules living or dead is purely coincidental." Mr. Peepers laughed conservatively. The children were silent. "I think," Mr. Peepers said softly, "that all stories should have points of humor." There was no response. Mr. Peepers thought for a moment. "I know you're sitting there," he said finally, "because I can hear breathing." The children whooped with laughter.

Snowbound

"Hey," Carl Dagny shouted happily, "that's Milton Berle!"

Mr. Peepers nodded. "Yes, Carl," he said glumly, "I know. . . .

"Anyway," he continued, "back to Homer and Max. They mounted their trusty steed, King of the Plains and, carrying several small picks and a bottle of hydrochloric acid for making rock tests, made their merry way over hills and dales and . . . hills . . ." Mr. Peepers giggled. The children did not. Mr. Peepers cleared his throat. He thought of another television joke, but decided he preferred silence. "Suddenly," he said, "Max straightened in the saddle and said: 'Homer, where are we?' Homer, always there with a ready answer, said: 'Lost, Max.' Max leaped from the saddle, quite disturbed by this change in events. He stared up at Homer with tired eyes. 'Homer,' he said, 'my eyes are tired.'"

Mr. Peepers yawned in spite of himself. Several of the children were snoring. Nancy Remington and Mrs. Gurney had their eyes closed. Only Wes Weskit was still with him.

"You see," Mr. Peepers said, yawning, "riding over dills and hales, and . . . hills . . . will make one's eyes tired."

Mr. Peepers was asleep. So were the children. Without knowing it, he had accomplished his task.

Two hours later Wes Weskit was shaking Mr. Peepers' shoulder. Mr. Peepers murmured ". . . so then Max and Homer said: 'Let's get another mule,' and . . ."

"Wake up, Rob," Wes whispered.

"Hm?" Mr. Peepers said, opening his eyes. "What's wrong, Wes?" he asked loudly.

Wes hushed him quickly. "Shhh. Come out into the hall."

Mr. Peepers

A sleepy Mr. Peepers tiptoed behind Wes Weskit out of the room of heavily breathing children. Even Nancy and Mrs. Gurney were asleep. Mr. Peepers wondered what time it was as Wes closed the door behind them. "What's wrong?" Mr. Peepers asked quietly.

"I've got to do something about Marge, amigo," Wes said. "Her train is due at ten-thirty. I've got to get to the depot and meet her or she'll be worried sick."

"But the blizzard and everything. . . ."

"Don't worry. I'll be okay."

"Gee," Mr. Peepers said. "She went to so much trouble to come to the party and now there isn't going to be a party."

Wes Weskit snapped his fingers. "I've got an idea. Suppose I round up a little chow in town, including a cake. We'll have Nancy's party right here."

"Oh, Wes," Mr. Peepers said, "you shouldn't go out in this storm. It's much too perilous."

Wes's upper lip stiffened perceptibly. "I'll make it," he said gravely.

"Well," Mr. Peepers said, "if you think you can."

"I think I can," Wes said, "and if I think I can, I can."

Mr. Peepers was filled with admiration. "I think you can, Wes. And look, as long as you're going to town, will you stop by my place and pick up the sweater I bought for Nancy? It's wrapped in brown and yellow paper with plastic rosettes pasted on the ribbon."

"What color is the ribbon?"

"Green."

Wes nodded. "Check. I won't miss it."

Mr. Peepers smiled. "I'll get my house key." He took the hammer and ruler down from atop the lockers. Three good

Snowbound

whacks on the steampipe sprung his locker door open. He reached into his coat pocket and got the key. He also gave Wes money for the food.

Wes saluted smartly and clicked his heels. "I'm off!"

"Good luck, Wes. Be careful!"

Wes waved good-by. He made his way bravely into the storm. Mr. Peepers ran to the window and watched him. The wind was blowing furiously. Wes had to lift his legs high and bend himself forward. Mr. Peepers bit his lip. The snow was swirling around Wes chaotically, impeding his progress at every turn. A few moments later he was out of sight. Mr. Peepers turned away from the window. He hoped that Wes wouldn't get into any trouble.

Preoccupied, he slammed his locker shut. The rest of the lockers sprang open. Mr. Peepers was amazed. He had never seen that one before. He closed the lockers one by one. His own locker sprang open. Mr. Peepers scratched his head. He didn't know where to begin.

He was standing by one of the hall windows an hour later when Nancy found him. He had used a window pole held horizontally to close all the lockers at once.

"Robinson?" Nancy said.

Mr. Peepers turned round. "Oh, hello, Nancy."

"Why were you looking out the window?"

Mr. Peepers shook his head. "Wes had to go out into the storm."

"Oh, good heavens," Nancy said, "why?"

"He had to go to the station to pick up Mar——Er . . . ah . . . he needed a clean shirt. I mean . . . Why don't we sit down?"

They sat together on a hall bench. Mr. Peepers clasped

Mr. Peepers

his hands together. He was very worried about Wes. Somehow he felt guilty about asking him to pick up Nancy's present and food and everything. He had visions of Wes slipping in the snow with a bag of frankfurters. Mr. Peepers sighed. It was a bad-luck day, all right. Nancy's party had been wiped out, and poor Wes was in danger. Mr. Peepers thought longingly about how nice everything would have been at the South Seas House of Italy. Pineapple pizza and leis, and the soft Hawaiian music of Giuseppe LaMotta and His Natives.

"What's the matter, Robinson?" Nancy asked.

Mr. Peepers tried to smile. "I can't help worrying about Wes."

"Oh, don't," Nancy said. "I'm sure he'll be all right." Mr. Peepers didn't look convinced. Nancy tried to think of something cheerful. "When are he and Marge getting married?"

Mr. Peepers smiled. "Early in March. Isn't it wonderful? She's going to be a March bride." Suddenly he felt better. He could almost see the wedding ceremony. All the men grinning and the women crying. Mr. Peepers' Grandmother had always said: "Weddings are for crying." But Mr. Peepers knew that that was just the feminine point of view. He looked at Nancy and smiled. He'd been thinking of her in a wedding dress; how pretty she'd look. He wondered if Nancy had ever pictured him as the groom type. "Do you like weddings, Nancy?" he whispered.

"Uh-huh," Nancy said, nodding. "I haven't been to one since last spring when my brother Paul got married."

"Oh?" Mr. Peepers said. "Was he a March bride, too? I mean . . . groom?"

Nancy smiled. "April first," she said.

Snowbound

"Oh, that's nice," Mr. Peepers said. "First fool of the . . . er . . . this'll be my first wedding."

"Really?" Nancy said.

Mr. Peepers nodded. He hoped that Nancy hadn't been offended by his slip of the tongue about her brother. He searched his mind desperately for something to say. "Hahaha," he laughed. "Yes, indeed . . . weddings. Do you like weddings?"

Nancy laughed too. "You just asked me that."

Mr. Peepers chuckled. "Uh . . . so I did." He tried to keep laughing, but it was very difficult. Finally he fell silent and rubbed his hands together. "I think," he said earnestly, "that everyone should have a wedding. I mean, a big one. My Mother and Dad . . . gee whiz, they had an enormous wedding."

"That's wonderful," Nancy said.

Mr. Peepers looked into Nancy's eyes. They were so beautiful. "Enormous," he said softly. "There were so many guests they had to have the ceremony in the high-school gymnasium. The local Methodist church wasn't big enough. In the middle of the service, a basketball fell on the minister's head. My sister told me all about it. I mean, Aunt Emma told her and she told me. . . ." Mr. Peepers felt transfixed by Nancy's eyes.

"Paul's wedding was lovely," Nancy whispered. "I was maid of honor."

"Gee," Mr. Peepers said, "I'll bet you looked lovely."

"Lovely," Nancy said. "The wedding, I mean. I wore pale yellow. Paul's wife wore white silk. She's quite pretty."

Mr. Peepers sighed. "You'd look lovely in white silk," he said softly.

"Thank you," Nancy whispered.

Mr. Peepers

For a long time they stared at each other. Finally Mr. Peepers felt obliged to break the silence. "My father wore spats," he said.

"That's nice," Nancy said.

Mr. Peepers nodded. "He made them himself out of his World War I Army leggings."

Nancy smiled. "I like men who can do things."

Mrs. Gurney entered the hallway suddenly. "Oh, Nancy, dear," she said, "I've been looking all over for you. Poor little Genevieve here has a sore throat. Can you take care of her?"

Genevieve indeed looked very forlorn. "Certainly, Mrs. Gurney," Nancy said. "Come along, Genevieve. We'll go down to the dispensary." She took the child by the hand and departed.

Mr. Peepers rose from the bench and peered out of the window again. He couldn't see a thing. He rubbed a space clear with his hand. The visibility was still poor. Suddenly Mr. Peepers squinted. It seemed to him that he could see something moving. He ran to the door and tugged it open. Several clots of wind-driven snow struck him in the face. They were followed by Wes and Marge.

"Wes! Marge!" Mr. Peepers cried. "You made it!"

"Shut the door, sport," Wes gasped.

Mr. Peepers obeyed happily. He could hardly believe it. "How did you manage?"

"Old man Leslie brought us up with his team," Wes said.

Marge threw her arms around Mr. Peepers. "Good to see you again, Robby. Where's Nancy?"

"Shhh!" Mr. Peepers cautioned. "She's down at the dispensary."

Wes grinned at him. "Well, be of good cheer, old-timer,"

Snowbound

he said, patting the bag he was holding. "I've got chili dogs and ginger ale and coffee and the sweater's in here too, just the way you wrapped it. Now, how's that for a message to Garcia?"

Mr. Peepers could hardly contain himself. "It's just wonderful, Wes," he said. He was too excited to think clearly. Nancy's lost party was reappearing with spangles. "Now let's see . . . uh . . . Wes, take Marge to your classroom and try not to run into Nancy."

"Check," Wes said.

"I'll take the bag," Mr. Peepers continued, "and try to fix my room up. Gee—we'll have that surprise party for Nancy yet."

Marge stamped her feet on the floor and slapped her arms together.

Mr. Peepers grinned at her. "Pretty cold out there, eh?"

"Cold!" Marge exclaimed. "Well, I just wish you could feel my hands!"

Humming happily, Mr. Peepers hurried to his classroom. He cleared the top of his desk and set the bag down. Then he emptied the bag and used four paper towels for place mats. Humming "Happy Birthday to You," he arranged the cardboard plates and forks. He opened a desk drawer and got out four envelopes; by tearing the seams, he made serviceable party hats out of them. He then put one on his head and hurried to the mirror. It looked excellent. He hurried back and placed the other envelopes on the plates. He leaned over to the water cooler, pressing the cup-dispenser button four times. Efficiency was of the essence. Mr. Peepers wanted everything arranged by midnight, and it was already ten minutes to. He undid the cakebox quickly, got a bayberry candle from his desk, stuck it in the center of the tiny cake and put the cake in the middle of the food and plates. He then leaned back to the cup dispenser to get the four cups, which now popped out one at a time. The dispenser did not work instantaneously, but through years of practice Mr. Peepers had learned to time it without error. He picked up his waste-paper basket, opened the window and filled the basket with snow. He set the basket on the dunce stool. Inserting the three bottles of ginger ale into the snow, he twirled them maître d'hôtel style until they were more than half immersed.

He stood back from the setup and grinned. The bayberry candle was a bit too thick for the little cake but, aside from that, everything looked as though it had been professionally catered. Mr. Peepers erased his blackboard and picked up the chalk. HAPPY BIRTHDAY, NANCY, he wrote, in letters large enough to fill the board.

After he got Wes and Marge he thought of something else. He took one of the paper napkins and placed it in a test tube. By a careful twisting and folding of the corners, he made it look like a single rose in a thin glass vase. Marge was astonished. "Why, that's marvelous," she said.

"Let's put on our party hats, honey," Wes said. They did, too. Then they laughed at each other. Mr. Peepers thought they looked very nice.

"It's four minutes to twelve, sport," Wes said.

Mr. Peepers nodded. He could hardly wait for the party to begin. After he had checked everything for last-minute oversights, he smiled and lit the cake candle. "Now you wait here," he said to Wes and Marge. As he left he switched off the lights.

He found Nancy in Mrs. Gurney's room. Everyone else

Snowbound

was asleep. Mr. Peepers breathed a sigh of relief. He hated to awaken people.

"Why, Robinson," Nancy whispered, "what are you doing prowling around in the middle of the night? It's almost midnight."

"I know," Mr. Peepers said gleefully. "Come with me."

"Where?" Nancy asked.

"To the Casbah," Mr. Peepers said.

Nancy was amazed. "Robinson, do you feel all right?"

"Oh," Mr. Peepers said, "now, never you mind. Come on."

When they arrived at the door to his classroom, Mr. Peepers smiled. "Now close your eyes," he said softly.

Nancy covered her eyes with her hands. Mr. Peepers opened the door and closed it quietly behind them. He led Nancy past Wes and Marge to behind the desk. Then he said: "You can open your eyes now, Nancy."

Nancy opened her eyes to see one candle burning in a dark room. "My goodness!" she said. "What . . . ?"

Wes switched on the lights. "Happy birthday," he whispered. So did Mr. Peepers and Marge.

Nancy nearly jumped. "Oh, Robby! And Wes!" She turned to Marge. "And you must be . . ."

"Marge!" Marge said. "Oh, I've heard so much about you, Nancy—Happy birthday!"

Nancy brushed at her eyes. "Oh, thank you, thank you," she said softly. "This is just wonderful. . . ."

Wes tapped Mr. Peepers on the shoulder. "The present, sport," he whispered.

"Oh, yes," Mr. Peepers said. He took the box from Wes and gave it to Nancy. "Happy birthday, Nancy."

Mr. Peepers

"Oh, Robinson," Nancy said. She undid the ribbon eagerly and took the top from the box. She took out the sweater. It was frozen solid. Nancy banged it on the table.

"My goodness!" Marge cried. "It's frozen. It must have been a damp day when you packed it, and . . ."

Mr. Peepers looked disappointed. Nancy embraced him. "But it's beautiful," she said. "Thank you."

Mr. Peepers smiled happily. A thank you from Nancy was worth more than any fancy celebration he could think of.

"All righty," Wes said, offering a cup of ginger ale to Nancy. "How about trying our bathtub champagne?"

Nancy curtsied. "I'd be delighted."

All four of them had a wonderful time at the party. Mr. Peepers was delighted beyond words. In fact, he thought it was the finest birthday party he had ever attended. Even if he did say so himself.

CHAPTER VI

The Automotive Age

ALL IN ALL, Mr. Peepers was very happy. It seemed to him that his relations with Nancy were developing into a relationship. In fact, he expected soon to see the day when an evening away from Nancy was a rare day indeed. Or evening, however one wanted to put it. In any case, it certainly looked as though Robinson J. Peepers was the one consistent male in Nancy's life. That was fine with Mr. Peepers. He was not a man to covet competition.

One bright afternoon, after partaking of the corner drugstore's weekly Athlete's Luncheon (vegetable steak, prune jello and dandelion tea), which he coaxed manfully down his throat every Wednesday, Mr. Peepers was making his

Mr. Peepers

lighthearted, preoccupied way back to school. He was thinking of Nancy, of what nice cheekbones she had. Mr. Peepers smiled now as his imagination re-created Nancy's smile. He wished that he could smile the way Nancy smiled. She really *smiled*.

All at once the spell was broken. Mr. Peepers' eye was arrested by some hopscotch lines on the sidewalk. Suddenly he felt studentlike again. Since there was no chalk about, he decided merely to run the course on one foot. He balanced himself with outstretched arms and took off like a gamesome ostrich. Hopping happily, wondering how long he could last, he had just negotiated the difficult 4, 5, 6, 7 quadrants and landed triumphantly in the 8 square when he looked up and saw Nancy staring at him. Mr. Peepers put down his bent foot and stiffened. Nancy was smiling, but he felt quite embarrassed. Some excuse was certainly necessary to explain his sudden attack of juvenility.

"Ah . . . Nancy," he said, deepening his voice, "a little experiment. Uh . . . I must speak to the students about drawing hopscratches on the salkwide, I mean—" Mr. Peepers cleared his throat—"hopscotches on the sidewalk."

Nancy smiled pleasantly. "Why?" she asked. "It's good exercise and they enjoy it."

Mr. Peepers thought for a moment. "Well," he said quickly, "someone might get hurt. That is . . . it's habit-forming."

Nancy looked at him strangely. "Really?"

"Well," Mr. Peepers said, blushing, "no, but . . ." He couldn't go on. He wished that something would happen to wipe out the whole incident. He wanted to start life afresh.

Nancy saw his discomfiture and apparently decided to

The Automotive Age

help him. "I should think you'd object more to the cartoons they draw."

Mr. Peepers grinned happily. He was delighted with the chance to prove his adulthood. "On the contrary," he replied, glancing at one of the cartoons, "I find they furnish a valuable insight into the workings of the child mind. Now this one here of a man kicking a refrigerator is obviously drawn by Peter Ginch, who will someday inherit his father's ice business. One can clearly see the hostility against electrification of home appliances."

Nancy stared at the drawing. "Robinson," she said sweetly, "that's not a refrigerator. That's you opening your locker."

Mr. Peepers took another look. Nancy was indeed correct. The cartoon figure had a hammer and ruler in his hands. Mr. Peepers sighed. The conversation had again descended to what he called the Blank Look and Ahem Level. He tried to think of an uplifting remark. Nothing occurred to him but "Oh, yes" and "No." Mr. Peepers decided to change the subject. He looked at the school clock.

"I have sixteen minutes before I must go in," he said. "Would you like to sit and talk?"

"Fine," Nancy said. "Shall we sit right here?"

Mr. Peepers felt a faint sensation of panic. Nancy had indicated the waiting bench for the city busses. "Well," he said carefully, "in about three minutes we can sit down here for nine minutes. Or perhaps it would be better if we got up at the end of eight minutes to give him a bit of leeway in case he's early."

Nancy didn't understand. "Who?"

"The bus driver," Mr. Peepers replied. "The bus is due

[141]

Mr. Peepers

in three minutes and the next one will be due in nine minutes. I wouldn't want him to think we were passengers."

"Oh," Nancy said.

"Of course," Mr. Peepers continued, "that doesn't prevent us from starting a conversation now and carrying it over to the bench and then continuing it after we get up. We'd merely have to talk a little louder as they go by."

Nancy smiled. "Whatever you say, Robinson."

"Or," Mr. Peepers added, "we can sit for the first minute and a half. I have been talking for thirty seconds, but that would still give the first bus a minute's leeway."

"Whatever you say, Robinson."

Mr. Peepers nodded happily. His careful study of the bus schedules had at last borne fruit. "I'd say let's sit."

They sat down. A bus came by and slowed to a halt. Mr. Peepers jumped up quickly. "You're early, Tyrone!" he cried, grinning desperately.

Tyrone's expression flattened. He pulled the door to a close and muttered something grouchy. With a roar of acceleration and a clashing of gears the bus drove on.

"Good luck on the route!" Mr. Peepers shouted, as the bus faded angrily into the distance.

"We'd better stand up," he said to Nancy. "It's too risky."

Nancy was already standing up. In fact, she was looking up and down the street, as though she were expecting someone. Mr. Peepers had uncomfortable visions—tall dark young men with footballs under their arms. "Er . . ." he said, "are you waiting for someone, Nancy?"

"Hm?" Nancy said. "Oh, yes. Freddie Willis is in town from San Francisco. He asked me to have lunch with him."

Mr. Peepers gulped quickly. His direct fears had been confirmed. "How nice," he said weakly.

The Automotive Age

Nancy smiled. "I haven't seen him for ages."

Mr. Peepers nodded. "I just finished my lunch," he said.

Nancy wasn't listening. "He said he had some sort of surprise for me."

"Vegetable steak and dandelion tea," Mr. Peepers said.

Nancy continued to look up and down the street. "I wonder what he's up to."

Mr. Peepers stared at the back of her neck. "The tea was cold."

At that moment a blatantly honking horn announced the oncoming of Freddie. He was behind the wheel of a brand-new blue sports car. It sped toward them and pulled to a screeching stop by the curb. Mr. Peepers recognized the car. There were photographs of it in the latest issue of *Futurama* magazine. It was a new British product known as the Jet-Healey Superflame: the only contemporary auto designed for a propeller.

"Freddie!" Nancy cried.

"Hi, Nancy!" Freddie shouted. He took off his goggles and grinned. Then he saw Mr. Peepers. "Oh, hello there, Peepers," he said curtly. "Well," he said expansively, looking at Nancy again, "what do you think of the new knockabout?"

"Oh," said Nancy, wide-eyed, "it's beautiful!"

Mr. Peepers felt very depressed. He wondered how he could ever compete with such glamour.

"Yup," Freddie continued. "I picked 'er up just before I left Frisco. She's only got twenty-five hundred miles on 'er. I chose this color 'cause it matches your eyes, Nan baby."

Mr. Peepers edged closer to the car. "My eyes are blue, too," he said. His Grandmother had always said: If you can't lick 'em, join 'em.

Mr. Peepers

Freddie nodded coolly. "Good for you," he said. "Hey, Nan," he added, pointing to the various dashboard features, "look here. She's got an overseas radio, an air conditioner, a heater, an instant-touch lighter and a compass."

"Wonderful!"

Mr. Peepers leaned lightly against the fender to look inside.

"Watch the paint, Peepers!" Freddie cried quickly. He took a handkerchief from his pocket and wiped the spot where Mr. Peepers had put his hand.

"Oh," Mr. Peepers said, "I'm sorry." He supposed he would have to give up on seeing the dashboard. He had read, however, about the custom-built water-injection system of the Jet-Healey and was curious to see how it connected with the carburetor. "May I look at the motor?" he asked timidly.

"Sure," Freddie said, winking at Nancy, "just press down on the lion's tongue."

Mr. Peepers smiled. The Jet-Healey was the only car he'd ever seen with a lion's head for a hood decoration. "It looks like the beginning of a Monogram movie," he said cheerfully.

"You mean M-G-M, don't you?" Freddie said.

"Oh, I suppose so," Mr. Peepers said. "I can never get those movie trade-marks straight." He pressed the tongue. The hood sprang up, and Mr. Peepers sprang back. Then he leaned forward and inserted his head carefully.

In the driver's seat, Freddie winked at Nancy again. Then he leaned on the horn.

Mr. Peepers' feet nearly left the ground. He struck his head on the top of the hood.

"Hey, Peepers!" Freddie shouted. "Watch the paint!"

The Automotive Age

"Sorry, Freddie," Mr. Peepers said, rubbing his head. He couldn't understand how such an accident had happened. The Jet-Healey seemed too well made for horn short circuits. He looked carefully around the motor. "I don't think I damaged anything."

Freddie chuckled. "Just maybe your head," he whispered.

Nancy Remington stared at him. "That wasn't funny, Freddie."

"Oh, come on, Nan," Freddie said, "no harm done."

Mr. Peepers closed the hood. "Certainly is efficient-looking in there."

"Well, that's what we pay for, Peepers," Freddie said. "Hop in, Nan. We'll go have some lunch."

"Fine," Nancy said. "Come on, Robinson. Take a ride with us."

"Well——" Mr. Peepers said.

Freddie Willis interrupted. "Peepers probably has things to do, Nancy."

"Oh, Freddie," Nancy said, "I'm sure he has time for a ride around the block. Come on, Robinson. Jump in."

"Nan," Freddie said, "I had sort of planned . . ."

"Well," Mr. Peepers said, "I . . . uh . . . do have things to do. I want to catch the bus driver on the return trip and apologize."

"What?" Freddie asked.

"Never mind, Freddie," Nancy said. "We'll be back soon, Robinson," she added. "We're just going to have some lunch."

"I know," Mr. Peepers said. "I've already had my lunch. I had vegetable steak and . . ."

Freddie started the car. "See you later, Robinson!" Nancy cried.

Mr. Peepers

Mr. Peepers stood there for a moment staring after them. "The tea was cold," he murmured. Then he looked at the school clock. There was still time to wait for Tyrone. As the bus came lumbering around the corner, Mr. Peepers flagged it down.

"Hi there, Tyrone," he said, smiling, as the door opened. "I just wanted to apologize for slowing you down before."

Tyrone put one hand to his forehead. "Give me strength," he murmured.

In the locker room, before class, Mr. Peepers took a couple of books from his locker. They both contained essays on the contradictions of organic chemistry. Mr. Peepers was giving a lecture that afternoon entitled "How Acids Can Be Alkaline, and Vice Versa."

Wes Weskit approached quietly from the rear and without warning slapped Mr. Peepers on the back. "Hiya, sport!" he said gaily.

Mr. Peepers disengaged his face from the locker door. He supposed it was going to be another of those physical-mishap days. Wes apologized profusely. Mr. Peepers shook his head. "That's all right, Wes," he said glumly.

"Gee," Wes said, "you look a little down, sport. What's up?"

Mr. Peepers sighed. "Oh, it's nothing, Wes." He didn't want to complain to Wes about his troubles. If there was one thing in life Mr. Peepers disapproved of it was complaining.

"Aw, come on," Wes said. "If you can't tell friends, you can't tell anybody. What's on your mind?"

Mr. Peepers hemmed and hawed. Wes was right, of

course. If a person had anything to complain about it was best for a person to complain to his friends. "Oh, well," he said, "Nancy and I . . . we . . ." Mr. Peepers hesitated again. Then he shook his head. He just didn't want to continue. Talking about it felt too much like complaining. "I don't want to complain, Wes."

"Well," Wes said casually, shrugging his shoulders. "If you say it's nothing, then that's good enough for me. I'd be the last chap in the world to pry. I'm not a pryer."

Mr. Peepers grabbed at the bait. He didn't want Wes to feel like a pryer. "Oh, you're *not* prying, Wes. As a matter of fact, I'd *like* to tell you."

Wes shook his head. "Only if you'd like to," he said, with an offhand gesture. "I'd rather cut my hand off than pry."

"Well," Mr. Peepers said, "it's only . . ." He stopped again. No matter what Wes said, it felt like complaining. Not only that, it was taking advantage of friendship to burden Wes with his problems. "I can't talk about it, Wes," he said finally.

Wes tried a shift in tactics. "Well, let's change the subject!" he said heartily. "Did you meet anyone during your lunch hour?"

"Yes," Mr. Peepers said. "Nancy."

"Uh-huh," Wes said. "Well, how are things going with you and Nancy?"

"I don't know," Mr. Peepers replied glumly. "Nancy and I . . ." Mr. Peepers halted. He couldn't understand how the conversation had come back to Nancy so quickly. "Well," he said, "we . . . uh . . . Oh, it's nothing, Wes."

Wes Weskit's back teeth ground slowly together. "Well," he said tensely, "if you can't tell friends, you can't tell anybody. Now, what's on your mind?"

Mr. Peepers

Mr. Peepers shook his head. "It's nothing really, Wes."

"Look," Wes said gravely. "I'd be the last chap in the world to pry. Let's change the subject."

Mr. Peepers smiled gratefully. "Thanks, Wes."

Wes could not speak. He managed a nod.

Mr. Peepers stared at him for a moment. He wondered if Wes were hurt at being left out of things. Wes was certainly too good a friend to keep secrets from. He decided to approach the problem from another direction. "Wes," he said carefully, "*I* don't want to pry, but—what do you think of Freddie Willis?"

Wes slammed his locker triumphantly. His lungs released several superfluous pounds of air pressure. "Ah-hah!" he said. "Back in town."

Mr. Peepers nodded. "With a new car."

"Uh-*huh!*" Wes said. He deliberated for a moment. "Nancy pretty impressed?"

"He took her out to lunch," Mr. Peepers said.

Wes shook his head dolefully. "That's a woman for you. That *is* a woman for you."

Mr. Peepers was a little disturbed by Wes's tone. He hoped Wes didn't think that Nancy was a woman. At least, not like other women. "Nancy's different, Wes." Then he thought about it for a moment. "Isn't she?" he asked.

"Oh, sure, sure," Wes said. "Nancy's different, but they're all alike. Except Marge. She's different."

Mr. Peepers tried to absorb the philosophy carefully. He realized how knowledgeable Wes was in such matters. "Nancy and Marge are different," he said slowly, "but they're all alike."

Wes nodded.

"But not Nancy and Marge," Mr. Peepers said. "Right?"

The Automotive Age

"Right!" Wes said. He stared at Mr. Peepers for a moment. "Still . . ."

"Yes?" Mr. Peepers said.

Wes spread his hands. "Well, that's a woman for you! Every time!"

Mr. Peepers was a little confused. "Let's change the subject."

Wes grinned at him, hoping he'd been a comfort. "Sure, sport."

There was a pause. Then: "Are cars very expensive, Wes?" Mr. Peepers asked.

"All depends," Wes said carefully. "Thinking about getting one?"

"Well, I . . ."

"You can use mine any time you want, sport," Wes said. "But it's nice to have one of your own. You can drive away for lunch. You can——"

"I'm not thinking of getting one just to impress Nancy," Mr. Peepers interjected.

"Oh, of course not," Wes said.

Mr. Peepers pursued the possibility. "I could use one in my work," he said gravely. "You know, for . . . well, hauling things . . . er . . . topsoil . . . rock specimens . . . people . . . seeing my mother . . . riding around . . . er . . . driving."

Wes nodded. "They're nice," he said. "I got my first car when I was—well, let's see—seventeen. I'll never forget it. It was a nineteen-twenty-nine job."

Mr. Peepers smiled. "They were swell."

"Right," Wes said. "It was a good year." He laughed. "What a car! No fenders, no top, no floor boards; self-starter was busted. I got it for twelve bucks."

Mr. Peepers

"Gosh," Mr. Peepers said. "That was a bargain."

Wes concurred. "I bought it from the original owners: an elderly couple who had smashed it up. They'd driven it into a causeway. Pretty fast, too."

Mr. Peepers nodded eagerly. "Sounds swell."

"It wasn't much to look at," Wes continued, "but Rob . . . the women . . . wouldn't . . . leave . . . me . . . alone!"

"My!" Mr Peepers said.

"I'll bet I drove at least seven different girls to school every day. It would be loaded. Jammed. Before I knew it, the old bus started rattling to beat the band."

Mr. Peepers nodded knowingly. "Body began to get a little loose. All that extra weight."

"Nope," Wes said. "Bobby pins. All over the car."

Mr. Peepers considered the possibility. Then he shook his head. "Nancy has short hair."

"You're lucky," Wes said. He smiled at Mr. Peepers. "Well, what do you think?" he asked gaily. "Gonna buy a car?"

Mr. Peepers deliberated for a moment. "I dunno, Wes. Cars are pretty expensive. I wonder if I could find a reckless elderly couple."

Wes shook his head. "That was one in a million. But listen—I know a spot. Any kind of car you want. Patton's Used Cars. You can get credit in a minute down there. They've got a sign right over the lot. 'Easy Credit—Just bring in an Honest Face.'"

Mr. Peepers nodded. He looked in the wall mirror. Then he turned back to Wes. "What do you think?"

Wes Weskit examined Mr. Peepers' face with care.

The Automotive Age

"Robby," he said earnestly, "If Diogenes had found you, he would have put out his lamp."

Later that afternoon when Mr. Peepers stopped by the water fountain, he overheard a conversation between two of the female students.

"Honestly, Sylvia," Marilee Dagny was saying, "I just couldn't make up my mind."

"Gosh!" Sylvia Gibson exclaimed.

"I like Bruce," Marilee continued, "but I also like Roger. I didn't know what to do. Both of them have been phoning, phoning, phoning."

"They're both adorable!" Sylvia said frantically. "How on earth did you make up your mind?"

"It was easy," Marilee explained, "once I found out that Bruce had a car."

Mr. Peepers choked slightly on his mouthful of water. He listened carefully to the rest of the conversation.

"Are you still seeing Bruce?" Sylvia Gordon asked.

"Yes, he's taking me to the dog races tonight."

"Well, gosh, Marilee," Sylvia said, "can I have Roger?"

"Sure," Marilee said.

That was the last Mr. Peepers heard. He peered around the corner of the hallway. The two girls were walking away arm in arm. But Mr. Peepers had heard enough. He had been granted a valuable insight into the workings of the female mind. He wondered if Mrs. Gurney might be able to add anything notable. He decided to pay her a visit.

In her English class Mrs. Gurney was reviewing a batch of poems recently written by the students. "Lester," she said to Lester Cohen III, "please remove your feet from Emily's chair!"

Mr. Peepers

Lester complied. He was wearing his older brother's combat boots. They made quite an earth-shaking sound as they struck the floor.

"Oh, good heavens," Mrs. Gurney said, startled, "in the future, Lester, could you please wear sneakers to school!"

"Yes, Mrs. Gurney," Lester said.

Mrs. Gurney smiled at him. "Bless you." She held up the batch of poems. "I have here last week's poems, and I must say you did a splendid job—splendid. Most of them are extraordin—extrord—They're splendid!"

She took the top one and set the rest down. "Suppose we read a few of them." She picked up her lorgnette and readied herself for reading. "Mmmm," she said, "this is a lovely one. 'My Brown Dog,' by Harold Golden. Ahem!

> 'My dog is brown
> We live in town
> Don't ever frown
> A king wears a crown
> My dog is brown.'"

Mrs. Gurney paused and stared at Harold. "Very nice," she said warmly. "The rhyming is very consistent. However, Harold, the meter leaves just a little to be desired. And perhaps the rhyming was a little *too* consistent. Nevertheless, a good try. Your effort was extraordin—splendid!"

Mrs. Gurney picked up the next poem. "Now, here's Marilee Dagny's. And very spirited, too. It's called 'Yahoo, Yahay!'

> 'Yahoo, Yahay!
> It's Spring today!

The Automotive Age

Let's go and play
With all our friends
From the corner drugstore.
They're swell kids.
Yahoo, Yahoo, Yahay!' "

Mrs. Gurney frowned. "Very nice, Marilee," she said, "Very . . . You sort of gave up in the middle, didn't you, dear? Well . . . good effort, good effort."

Mrs. Gurney saw Mr. Peepers standing in the doorway. She waved at him brightly. "Now, class," she said, "here's one by Walter Murdock. At first glance it seems rather familiar. The title is different, I'll admit, but it does seem familiar." Mrs. Gurney cleared her throat. " 'Things That Grow,' " she said, "by Walter Murdock. Ahem!

'I think that I shall never see
A poem lovely as a tree
A tree that may in summer wear . . .' "

Mrs. Gurney paused and looked at Walter. "Are you sure you wrote this, Walter?" she asked. Walter nodded. "You did," Mrs. Gurney said flatly. "I'd like to see you after school. Now, then . . . here's Leonard Gorf's." She smiled at Leonard. "I might have known there'd be a military motif, Leonard," she said warmly. "Bless you! Ahem . . . it's called 'The Big Guns Boom' . . ."

The school bell bonged. Mrs. Gurney started. Then she lowered her lorgnette. "That will be all, class," she said.

The children filed from the classroom, jostling, whispering and making jokes about each others' poems. Leonard Gorf passed by Mrs. Gurney's desk, looking disappointed.

Mr. Peepers

"Don't fret, Leonard," Mrs. Gurney said. "Your guns will boom tomorrow. Er . . . bless you."

As Mr. Peepers stepped toward her, Mrs. Gurney put one weary hand to her forehead. "Oh," she said, "it's been a trying day, Mr. Peepers, a trying day." She lowered her hand and shook her head. "Trying," she added. "Now, then," she continued cheerfully, "what did you wish to see me about?"

"Well," Mr. Peepers said timidly, "I wanted to get your feelings about cars."

Mrs. Gurney's eyes widened. "Well, I . . . er . . . there seem to be a great many of them."

"No, no," Mr. Peepers said. "What I mean is . . . uh . . . when Mr. Gurney was courting you, before you were married . . . did he have a car?"

Mrs. Gurney smiled. "He had a buggy," she said nostalgically, "And what a buggy! The very first thing that caught my eye about Mr. Gurney was his buggy whip."

"Really?" Mr. Peepers said. "His buggy whip?"

Mrs. Gurney nodded. "He picked up my handkerchief with it!" she said gaily. Then she tittered girlishly. "He was a caution. Full of balderdash! Why do you ask me this, Mr. Peepers?"

Mr. Peepers made a few embarrassed gestures. "Well, I . . . uh . . . was just wondering—did the fact that Mr. Gurney have a buggy make a difference?"

"Oh my, yes," Mrs. Gurney said. "So full of balderdash!"

Mr. Peepers grinned. "I imagine a car does give a man dash," he said. "Balderdash."

Mrs. Gurney concurred happily. "Most certainly. Most."

Mr. Peepers made a mental note of that and continued. "I also wanted to get your feeling about credit."

The Automotive Age

"Well," Mrs. Gurney said, "I've always felt that credit should be given where credit is due. It's only fair . . ."

"No," Mr. Peepers said. "What I mean is—do you think I have an honest face?"

The question paralyzed Mrs. Gurney for a moment. She stood staring at Mr. Peepers with her head trembling. Then she coughed. "Eejaboo, Mr. Peepers," she said.

At four o'clock that afternoon, Mr. Peepers stood tentatively before a huge sign reading: PATTON'S USED CARS. EASY CREDIT—JUST BRING IN AN HONEST FACE. He touched at his features idly with his fingers. There was no one in sight. Close to the entrance there stood a cream-colored, low-axled Jaguar with the top down. Mr. Peepers looked at it, holding his breath. There was a '33 Terraplane with a mashed-in grille standing right next to it. Mr. Peepers decided to concentrate on the older car. He appraised it carefully for a moment. Then he took hold of the door handle. The handle came off in his hand. He tried to get it back on, but couldn't. He reached inside the door to open it from within. The inside handle came off in his hand. Mr. Peepers began to feel nervous. He wondered if there were anyone around. He tried again to fit the outside handle on, and succeeded. He exhaled with relief and tossed the inside handle onto the back seat.

Glancing around again, Mr. Peepers stepped carefully into the Jaguar. It was quite an experience. The upholstery was red leather, the dashboard mahogany. Mr. Peepers hunched over the wheel and grinned. He wished he had a pair of goggles, like Freddie Willis.

"She's a honey, ain't she?" he heard a soupy voice say.

Mr. Peepers started. He looked up and saw a man in coveralls. Mr. Peepers scrambled out of the car, barking his

Mr. Peepers

shin. The salesman, a dark, gimlet-eyed man, put a hand on Mr. Peepers' shoulder.

"A-1 condition," he said emphatically. "A car to suit the king's taste. Look at those tires."

Mr. Peepers glanced at the white-wall tires and wire wheels. The salesman kicked sharply at one of the tires. "A-1 shape," he said. "Go ahead—give it a kick."

Mr. Peepers shook his head. The salesman's kick had left a small black smear on the tire. "Oh, I'd rather not," said Mr. Peepers.

"Go ahead," the salesman said sincerely. "Kick 'er."

Mr. Peepers tried to smile. "No, really. I'm just looking."

"C'mon," the salesman said, his face incredulous. "Give it a kick!"

Mr. Peepers began to back away. "No, honestly. I . . ."

The salesman grabbed hold of Mr. Peepers. "You've got to give it a kick!" he said fiercely.

Mr. Peepers showed his teeth in a strained grin. "Well," he murmured, "maybe a small one."

He looked at the tire and nudged it with his toe.

"Well?" said the salesman.

"They kick nice," Mr. Peepers said.

The salesman put a hand on Mr. Peepers' shoulder. "She's got a hundred and sixty horses," he said intimately, "and she'll do a hundred and twenty miles an hour."

Mr. Peepers inhaled in amazement. "Oh, my, I'd never drive that fast."

"Maybe not," the salesman said, "but it's nice to know those horses are under the hood if you need 'em."

Mr. Peepers strolled around the car, staring at every feature. "How much is it?"

The salesman folded his arms. "I can put you in this car

The Automotive Age

for . . . mmm . . . tell you what—you're a man with an honest face. For you, a deal!" He glanced around the lot. "Don't tell the boss!" he whispered. "Fifty-five hundred dollars. . . . How about that? I'll give up my commission."

Mr. Peepers repressed an outcry. "That's very nice of you," he said, "but I . . ."

The salesman spread his hands. "She's ready to go!"

"Well," Mr. Peepers said, "I . . ."

"Yes or no," the salesman said.

Mr. Peepers thought fast. "Er . . . I wouldn't want you to deceive the boss," he said.

"Look, buddy," the salesman said, "I like to do business with nice people. And you're *nice* people. . . ."

He put his arm firmly around Mr. Peepers' shoulders, fixed his shining, gimlet eyes on Mr. Peepers' blinking ones, and shook him gently. "Pal," he said. "I *like* you. . . ."

Mr. Peepers reddened. "Awfully nice of you."

"You're my kind of guy," he said, his voice reverberating.

Mr. Peepers, hypnotized to a point of fantasy, stared longingly at the Jaguar. For a moment he saw himself speeding down a highway in a white pilot's cap with goggles. A mere fifty-five hundred dollars, he thought. A bagatelle. I'm no skinflint. If I sell all my clothes, insurance and savings bonds, I'll be able to pay. Suddenly Mr. Peepers woke up from his daydream, horrified. He shook his head vigorously and slipped from under the salesman's arm. "Er . . . listen," he said, "I think I'd better look at something less expensive."

The salesman snapped his fingers. "You're the doctor!" he cried, turning about briskly and giving the old Terraplane a whack on the fender. "Now here," he said, "is a

Mr. Peepers

dandy for you. Just look at that paint. That is the original paint job. This car has only had one owner in its entire history."

"Oh?" Mr. Peepers said, impressed.

"That's right," the salesman said, "the Peerless Cab Company."

The salesman grabbed the door handle and tugged. The handle popped off in his hand. The salesman laughed.

"Hahaha!" he exclaimed. "First time that's ever happened." He looked at Mr. Peepers. "Think nothing of it. You can open it from the inside."

Mr. Peepers hoped the salesman wouldn't guess whose fault it all was. He thought he might be charged for damages. The salesman reached happily inside. His expression changed as he found no door handle. He shrugged and opened the back door instead.

"Look at that back seat!" he shouted.

Mr. Peepers obeyed. "Nice."

The salesman spotted the door handle lying on the back seat, where Mr. Peepers had thrown it. He picked it up quickly and showed it to Mr. Peepers. "Loaded with extras!" he cried. "She's a dandy!"

He saw Mr. Peepers staring at the mashed-in grille. "I mean," he conceded, "she's a dandy for the shape she's in. I'll admit she could use a little work. I'll have the mechanic hammer that grille out for ya——"

Mr. Peepers interrupted. "What year is this car?" he asked.

"My boy," the salesman said pontifically, "age means nothing if a car's got character."

Mr. Peepers thought for a moment. "How much is it?"

The salesman rubbed his hands together. "I can put you

The Automotive Age

in this car," he said, "for . . . tell you what. You're a man with an honest face. For you . . . a deal!"

Mr. Peepers looked around suspiciously. "What about the boss?"

"Never mind," the salesman said. He pointed to the car and whispered. "One hundred and twenty bucks." Mr. Peepers looked doubtful. The salesman held up the door handle. "I won't charge you for the extras."

Mr. Peepers scratched his head. "A hundred and twenty, eh?"

"That's just to you. You know why?"

Mr. Peepers smiled. "You like me."

"Not only that," the salesman said. "You're my kind of guy."

"Well," Mr. Peepers said, "let's see—what would the down payment and monthly payments amount to?"

The salesman took a small book from his pocket and thumbed through it. "Let's see now. I can put you in this car for thirty-seven dollars and—" he glanced at Mr. Peepers—"I'll figure this on a six months' contract. Okay?"

Mr. Peepers didn't know what he meant. "Fine," he said cheerfully.

The salesman looked at his book again. "I can put you in this car for thirty-seven dollars down and . . . fourteen dollars and twenty-two cents a month. Interest included."

Mr. Peepers took a pencil and paper from his pocket. "Fourteen twenty-two," he said. "Let's see: I pay thirty dollars a month for rent . . . and . . . uh . . . seven dollars a month for laundry . . . Hmmmmm . . ."

"Well?" the salesman said.

"If I can cut down on one luxury," Mr. Peepers murmured, "I might be able to do it." Mr. Peepers thought hard

[159]

Mr. Peepers

for a moment. "I'll just subdue my craving for peanut brittle," he said, "which will automatically cut down my consumption of dental floss."

"That ought to do it," the salesman said. "Shall we call it a deal?"

Mr. Peepers looked at his figures again. He had miscalculated slightly. He would have to surrender his after-lunch gum ball, too. "Let me think it over a little more," he said.

"You're the doctor," the salesman said, "and I'm with *you*; but make up your mind pretty quick. This car is priced to move." He pushed the car surreptitiously. The car jostled from side to side. "See what I mean?" He took a folded paper from his pocket. He handed it to Mr. Peepers. "All right, dad," he said lustily. "Now, here's yer application for credit. Just take it home with you; look it over at your leisure. When you're ready to make a deal, tear off the top of your neighborhood bus sign and send it in with the papers. . . ."

Mr. Peepers looked pale. "Oh, dear, I couldn't . . ."

The salesman's expression stiffened. "Just a joke, son. Bring it in when you're ready."

"Oh, thank you," Mr. Peepers said. He unfolded the paper. It was nearly two feet long. "Gosh," he said, frowning, "there's an awful lot to fill out here to get credit. The sign says all you need is an honest face."

The salesman shrugged his shoulders. "Very true. All the paper does is prove it. Get what I mean?"

The following morning on the way to school Mr. Peepers saw Freddie Willis's Jet-Healey zoom up to the curb. Mr. Peepers stepped back into a doorway. The car door opened and Nancy emerged.

The Automotive Age

"Thank you for the ride, Freddie," Mr. Peepers heard her say.

"My pleasure, honey," Freddie said. "See you later. Just watch this pickup."

The Jet-Healey roared away rapidly, with Freddie's voice echoing: "Excuse my dust!"

Mr. Peepers stepped out from the doorway. "Hello, Nancy."

"Why, Robinson," Nancy said, "What were you doing— hiding?"

Mr. Peepers was very embarrassed. He didn't know Nancy had seen him. "Er . . . no. I like doorways. I mean . . . Isn't it a lovely day?"

Nancy nodded. "It certainly is," she said. "Lovely."

"Yes," Mr. Peepers said, "it certainly is." He looked at the school clock. "Er . . . would you like to sit in the sunshine for a few minutes? We still have time."

"Fine," Nancy said. She smiled warmly. "How long can we sit on *this* bench?"

Mr. Peepers laughed. "There's no limit. This bench isn't a bus stop."

There was a long pause while Mr. Peepers touched at the used-car application in his pocket. "Freddie's car certainly is nice," he said.

"I suppose so," Nancy said casually. "What time are you picking me up for the movie tonight?"

Mr. Peepers didn't really hear the question. He was too preoccupied with cars, gum balls and peanut brittle. "Enjoy your lunch yesterday?" he asked.

Nancy sighed. "Not very much. All Freddie talked about was the new car. Same time for the movie tonight?"

Mr. Peepers

Mr. Peepers sighed. "It is a nice car," he murmured, "and Freddie's really a nice person."

"Robinson," Nancy said, smiling, "you're not listening to me."

Mr. Peepers emerged from his trance. "I'm sorry, Nancy. What did you say?"

Nancy inhaled. "Will you pick me up at the same time as usual for the movie tonight—seven o'clock?"

Mr. Peepers exhaled. "Nancy," he said nervously, "it would be nice if I had a car, wouldn't it? Then we wouldn't have to leave so early. As we know from bitter experience, the bus schedules are not too dependable."

Nancy shook her head. "No, Robinson," she said, "I've decided I don't like cars. Or Freddie Willis, either." She took Mr. Peepers' hand. "Besides, if you had a car we wouldn't be able to play our transfer game."

Mr. Peepers could hardly believe his ears. "Oh, well," he said, grinning, "I'd probably win, anyway."

"Is that so?" Nancy said. "Well, I'll take even."

"Okay. I'll take odds. Agreed?"

"Okay."

"You say," Mr. Peepers said, "that an even number of people will ask for transfers, and I say an odd number of people will ask for transfers."

"That's right," Nancy said.

Mr. Peepers removed the used-car paper from his pocket. "And the loser," he said, "buys the peanut brittle." He began to tear the paper up.

"What's that you're tearing up, Robinson?" Nancy asked.

Mr. Peepers smiled. "It's an application for an honest face."

Later Mr. Peepers bought a whole week's supply of gum

The Automotive Age

balls at the corner drugstore. Nancy had told him he was much more fun than Freddie Willis, with or without a car. Mr. Peepers thought that called for a little celebration and insisted on buying the peanut brittle, too, even though Nancy had lost the transfer game. At the movie that night they consumed all the peanut brittle and three and a half gum balls apiece. The count worked out that way because they shared the last one.

CHAPTER VII

The Thecla Titus

THE FIRST WARM DAY of spring arrived on a Friday. Mr. Peepers took immediate advantage of the opportunity. He announced "Specimen-Collection Week End" to the students. The students groaned. Mr. Peepers smiled. He never paid much attention to student groaning. He had often referred to it as "a natural outgrowth of youthful unwillingness."

"Just bring in a specimen," he said to the class, "identify it and tell us all about it."

Carl Dagny asked an impertinent question.

"No, Carl," Mr. Peepers said firmly. "You certainly may not borrow a test tube." He dismissed the class. The children filed glumly from the classroom.

The Thecla Titus

Mr. Peepers was amused by their chagrin. He wanted the children to take advantage of spring—by force, if necessary. Mr. Peepers believed in taking advantage of things. He did not make an exception of Wes Weskit. He asked him along for a Sunday woods junket, believing that Wes would prove of great value as associate collector.

He also thought it would be good for Wes to have an outing. A few days before, Wes had remarked with some asperity: "The Board of Education won't let me get married." He meant that the school had denied his application for a leave of absence until after Easter holidays.

"Perhaps they need you to help paint the eggs," Mr. Peepers suggested, but Wes didn't seem to find any humor in the thought. Mr. Peepers could sympathize with Wes's disappointment. It reminded him of the time he had waited nearly four months for a tadpole to develop into a frog. When the great day at last arrived Mr. Peepers was so exhausted he could not enjoy the experience. He wanted to keep Wes cheery company as much as possible until after Palm Sunday. He knew what it was like to have one's dream postponed.

By four o'clock that Sunday afternoon Mr. Peepers' pockets were brimming with wild ferns, liverwort and mushrooms. He looked forward to Monday's class with great anticipation. He smiled as he heard Wes Weskit's feet plunging through the undergrowth at some distance. "Are you all right, Wes?" he called.

"Rob!" Wes answered, sounding frightened. "Where are you?"

"I'm right over here, Wes," Mr. Peepers cried. "Just follow my voice. Be sure you walk around the——"

He was interrupted by a sound of splashing and a stran-

[165]

Mr. Peepers

gled outcry. It occurred to him that Wes had not been properly apprized of Walker's Bog. A moment later Wes appeared through the bushes dripping wet and festooned with brambles.

"That was Walker's Bog," Mr. Peepers said.

Wes nodded. "Thanks," he said.

Mr. Peepers gazed at the silver birches and the hawthorn. "Isn't nature beautiful, Wes?"

Wes pulled a thorn from one finger. "Yes," he said, wincing, "beautiful."

Mr. Peepers nodded. "I wish we came specimen hunting more often."

Wes showed him a palmful of thorns. "Do you want any of these?"

Mr. Peepers shook his head. "No, Wes. You keep them. They're nice souvenirs."

Wes's head began to quiver. "Thanks a bushel," he said darkly. "You're a pal."

Mr. Peepers smiled and looked into his specimen box. "All right, Wes," he said generously. "I guess I have enough."

Wes stomped eagerly toward the roadway. Mr. Peepers followed, sneaking last-minute glances at a clump of red clover here and a pasqueflower there. He had just completed a swift perusal of some advanced blight on a sycamore when he spotted something amazing on a near-by rock. "Oh, my," he murmured, adding quickly: "Wait a minute, Wes. Come here!"

Wes tramped back grumpily. "What is it?"

Mr. Peepers pointed to a gloriously colored butterfly.

"Say," Wes said, momentarily entranced. "That's a handsome butterfly."

Mr. Peepers was astonished. "I've never seen one like that before."

They stepped closer. Mr. Peepers bent down. Wes joined him, whispering: "Rare, eh?"

"I suppose," Mr. Peepers whispered.

Wes's voice hushed to near inaudibility. "Have you got your butterfly net?"

Mr. Peepers shook his head. "No," he whispered. "It's home full of dirty laundry."

"Oh, no!" Wes cried. Then he caught himself. "Oh, no," he whispered.

Mr. Peepers waved Wes silent. "Perhaps I can catch him by hand," he murmured.

"Steady now," Wes said.

Mr. Peepers extended his hand. His finger tips had very nearly touched the butterfly's wings when he pulled them back.

"What's wrong?" Wes whispered.

"He was looking this way."

They sat silently for several seconds until Wes began to grow impatient. "Look, Rob," he whispered, but Mr. Peepers shushed him. Then Wes got an idea. "Why don't I go around the other side," he suggested, "and distract him?"

"All right," Mr. Peepers whispered. "If you want to."

Wes Weskit winked. "I'll go *around* the bog."

Mr. Peepers kept a patient eye on the butterfly. In the distance, he could hear Wes's careful footsteps sneaking through the brush. Then he heard Wes's voice.

"Oh, nooooo!!"

Which was followed by a splash and the sounds of violent threshing. The butterfly fluttered its wings. Mr. Peepers grabbed quickly. He had it.

Mr. Peepers

"I've caught it, Wes!" he cried.

There was no response.

Mr. Peepers rose from his haunches and peered through the underbrush. "Wes?" he called.

Wes emerged suddenly from some thick foliage. He was again soaking wet. He was also well decorated with cockleburs and fronds. He grinned tensely at Mr. Peepers.

"I'm the outdoor type," he said.

The following morning Mr. Peepers transferred the butterfly to a bell jar, intending to display the little prize to his students. He proudly set up a display table next to his desk. On it he placed the bell jar and his specimen box, the combination making, he felt, an extremely worth-while exhibit.

As for the students, they had done very well too. Even Walter Murdock brought in a specimen.

"All right, class," Mr. Peepers was saying, as Carl Dagny helped Walter back to his seat with the tree trunk, "who else has some nature specimens? Lester?"

Lester Cohen III came to the front of the classroom. He had a box in his hands. "Well, Mr. Peepers," he said haltingly, "I did like you told us. I went out in the country to look for some leaves and plants and junk and . . . uh . . . here it is."

Mr. Peepers was a little disappointed. "The assignment, Lester," he said, "was to identify the specimens and then tell us about them."

Lester looked indignant. "I know what they are."

"Very well," Mr. Peepers said. "Continue."

Lester placed the box on the table. He pulled out a rock. "This is a rock."

The Thecla Titus

Mr. Peepers stared at Lester. "And . . . ?" he said.

Lester stared back at him.

"And?" Mr. Peepers repeated.

Lester shrugged his shoulders. He reached into the box and pulled out another rock. "This is another rock."

Mr. Peepers sighed. "Lester," he said, "you don't seem to follow me. Can't you tell us what kind of rocks these are?"

Lester glanced at the rocks. "Well, they're . . . uh . . . uh . . ."

"Yes?" Mr. Peepers said.

"They're stones!" Lester cried.

Mr. Peepers decided to deal firmly with Lester. "Lester, if you had paid any attention during Igneous Rock Week, you'd have very easily noticed that these are igneous rocks." Mr. Peepers picked up one of the rocks. "See?" he said. "You can tell by the crystalline structure."

Lester looked blankly at the rocks. "Yes, sir," he mumbled.

"What else did you find, Lester?" Mr. Peepers asked.

"That's all," Lester said.

Mr. Peepers frowned. "You didn't really go to the country at all, did you?"

Lester's face got very red. "No, sir, I didn't."

Mr. Peepers nodded knowingly. "Where did you get these rocks?"

"From Walter Murdock," Lester said.

"Oh?" Mr. Peepers said.

"He threw 'em at me," Lester said.

"Take your seat, Lester," Mr. Peepers said. "We shall discuss another assignment for you after class."

Mr. Peepers smiled at the students. The time had come

Mr. Peepers

for his personal exhibit. "Right now, class," he said, "I'd like to show you some of my specimens." Mr. Peepers reached into his specimen box. "This," he said happily, "is a spruce bough. I found it in the woods near Walker's Pond. Isn't it charming?"

The students were silent. Mr. Peepers cleared his throat.

"Contrary to popular belief," he continued, "the spruce is a flowering plant. It has ovules, stamens and pistils . . . contrary to popular belief." Mr. Peepers leaned forward. He wanted to impress the point upon the children. "It's really difficult to comprehend," he said, "why there are still people who do not believe this. Even though the facts have been published time and again in publications like *Petal and Stem, How Does Your Garden Grow, Gardening without Fear,* and a fine nature book by Tennessee Dingle called *Way Down Yonder with the Compost*—all internationally known publications. Yet, the false propaganda persists. Oh, well . . ." Mr. Peepers dropped the subject. The students didn't seem impressed by the injustice of it all. He smiled and picked up another specimen. "This," he said, "is a sprig of white clover. The family is normally friendly to man. It includes peas, beans, alfalfa and other sources of vegetable protein. But, like many families, it has its wayward members, too: most notably the milk vetch, the dreaded locoweed of the West." Mr. Peepers frowned and shook his head. "A very bad weed," he said darkly, "very bad." He replaced the clover in the box. Then he proudly indicated the bell jar. "And now, class," he announced, "the find of the day." He scratched playfully at the glass surface. The butterfly fluttered its wings. "Of course," Mr. Peepers said, smiling, "you can see it's a butterfly. I caught him

The Thecla Titus

yesterday near Walker's Bog with the expert assistance of Mr. Weskit. We must give credit where credit is due, mustn't we? Of course we must. Isn't he a beauty? I have never encountered this particular species before. Hence I'm somewhat elated. If you'd like, you may come to the front of the class and——"

The school bell bonged. Mr. Peepers glanced at his desk clock. "My," he murmured, "time does fly. . . ." He looked at the children and smiled. "Well," he said brightly, "we shall discuss our winged friend a little more thoroughly tomorrow. Class dismissed."

After the students had left and Mr. Peepers finished straightening up his desk, he sat down contentedly with his chin in his hand and smiled at the butterfly. The butterfly flopped its wings lazily against the inside of the jar.

"You're beautiful," Mr. Peepers murmured. The butterfly fluttered crazily inside the jar, up and down and sideways. "I wish you could tell me who you are and where you came from," Mr. Peepers whispered. "I've written to the Midwestern Society of Lepidopterists about you. Perhaps they'll tell me who you are."

Mrs. Gurney, dumfounded, stood by the door. She had entered Mr. Peepers' classroom a moment before. Looking hurriedly right and left, she wondered anxiously with whom Mr. Peepers was talking. Then she heard him laugh.

"Here, here!" he was saying, his eyes fascinated by the butterfly. "Don't wave your antennae so much—you'll get dizzy."

Mrs. Gurney's head trembled. She wondered if Mr. Peepers were conducting some sort of supernatural rite. She tiptoed to behind his desk and gazed at the bell jar. Mr.

Mr. Peepers

Peepers was still murmuring, but his words were unintelligible. Mrs. Gurney stared at the haphazard fluttering inside the bell jar.

"Mr. Peepers," she said nervously, "are you talking to a moth?"

Mr. Peepers looked over his shoulder and smiled. "Oh, hello, Mrs. Gurney," he said. "No, this isn't a moth. This is a butterfly. Butterflies are Rhopalocera and moths are Heterocera."

Mrs. Gurney's head trembled furiously. "Of course they are, dear," she said. "Uh . . . not a moth, you say?"

"Oh, no," Mr. Peepers said. He pointed to the butterfly. "If you will observe the antennae, you'll see that they're club-shaped at the end. That's how we distinguish a butterfly from a moth."

"Splendid," Mrs. Gurney said. She was much relieved. Mr. Peepers' relaxed manner had soothed her nerves somewhat. She peered carefully into the bell jar, and the butterfly made what seemed to be friendly gestures.

"I think he likes you," Mr. Peepers said. "He's waving his antennae at you."

Mrs. Gurney was overcome with gratitude. "Ohhh," she cooed. "Bless him." She put both hands to her forehead and wiggled her index fingers. "Eejaboo!" she cried.

The butterfly seemed to reciprocate.

"My, that's wonderful, Mrs. Gurney," Mr. Peepers said. "You must have club-shaped fingers."

Mrs. Gurney continued waving. "Yes," she said proudly. "Oh, my . . . he's a friendly little thing."

"Yes, he is," Mr. Peepers said. "We've become quite attached. He's very rare, you know. I couldn't find him classi-

The Thecla Titus

fied in any of my entomological encyclopedias. However, I can tell from his size that he belongs to the family Lycaenidae."

Mrs. Gurney stopped waving. "Really?"

Mr. Peepers nodded. "And the neuration of his wings indicates that he belongs to the genus Thecla."

Mrs. Gurney was spared a reply by the entrance of a Western Union messenger. He was a white-haired old gentleman whose head trembled perceptibly. Mrs. Gurney felt instantly drawn to him. In his hand the old man was clutching a telegram.

"You Mr. Peepers?" he asked.

"That's correct," Mr. Peepers said.

"Got a telegram for ya."

Mr. Peepers opened the envelope quickly. Mrs. Gurney and the messenger crowded together, peering over his shoulder.

"Somebody sick?" the messenger asked.

"No," Mr. Peepers said. "This is from the Midwestern Lepidopterist Society."

"Are *they* sick?" Mrs. Gurney asked.

"It's about the butterfly," Mr. Peepers said.

"Oh," the messenger said. "The butterfly's sick."

"No," Mr. Peepers said. "Nobody's sick at all. The society——"

The messenger was indignant. "Then why did they send a telegram," he said, "if nobody's sick?"

Mr. Peepers sighed. "The society," he said, "believes I have a *Thecla titus*."

Mrs. Gurney looked startled. "Oh," she said, "then *you're* sick!"

Mr. Peepers

"No, no," Mr. Peepers said, with a hint of strain. "The *Thecla titus* is this butterfly. The society is sending some people down today to see it first hand."

The old messenger scowled and peered into the bell jar. "Hmp," he said.

"Like it?" Mr. Peepers asked.

The messenger shrugged. "I can take butterflies or leave 'em alone." He looked at Mrs. Gurney and winked. "But you're kinda cute," he said. "Look me up at the office sometime."

Mr. Peepers got busy tidying up his desk. "I guess I'd better get things ready before the people arrive," he said. "This is quite an occasion. They may be here any moment." He stood up and adjusted his suit jacket. "Do I look all right, Mrs. Gurney?"

Mrs. Gurney backed off a step. "Hmmm," she said. "You have a spot on your tie, Mr. Peepers."

"Oh, yes," Mr. Peepers conceded. "It's tomato soup, I believe. The corner drugstore had a special on it this afternoon: two bowls for a quarter. Howard Fulgit, the counterboy there, told me the cellar was so overstocked with tomato soup they didn't have room for lentil soup. I don't like soup at all but I always like to help tradesmen out, so I ate two bowls. It was terrible."

Mrs. Gurney tried not to smile. "You have a highly developed sense of social responsibility, Mr. Peepers."

"Thank you," Mr. Peepers said. "Well, I have another tie in my locker. Would you excuse me, Mrs. Gurney? I'll be right back."

"Of course, Mr. Peepers," Mrs. Gurney said. "Of course." She was secretly delighted to be left alone with the Ly— Thec—the butterfly. As the door closed behind Mr. Peepers

The Thecla Titus

she tiptoed to the bell jar and peered inside. "Oh, my," she murmured, making sympathetic faces. "You don't look very well to me. I wonder if you've had enough to eat today. Would you like a flower?"

The butterfly did not respond.

"Oh," Mrs. Gurney said. "Probably you don't speak English." She waved her index finger again like antennae. The butterfly waved back. "How sweet," Mrs. Gurney said. "I'll get you a flower."

She plucked a daisy from Mr. Peepers' window box and, waving the flower, returned to the bell jar. The butterfly flew ecstatically from one side of the jar to another. Mrs. Gurney smiled blissfully and lifted the lid. The butterfly made a hurried exit.

"Oh, no!" Mrs. Gurney cried. "Don't fly away! Come back!"

The butterfly stopped at the window sill. Mrs. Gurney made a frantic way toward it, endeavoring to control herself. "Now don't be frightened," she whispered desperately. "There's nothing to fear." She set down the flower and put her hands to her forehead. Wiggling her forfingers nervously, she mumbled: "Come to Mrs. Gurney, dear. . . . Mrs. Gurney's a nice lady. . . ."

She interrupted herself to make a grab for the butterfly. The butterfly escaped her grasp and flew away. Mrs. Gurney gasped. "Oh, dear," she said. "Oh, dear."

Two minutes later, when Mr. Peepers returned, Mrs. Gurney was still leaning out the window, calling "Yoo-hoo . . . Come back, little butterfly. . . . Come back!"

"What's wrong, Mrs. Gurney?" Mr. Peepers asked, suspecting the worst.

Mrs. Gurney turned to him and bit her lip. Her head

was trembling very badly. "I was only going to feed him, Mr. Peepers," she murmured, "and he . . . he flew away."

"Oh, dear," Mr. Peepers said.

"That's what I said," Mrs. Gurney said, "oh, dear."

Mr. Peepers scratched his head. "What'll I do? The people from the society will be here any minute. What can I tell them? Oh, dear."

"Oh, dear," Mrs. Gurney replied, crestfallen. "I'm sorry, Mr. Peepers."

"It wasn't your fault, Mrs. Gurney," Mr. Peepers said. "You meant well. I always say there's no use crying over spilled milk."

Mrs. Gurney stared at the floor. "I didn't spill any milk, Mr. Peepers," she said softly. "It was just this flower." She held up the limp daisy. "I wanted him to eat this because he looked so thin."

"I understand," Mr. Peepers said. He took the flower and dropped it into the waste basket. "Please don't worry about it. We'll think of something."

Mrs. Gurney's face brightened slightly. "Perhaps the butterfly will come back."

Mr. Peepers shook his head. "I doubt that. The butterfly isn't known for its homing instinct."

At that moment Carl Dagny entered the classroom. "There's a bunch of people to see you, Mr. Peepers," he said. "They're down at the office. There's a guy with a camera and everything."

Mr. Peepers sighed. "You may as well tell them to come up, Carl."

"Okay," Carl said.

Mr. Peepers looked at Mrs. Gurney. "Oh, dear," he said.

"Oh, dear," Mrs. Gurney said. Then a thought seemed to

occur to her. She began opening and closing Mr. Peepers' desk drawers. At last she secured a medium-sized cloth. She draped it cermoniously over the bell jar.

"What's that for?" Mr. Peepers asked.

Mrs. Gurney laughed triumphantly. "Oh, Bernice Gurney," she said, "you're so clever." She gazed proudly at Mr. Peepers. "We'll say he's taking a nap!" she exclaimed. "And mustn't be disturbed."

Mr. Peepers was not enthusiastic. "It won't work," he said. "They'll want to peek."

Mrs. Gurney nodded, removing the cloth. "Even the walls have ears."

The door to the classroom burst open. Four men entered briskly: three of them with broad smiles and Homburgs; the fourth with a crumpled, gray suit, an expression to match, and a Rolleiflex camera. Mr. Peepers assumed that he was the newspaper representative.

"Come in, gentlemen," Mr. Peepers said gaily, trying to keep up appearances. "I'm Robinson J. Peepers."

The most prosperous-looking member of the group stepped forward. He had a tiny waxed mustache and was wearing pin-striped trousers. He removed his Homburg and extended his hand. "Anderson P. Henderson," he said suavely.

Mr. Peepers recognized the name at once. "Oh, yes," he said. "You're the famous butterfly collector."

Mr. Henderson responded with a military nod. "Correct," he said. He turned crisply to his associates. "This is Mr. Peepers, gentlemen." The two men nodded. Mr. Henderson immediately returned his attention to Mr. Peepers. "And Mr. Peepers, this is Dr. Hudson. Dr. Hudson, Mr. Peepers." Dr. Hudson removed his Homburg. Mr. Peepers bobbed his head. "And Dr. LaPlanche," Mr. Henderson said, "Mr. Peepers. Mr. Peepers, Dr. LaPlanche." Dr. LaPlanche removed his Homburg. Mr. Peepers bobbed his head. Mr. Henderson cleared his throat. Mr. Peepers tried to introduce Mrs. Gurney, but Mr. Henderson ignored him. "These men," he said to Peepers, "are from the Entomological Society."

Mr. Peepers found Mr. Henderson's briskness a little alarming. "How do you——" he began, but Mr. Henderson interrupted.

"And now, Peepers——" he said, but the cameraman interrupted him, shifting gum from one side of his mouth to the other.

"Will you hold it for a group shot, please?" he said.

Mrs. Gurney hurried to a mirror. Mr. Henderson flung an arm around Mr. Peepers' shoulders and grinned. Mr. Peepers stared at him and tried to duplicate the grin. The effort made his mouth ache. The cameraman's flash bulb exploded just as Mr. Peepers was shaking his head. Not only that, the burst of light affected his eyes adversely. He didn't see well for several seconds. The cameraman put away his camera and made for the door. Mrs. Gurney completed primping and smiled at him. The cameraman smiled back. "Terrific," he said, and departed. Mrs. Gurney looked disappointed. She loved to have her picture taken.

Mr. Henderson rubbed his hands together and stared eagerly at Mr. Peepers. "Well?" he said. "Shall we examine little *Thecla titus?*"

Mr. Peepers looked at Mrs. Gurney. Mrs. Gurney looked at Mr. Peepers. "Er . . . let's have lunch!" she said.

The three men glared at her. "We've eaten, thank you," Mr. Henderson replied. "May we see the butterfly now?"

The Thecla Titus

Mr. Peepers cleared his throat. "Well . . . I . . ."

Mrs. Gurney leaped bravely into the breach. "I turned it free!" she shouted.

The three gentlemen spoke as one. "Wha-a-a-a-t?"

"Well, I . . ." Mrs. Gurney said. "No nation can survive . . . Are you *sure* you've had lunch?"

Mr. Henderson stared at Mr. Peepers. "Is it true, sir?" he queried. "Has the quarry escaped?"

Mr. Peepers hung his head. "Yes, sir," he said. "We were only going to——"

He was interrupted by the *Thecla titus* itself. It flew loopingly through the window and alighted on his shoulder.

"Aaahhhhh!" the three gentlemen said.

Mr. Peepers looked at the butterfly and smiled. He lifted his hand to his shoulder.

"Shhhhhh!" Mr. Henderson said.

"Shhhh!" the two doctors said, glaring at Mrs. Gurney.

"Shhhhh!" Mrs. Gurney said, glaring back at them.

Mr. Peepers lowered his hand. The hushing sounds had made him nervous. "Please," he whispered. "It's really very simple."

"Simple," Mr. Henderson repeated.

Mr. Peepers smiled at the butterfly. Mr. Henderson interrupted him. "Peepers . . ." he whispered.

"What?" Mr. Peepers said.

"Don't you have a pocket net?"

Mr. Peepers shook his head. "I'll catch him with my hand." Again he raised his hand to his shoulder. He had very nearly touched the butterfly when the door was flung open.

"Hi, everybody," Wes Weskit said.

Everyone responded with a horrified "Shhhh!" except

Mr. Peepers

Mr. Peepers. He was too busy. He had decided to approach the butterfly by walking his fingers deceptively along his shoulder.

Mrs. Gurney watched the process, hypnotized. She could hear her heart thudding furiously in her breast. She glanced wide-eyed at Wes Weskit. "Isn't this exciting?" she whispered.

"Shhhhhh!" everyone answered.

Mr. Peepers secured the butterfly in a sudden skillful fillip. Everyone exhaled. Mr. Henderson applauded. Mr. Peepers smiled gratefully. He put the butterfly back in the bell jar as the three specialists crowded around. For several seconds they exchanged unintelligible mumbles, while Mr. Peepers, Mrs. Gurney and Wes waited. At last Mr. Henderson exchanged a look of certitude with Dr. LaPlanche, who was breathing heavily. Then he turned to Mr. Peepers.

"This is the *Thecla,* Peepers," he said huskily. "I've only seen one other."

Mr. Peepers blinked his eyes. "Really?"

"Correct," Mr. Henderson said. "In the Bellissima Collection in Greenland."

"It's beautiful," Dr. Hudson said, almost tearfully.

"Bellissima!" Dr. LaPlanche added.

"Peepers," Mr. Henderson said, "I'm prepared to offer you a tidy sum for the *Thecla*: three hundred dollars."

Mrs. Gurney and Wes Weskit gasped. Mr. Peepers stood stock still, with his mouth open. "Oh, my," he said.

"I'll expect you to mount it for me, of course," Mr. Henderson said.

Mr. Peepers was startled. "Mount it? You mean—I'll have to kill it?"

Mr. Henderson chortled. "They're rather difficult to

mount live," he said. The two doctors joined him, as they all laughed merrily.

Mr. Peepers frowned. He couldn't see himself killing the butterfly. Not that the process was completely new to him. He had mounted butterflies for the Junior Lepidopterist Society as a youth. In fact, he still had mounting tools in his desk. But, as his Grandmother had so often said, youth is callous, and Mr. Peepers could no longer think of killing mobile things without a twinge of conscience.

"You'd better let me think it over for a few minutes," he murmured. He walked dejectedly to the other side of the room. Wes and Mrs. Gurney joined him. For a few moments no one said anything. Mr. Peepers was thinking that if the *Thecla was* so rare it should be allowed to live and multiply. The near extinction of the buffalo struck him as a deplorable example of avarice and profligacy. He did not wish to contribute to the annihilation of a species. It wasn't worth three hundred dollars.

Wes Weskit watched him carefully. Finally he could contain himself no longer. "Gee whiz, sport," he whispered, "three hundred dollars is a lot of money. I don't know what you're waiting for."

Mr. Peepers shook his head. "I don't know, Wes," he said. "Such a rare specimen should be allowed to live and multiply. Then, next year, there'd be more of them."

Wes spread his hands. "But even if they *do* multiply," he insisted, "how'll you know where to find this one?"

Mr. Peepers didn't know. "Perhaps he'll keep in touch," he said, smiling. "Besides, I've become quite fond of him."

"But, sport," Wes said, "just think of what three hundred dollars means. You could buy a new mattress and get rid of that one with the dent in it."

Mr. Peepers

"Oh, I'm used to that dent now," Mr. Peepers replied. "It just fits my right shoulder."

Mrs. Gurney offered a suggestion. "You could buy a new suit of clothes," she said softly.

Wes nodded. "That's right, ace."

Mr. Peepers looked down at his suit. "Isn't this suit all right?"

"Oh, sure," Wes said, "it's fine, but . . ."

"I always thought it looked pretty good."

"It does, it does," Wes said. "But . . . well, look, you've got a brown suit. Right?"

"Right."

"Now suppose," Wes persisted, "just suppose that your mother or someone gave you a pair of black shoes. I mean, these things do happen. If all you've got is a brown suit, you're finished. Those black shoes would just lie there and rot!"

Mr. Peepers smiled. "I don't like black shoes, Wes."

Wes gave up. "Just thinking of you, sport."

"You do what you think best, Mr. Peepers," Mrs. Gurney said. "If it bothers you to hurt your little friend, there's nothing to be done about it. But still . . . three hundred dollars . . . Oh, dear!"

Mr. Peepers smiled gratefully. "Thanks," he said. "Both of you. I suppose you're right."

He walked over to Mr. Henderson, who was making faces at the butterfly. The butterfly seemed to be laughing. Mr. Peepers stared at it wistfully.

"Well," Mr. Henderson said, "have you made up your mind, Peepers?"

"Just about," Mr. Peepers said. "It seems sort of silly to

The Thecla Titus

turn down three hundred dollars. When would you want the *Thecla titus*?"

"If you can do it this afternoon, fine."

"Very well," Mr. Peepers said. "You're at the hotel?"

"That's right," Mr. Henderson said. "Let me know when you finish." He addressed his companions crisply. "Gentlemen?" The two doctors replaced their Homburgs. Mr. Henderson bowed to Mrs. Gurney and the doctors did likewise. All three departed.

Mrs. Gurney bent over the bell jar and made imitation antennae once more with her forefingers. "Good-by," she whispered. Wes Weskit tapped her on the shoulder. They both left quietly.

Mr. Peepers was alone with *Thecla titus*. He took his mounting tools from the desk drawer, along with some chloroform and cotton. He saturated the cotton slowly. Then he lifted the lid of the bell jar and began to insert the soaked cotton. The butterfly fluttered about and Mr. Peepers halted.

"I wish you wouldn't look at me like that," he said.

He started to insert the cotton again, but he couldn't complete the action. The butterfly looped foolishly in the jar. Mr. Peepers decided to try logic. "You wouldn't want those black shoes to rot in the closet, would you?" he asked.

The butterfly flopped its wings against the sides of its enclosure.

"What are black shoes to a butterfly?" Mr. Peepers conceded. "Especially to a brown butterfly."

He replaced the lid to the bell jar, thinking that the time had come to deal with the realities of the situation: to talk to himself like a Dutch uncle. After all, he reasoned,

Mr. Peepers

butterflies are chloroformed and mounted every day. It is part of the study of science. If I don't do it, someone else will. The money would come in very handy. I could buy my mother a music box, the kind she's always wanted: a model of the Eiffel Tower that plays Hawaiian songs. I could make a contribution to the Anti-Butterfly-Mounting Society, thereby sacrificing one butterfly to save many more. I could buy a pair of brown and white shoes. All my life I've wanted a pair of brown and white shoes.

Mr Peepers braced himself. He stared sternly at the butterfly. "Brace yourself," he said. He resaturated the cotton with enough chloroform to kill a buffalo. He took the lid completely off the bell jar. He poised the wad of cotton. For a moment he lingered, paralyzed in his position as destructive mercenary. The butterfly seemed to be looking up at him. Mr. Peepers drew in his breath and dropped the cotton. He scooped the butterfly into his palms and hurried to the window. Then he opened his hands and waved them gently. The butterfly fluttered gracefully into the distance, increasing altitude as it disappeared.

"Come back and see me next spring!" Mr. Peepers called. The butterfly's wings waved quickly, as though it had heard him. Mr. Peepers smiled and cupped his hands around his mouth. "Have lots of children!" he called.

CHAPTER VIII

Freedom of the Press

H E WISHED the same for Marge and Wes Weskit. They were married, at last, on the eleventh of April. Mr. Peepers and Nancy Remington, in their respective capacities as best man and maid of honor, accompanied the betrothed pair to Chicago.

The wedding went off without a hitch. Except, perhaps, for the moment when Mr. Peepers appeared in the vestry clad in top hat, pearl-gray tie and striped trousers. Wes Weskit looked at him as though he'd gone mad. "Didn't I tell you, ace?" he cried. "We're all wearing blue suits."

Mr. Peepers had to return the suit to the renting tailor. Luckily the shop was near by and there was time. However, the double-breasted affair they gave him instead was a

Mr. Peepers

trifle large. In fact, Mr. Peepers had some difficulty presenting the ring on cue. The coat sleeves overlapped his fingers, impairing his dexterity severely. But all minor mishaps had been forgotten by the time Marge and Wes boarded the midnight express for Sun Valley.

As the train began pulling out, something crucial occurred to Mr. Peepers. "Oh, Wes!" he cried, shouting through the closed window of the newlyweds' compartment and beginning to jogtrot beside the train. "I forgot to tell you! You were married on the Two Hundred and Sixty-third Anniversary of the Crowning of William and Mary in London!"

Since Wes was a history teacher, Mr. Peepers thought the information wonderfully appropriate. He had memorized it carefully before leaving Jefferson City. Wes, however, didn't seem to understand him. The train made its slow, chugging way out of the station with Wes's nose pressed firmly sideways against the window. There was a puzzled expression on his face. "William and Mary!" Mr. Peepers shouted. "William and Mary!" But the train was gone.

Mr. Peepers turned to Nancy, a little abashed. "I forgot to tell him earlier."

Nancy smiled at him. "It's all right, Robinson. You can tell them when they get back."

Ten days later in Jefferson City Mr. Peepers was gazing happily at a colorful photograph on the front of a post card, his first news from the honeymoon couple since their departure. Beneath the picture an advertising blurb proclaimed proudly: SUN VALLEY IS ONE OF AMERICA'S MOST BREATHTAKING AND POPULAR VACATION RESORTS. Mr. Peepers nodded and turned over the post card. *Dear Sport,* Wes's message read, *They say that Sun Valley is one of America's most*

Freedom of the Press

breath-taking and popular vacation resorts. Mary sends her love. William.

Mr. Peepers knew that Wes would be returning to school within a day or two. Marge had telephoned Nancy to ask if the apartment they'd rented would be ready by the week end. Mr. Peepers smiled, thinking of all the fun they'd be having in the future. If he had three dreams in life, they were to see Wes settled down, to settle down himself, and to do a good job at the school. One of those dreams was now realized. As for the second, it was, as his Grandmother might have put it, quickening. The third, however, was another matter.

Mr. Peepers sometimes felt a twinge of anxiety concerning his position at Jefferson Junior High. Though there was no tangible evidence to support his concern, he often wondered just how valuable he was to the students and the school. Mr. Sidfern, the school superintendent, was scheduled to make an inspection that very afternoon. Mr. Peepers' palms perspired a bit whenever he thought of it. But above all he wanted to be more closely related to the students, particularly to school activities outside his own classroom. Furthering the latter wish, he had nearly completed a pleasant and illuminating week with the school newspaper. In Wes's place he'd been appointed faculty adviser for the end of April and the month of May. His first week's assignment was with the Jefferson Junior High *Spectator, Reporter and Observer*—WE SEE EVERYTHING. Mr. Peepers had found it a humbling experience. Young Homer Jansen, who edited the paper, was a bright young man of extraordinary capacity. In fact, it was hard for Mr. Peepers to believe that anyone less than five feet tall could attain, when necessary, such stature.

Mr. Peepers

On the day the "Specrepserver" (which was what Homer called it) went to press, Mr. Peepers dropped by the school printing room.

Homer Jansen stood up cheerfully and greeted him. He had a pencil tucked behind each ear. "It's sure been fun working with you this week, Mr. Peepers," Homer said, among other things.

Mr. Peepers felt very gratified. "Thank you, Homer. It's been fun for me, too. This is my first turn as faculty adviser."

"Well, you've been jim-dandy," Homer said, in his best professional manner. "You must have worked on a newspaper before."

"Well," Mr. Peepers said modestly, "at one time I almost took the job of garden editor with my home-town newspaper."

"Why didn't you, Mr. Peepers?"

"The paper made a last-minute policy change," Mr. Peepers replied. "Instead of gardening, they devoted the space to a column on croquet. It was called 'From Wicket to Post with Henrietta Mallet.'" Mr. Peepers smiled at Homer. "A pen name," he explained.

Homer adjusted his green eyeshade. "What was her real name?"

"Ralph Smith," Mr. Peepers replied. "He used the other name so the boys at the Fergus Garage wouldn't know. Ralph was an excellent mechanic."

Homer stared blankly at him. "Well," he said finally, with his customary heartiness, "so long and thirty, Mr. Peepers. I have to finish up the lead headline." He turned his head in another direction. "Copy boy!" he shouted.

Mr. Peepers decided to leave Homer to his duties. At a near-by desk Arabella Simpkins was working on the social

Freedom of the Press

column. Mr. Peepers thought it might be nice to pay her a visit. "How's it going, Arabella?" he said pleasantly.

Arabella finished pecking at her typewriter and smiled. She pulled the sheet from the roller and showed it to Mr. Peepers. Mr. Peepers read it aloud proudly. " 'Locker-Room Listenings,' " he announced, " 'by Arabella Simpkins.' " He nodded to Arabella. "Very nice title, Arabella."

"Thank you," Arabella said.

Mr. Peepers read the rest of the column. " 'We ought to have more talent programs like the one given in the auditorium last Thursday. Everyone said they liked it very much—especially the violin and xylophone challenge number.' " Mr. Peepers glanced at Arabella. "It was thrilling, wasn't it?"

"It gave me chills," Arabella said.

Mr. Peepers perused a little more of Arabella's column. "Well," he said, "this is interesting. 'Rumor is around that the silver slave bracelet given to Linda Shelton by Walter Murdock is nothing but his bicycle clip with the paint scraped off. For shame, Walter.' " Mr. Peepers smiled in spite of himself. "Are you positive of this, Arabella?"

"Oh, sure," Arabella said happily. "Read the next article."

Mr. Peepers nodded. " 'There was much excitement,' " he read, " 'in front of school yesterday when Walter Murdock skinned his knee. He got his trouser leg tangled in his bicycle sprocket!' " Mr. Peepers looked at Arabella again. "My, my," he said, "you're really letting Walter have it, aren't you, Arabella?"

Arabella nodded vehemently. "He'll never break a date with *me* again!"

Mr. Peepers cleared his throat. He thought of cautioning

Mr. Peepers

Arabella against vengeful tendencies, but decided that silence would be more persuasive. "Incidentally, Arabella," he said, "has Tommy Sparks finished the editorial column yet?"

"He's still working on it, I think."

Mr. Peepers nodded gravely. "Well," he said, "I hope we can get the paper completed before noon. We're having final term inspection by the school superintendent today and I'd like to get my science room in order."

"We'll get it finished," Arabella said. "I only have a couple more articles to write."

Tommy Sparks, a curly-haired young man with alert eyes, approached Mr. Peepers energetically. He had a piece of paper in his hand. "Hi, Mr. Peepers," he said intensely. "I finished my editorial."

Mr. Peepers was always a little alarmed by Tommy's driving inner force. It reminded him of an overaccelerating engine. "Well, that's fine, Tommy."

"Boy!" Tommy replied. "I really let 'em have it. I did a whole column on that new rule that stops the kids from sitting on the grass at lunchtime."

Mr. Peepers took the paper from Tommy's eager hands and read it over silently. It was rather virulently written: sprinkled through with phrases such as "this autocratic trampling on students' rights" and "Nature Belongs to All!" Mr. Peepers could not quite keep his face from setting into an expression of disapproval.

Tommy's cheerfulness faded slightly. "Did I get too rough, Mr. Peepers? I'll change it if you want."

Mr. Peepers shook his head. He didn't think it was his job to censor the students' opinions. The whole idea behind having a newspaper was to allow the boys and girls to ex-

Freedom of the Press

press themselves, even if they were wrong. "Well," he said, blinking, "are you sure this is the way all the students feel about it?"

Tommy nodded vigorously. "Oh yes, Mr. Peepers. I talked to every kid I could get my hands on before I wrote it. Student Council and everybody. They'll back me one hundred per cent."

"I'm with you all the way, scoop," Homer Jansen interjected.

Mr. Peepers cleared his throat. He hoped there wouldn't be repercussions, but he could not see himself interfering with the students' rights. "Then we'll print it," he said firmly. "It's your newspaper."

Tommy smiled gratefully. "Excuse me, Mr. Peepers," he said. He walked away, calling: "Get the front page ready, Emily."

Mr. Peepers stared after him for a moment. Then he shook off his apprehension. "All right, everybody," he said, "I'd like to have your attention, please."

Homer Jansen shouted to the other students: "Stop the presses!"

Mr. Peepers pointed to the clock on the wall. "As you can see," he said, "time is relentless. Let's see if we can have the paper out by noon. I want the room cleaned up and in order by the time the superintendent makes his inspection. Keep up the good work. When I return, I'll have the long arm of the law, in the person of Mr. Sidfern, with me. I hope you'll be ready for him."

"We'll be ready, chief!" Homer Jansen shouted.

The rest of the staff set up a cheer for Mr. Peepers, who smiled gratefully and made his way to the door. With his hand on the knob, he turned back to the grinning children

Mr. Peepers

and lifted his free hand high. "Don't forget," he said firmly. "Do a good job. Remember our motto: *'Machina mimiographica est gladio fortior.'* Or, 'The mimeograph machine is mightier than the sword!'"

Later, when everything was in order in his own classroom, Mr. Peepers had the students get cleaned up in the washroom and reseat themselves at their desks. He had begun to feel a little nervous. Mr. Sidfern was something of a bogyman to him. Mr. Peepers wanted his approval very badly. He always had visions of Mr. Sidfern speaking against him at closed meetings of the school board, saying things like: "Peepers is a dried-up little eccentric. He shouldn't be in a supervisory position with children. He should be left alone somewhere in a dark room to compose botanical encyclopediae." Mr. Peepers smoothed down his cowlick with one hand and glanced anxiously at the classroom clock. He hoped the children would behave themselves; especially Walter Murdock. It was on such unpredictables as Walter Murdock, Mr. Peepers felt, that the fate of many a schoolteacher turned.

"Now, class," Mr. Peepers said, trying to ignore his fears, "when Superintendent Sidfern enters our room, I will nod my head like this." Mr. Peepers demonstrated with a cleanly defined nod. "That will be the signal for you to rise. When I nod again, in the same fashion, you will all say in unison: 'Good afternoon, Superintendent Sidfern.' Then, when I nod the third time, you may take your seats. Is that clear?"

The students showed no sign of Yes or No. They had what Mr. Peepers called their "unit face" on. Mr. Peepers shud-

Freedom of the Press

dered, thinking of all the mishaps they could cause with Mr. Sidfern. "How many don't understand?" he asked as calmly as possible.

Gradually four hands appeared in the air, one by tentative one.

Mr. Peepers counted them aloud. "One, two, three, four. Well, class," he said, "if you'd only pay atten——"

He was interrupted by a fifth, eager hand. It belonged to Elwood Hamper.

"Very well, Elwood—five," Mr. Peepers said. "Now, students, I suggest to those who don't understand that they simply follow the rest of the class. Shall we try it once?"

Mr. Peepers made a pronounced nod. The students rose as one to their feet. Mr. Peepers breathed a sigh of relief. He made a second nod. The students said in remarkable unison: "Good afternoon, Superintendent Fidsern."

Mr. Peepers was aghast. "No, class, no," he whispered. "Sidfern. Sidfern. Now, let's try it again." He nodded. The children spoke as one: "Good afternoon, Superintendent Sidfern." Mr. Peepers made a final, pronounced nod and the children sat down.

"Very good," Mr. Peepers said. "Now—let's try it once more. . . ."

He did not hear the door open. Nor did he see Superintendent Sidfern enter the classroom. And, of course, he was not aware that the superintendent was standing right behind him as he nodded his head. The children rose. Mr. Peepers nodded again.

"Good afternoon, Superintendent Sidfern," the students chimed.

"Good afternoon, boys and girls," the superintendent replied in a great, booming voice.

Mr. Peepers

Mr. Peepers' expression became very severe. "All right," he said to the class. "Who said that?"

The children were paralyzed with horror.

"I did," the superintendent replied.

Mr. Peepers was really angry. "You are trying to make trouble, Walter Murdock," he said.

"No, no, Peepers, I said it," the superintendent said, tapping Mr. Peepers on the shoulder.

Mr. Peepers' head came near to breaking off relations with his neck. "Oh!" he said, startled at seeing the red-faced, imposing figure of the superintendent. "Mr. Sidfern! . . . Well . . . ah . . . hello." Mr. Peepers cleared his throat and told the class to sit down.

"Well, Peepers," Mr. Sidfern said, his face critical, "how's everything going?"

"Fine, thank you," Mr. Peepers said nervously.

"Getting ready for examinations?"

Mr. Peepers nodded. The students stood up. "Er . . . sit down please, class," Mr. Peepers said.

"Your room looks very orderly," Mr. Sidfern said, running one finger over the nearest window sill. "You're doing a fine job. Place looks tiptop. Getting enough supplies?"

Mr. Peepers nodded. The students stood up. Mr. Sidfern's jowls responded with a slight flutter of surprise. Mr. Peepers' heart sank. "Uh . . . take your seats please, class," he said hoarsely.

Unbelieving, Mr. Sidfern stared at the pupils. "Active group," he said.

Mr. Peepers was too nervous to control himself. He nodded again, while saying: "Yes."

The students stood up.

Mr. Peepers tried to wave them down. "Er . . . class,"

Freedom of the Press

he said, "the . . . uh . . . signals are off. Please remain in your seats."

Superintendent Sidfern frowned in dismay. "What in the world is wrong with your students, Peepers?"

Mr. Peepers stammered his way through a quickly invented excuse. "It's . . . uh . . . Well, I have . . . They get up when I nod. It's an exercise period. I mean . . . discipline."

"Never mind," Mr. Sidfern said curtly. He strolled down one of the aisles. Mr. Peepers followed hurriedly. Unfortunately, Mr. Sidfern stopped first beside dangerous Walter Murdock. Mr. Peepers held his breath.

"What's your name, young man?" Mr. Sidfern asked.

"Walter Murdock, sir," Walter replied, straight-faced and crisply.

Mr. Sidfern smiled benignly. "Everything all right with you, young man?"

"Sure," Walter said blithely. " 'Cept for one thing." He pulled up his pants leg to show his skinned knee.

"Well," Mr. Sidfern said, "skinned knee, eh? How'd that happen?"

"I'm engaged," Walter said.

The superintendent stared at the young man for a good ten seconds. "You're what?"

Mr. Peepers thought it might be good policy to interrupt before Walter complicated things further. "Well, you see . . . uh . . . Walter had a bicycle clip and he . . . uh . . . Well, he scraped the paint off and gave it to a young lady. The bicycle clip, of course. . . . Naturally he didn't give her the paint. It was sort of . . . Well, it was in the school paper. . . . Excitement in front of the school and . . . Well, he . . ."

Mr. Peepers

Mr. Sidfern was staring at Mr. Peepers as suspiciously as he had at Walter Murdock. Mr. Peepers realized that he had failed to make sense out of Walter's little saga. He cleared his throat, trying to conceal his embarrassment. "Er . . . would you like to see some clean test tubes?" he asked.

Mr. Sidfern frowned at him. "In a moment," he said. He passed on to the next desk. Elwood Hamper, grinning as usual, was standing beside it, erect and cheerful.

"What's your name, young man?" Mr. Sidfern asked.

"Elwood Hamper!" Elwood replied proudly.

Mr. Peepers corrected him in a whisper. "Sir!" he added.

Elwood grinned at Mr. Sidfern. "Sir Elwood Hamper!" he said.

Mr. Sidfern's jowls quivered and danced. Mr. Peepers tried to laugh. "Elwood has a rather advanced sense of humor," he explained.

Mr. Sidfern gazed at Mr. Peepers coldly. He did not seem amused. Mr. Peepers stopped smiling and shrugged his shoulders. Mr. Sidfern nodded. He returned his attention to Elwood.

"Tell me, Elwood," he said, "what have you learned in General Science?"

Elwood's grin faded slightly. He couldn't seem to find an answer to the question.

"Wouldn't you rather ask Marilee Dagny?" Mr. Peepers suggested.

"No," Mr. Sidfern said firmly. "I want Sir Elwood Hamp —this young man to tell me." He looked at Elwood again and softened his tone. "Just what do you study here in General Science?"

Freedom of the Press

Elwood's grin returned. His eyes were glassy with glee. "Rocks!"

"Geology," Mr. Peepers whispered.

"Yea, bo," Elwood said happily. "Geography!"

Mr. Peepers leaped instantly into the breach. "Suppose you tell Superintendent Sidfern how many kinds of rocks we studied."

Elwood held up three fingers. "Three," he said.

"And, of course," Mr. Peepers said quickly, "Elwood knows that the three rocks are igneous, sedimentary, and metamorphose. Don't you, Elwood?"

Elwood grinned more broadly than ever.

"Dont you, Elwood?" Mr. Peepers repeated.

Elwood shrugged his shoulders. "Sure," he said.

"Sit down, Elwood," Mr. Peepers said.

Mr. Sidfern approached Marilee Dagny. Mr. Peepers breathed a bit more easily. "What is your name, young lady?" Mr. Sidfern said.

"Marilee Dagny, sir," Marilee answered brightly.

"Can you tell me what kind of rock marble is?" Mr. Sidfern asked.

"I'd be happy to, sir," Marilee said. "Marble is metamorphosed limestone. Limestone is composed of minute shells and other calcareous parts of marine animals deposited on the bottom of shallow seas millions of years ago. When other layers of materials were deposited on top and the sea bottom was lowered through folding of the earth's surface and ever-increasing——"

Mr. Sidfern coughed loudly. "Very good, young lady," he said. "Shall we move on to the other departments, Peepers?"

[197]

Mr. Peepers

"Yes, sir," Mr. Peepers said. He could have embraced Marilee Dagny. "Leonard," he said to Leonard Gorf, "you may be monitor while I'm gone. Class, I will be gone for a few minutes and I want you all to be quiet in the interim." He nodded again to impress the point on the students.

"Good afternoon, Superintendent Sidfern!" Elwood Hamper shouted.

Mr. Peepers winced and closed the door quickly. He was happy to have emerged from the ordeal with a whole skin. He escorted the superintendent through the scrubbed-down hallways, the newly inventoried school library, and also demonstrated the lately adopted student filing system, all of which had been supervised by Mr. Peepers during his first week as faculty adviser. The superintendent seemed pleased. Mr. Peepers hoped that the tidiness of everything might placate what he regarded as Mr. Sidfern's prejudice against him. When at last they arrived at the pressroom of the school paper, Mr. Peepers was relieved to see that all activity had ceased and that the students were seated quietly behind their desks waiting for inspection.

"Very efficient-looking operation, Peepers," Mr. Sidfern said. "Yes, indeed, you've done a fine job this week."

"Thank you, sir," Mr. Peepers said.

Mr. Sidfern stopped in front of Arabella Simpkins' desk. "What is your name, young lady?"

"Arabella Simpkins, sir."

"And what is your job on the school paper?"

"I write the social column, sir," Arabella said.

Mr. Sidfern looked surprised. "Social column?"

Mr. Peepers decided not to leave the explanation up to Arabella. He envisioned the entire embarrassing incident

Freedom of the Press

concerning Walter Murdock's knee being dredged up into another moment of chaos. "Er . . . you know, sir," he said, "who's going with what girl . . . ah . . . entertainment, parties, skinned knees . . . er . . . bicycle clips—things like that."

Mr. Sidfern looked bewildered. "Yes, yes, of course."

Mr. Peepers piloted the superintendent to Homer Jansen's desk. "This is our editor, Homer Jansen," he said. "This is Mr. Sidfern, Homer."

They exchanged how-do-you-do's and Mr. Sidfern made his way to the mimeograph machine. Tommy Sparks was standing beside it, smiling. Mr. Peepers quietly crossed his fingers behind his back as Mr. Sidfern thumbed idly through the foot-high stack of separate sheets.

"That's this week's edition, sir," Tommy Sparks said. "Hot off the press."

Mr. Sidfern nodded, examining the front page with interest. "Hmmmm," he said. "Very well done, too."

"Thank you, sir," Tommy said.

Mr. Sidfern picked up the editorial page. "Well," he said, "editorials, too, eh?"

Mr. Peepers held his breath for a moment. "Oh, yes," he said, "everything's authentic."

Mr. Sidfern was reading the editorial. Mr. Peepers observed his facial expressions very carefully. After a moment of colloidal suspension, he saw Mr. Sidfern's attitude metamorphose from interest to concern. Mr. Sidfern beckoned Mr. Peepers to one side, away from the eager ears of Tommy Sparks and Homer Jansen.

"Peepers," Mr. Sidfern said, "what's this?"

Mr. Peepers assumed a bland expression. "Sir?" he said softly.

Mr. Peepers

Mr. Sidfern tapped at the page with one finger. "This editorial criticizing the rule prohibiting the students from sitting on the grass."

Mr. Peepers tried to look deprecating. "Oh, that's a mere . . ."

Mr. Sidfern shook his head. "I think you'd better delete it, Peepers. You know, criticizing the administration and all that sort of thing."

"But, sir," Mr. Peepers said, "the students have a right . . ."

Mr. Sidfern placed a hand on Mr. Peepers' shoulder. "You've done a good job this week, Peepers," he said warmly. "A fine job—sterling!"

"But, sir . . ." Mr. Peepers said.

"Have this little matter taken care of at once and I'd say everything was top-notch."

"But, sir . . ." Mr. Peepers said.

Mr. Sidfern patted him on the back. "Good boy," he said. "Stout fellow."

"But, sir . . ." Mr. Peepers said. Mr. Sidfern, however, had left the pressroom.

Later, in the science room, Mr. Peepers discussed the problem with Harvey Weskit, who had just returned to the school from his honeymoon. Mr. Peepers was feeding his pet white mouse, whom he called Louis after the famous Dr. Pasteur. Louis, who was often temperamental, snapped and snarled at each morsel Mr. Peepers fed him. The feeding was slow and patient because Mr. Peepers disapproved of Louis' tendency to bolt his food. Wes Weskit jumped slightly as Louis thrust his voracious head through the small bars of his cage. Mr. Peepers, however, was so used

Freedom of the Press

to Louis that he hardly noticed. Wes Weskit found it difficult to listen to what Mr. Peepers was saying. He was too entranced by Mr. Peepers' indifference to Louis' snapping and snarling.

"And then," Mr. Peepers was saying, "Mr. Sidfern told me to take the article out of the paper, Wes."

Wes Weskit shook off his hypnosis and concentrated on Mr. Peepers' problem. "Appalling," he said.

Mr. Peepers put another morsel of mouse food between his thumb and forefinger. Louis snapped avidly at it. "It isn't fair, Wes," Mr. Peepers said. "The students have a right to express themselves, even if they're wrong."

Wes Weskit moved his head slowly from side to side. "It's a pure case of freedom of the press, sport."

"That's what I say," Mr. Peepers said, as Louis made small sounds of chomping and chewing.

Wes Weskit cleared his throat. "Thomas Jefferson," he said gravely, "had something to say along those lines. It went something like this, and I quote: 'No Government ought to be without critics; and, where the press is free, none ever will.'"

Mr. Peepers nodded. "Thomas Jefferson."

Wes Weskit was amazed. "Right! How'd you know?"

Mr. Peepers looked at his friend. "You just——" he began, but Wes interrupted.

"Oh, yes," Wes said, "I just told you. Well, what are the plans, ace? You gonna take it out of the paper or not?"

Mr. Peepers moved his fingers away from Louis' mouth. The greedy mouse had tried to bite them. "I don't know, Wes," he said, offering the morsel to Louis again. "If I did take it out, I'd never feel right about it."

"You're going to lose a finger," Wes said.

Mr. Peepers

Mr. Peepers smiled. "I don't think so, Wes. Louis' little threats are meaningless, really."

Wes Weskit thought for a moment. "Know what I'd do if I were you?"

"What?"

Wes raised his eyebrows pontifically. Then he began nodding. " 'Course," he conceded, "the thing is I'm not you."

Mr. Peepers decided to attend to Wes carefully. He brushed the crumbs of mouse food from his fingers. He thought that Louis should go on a diet, anyway. The mouse was getting unconscionably fat. "I know," Mr. Peepers said, "but if you *were* me, what would you do?"

"And I don't want to confuse you," Wes said, "by a hypothetical situation."

Mr. Peepers shook his head. "I'm not confused."

"Right," Wes said. "So, if I were you——"

"Hypothetically," Mr. Peepers said gravely. "Because you're not me."

"Right."

"And," Mr. Peepers added, "conversely, I'm not you."

"Right," Wes said. He started to go on, but stopped abruptly.

"Go ahead," Mr. Peepers said mildly. "I'm not confused."

Wes nodded. "I know, I know. But I've forgotten what I wanted to say." After a moment's reflection, he continued. "Well, that's what I'd do if I were you. And, I think, what Thomas Jefferson would do, too—if he were you, instead of me."

Mr. Peepers frowned slightly. "Well . . ."

"Do you follow me?" Wes asked.

Mr. Peepers was stunned. "Uh-huh."

Freedom of the Press

"Well," Wes said, smiling broadly, "need I say more, sport?"

Mr. Peepers airily returned Wes's smile. "Thanks a lot, Wes."

Wes Weskit leaned over and gripped Mr. Peepers' shoulders firmly with both hands. "Don't be afraid," he said.

After he left, Mr. Peepers thought for a moment about Wes's advice. It seemed to him that something had been left out somewhere. He removed the now placid Louis from his cage and gently stroked his head. He wondered if it might mollify the superintendent to be presented with a gift of some kind. He looked at Louis. "How would you like to belong to the superintendent of schools?" he queried. Louis snapped savagely at one of his fingers.

Mr. Peepers took a bus to Melton the following afternoon. He wanted to discuss the problem further with Mr. Sidfern. He had decided not to eliminate the students' editorial, no matter how much Mr. Sidfern might hold it against him. Somehow he thought there must be a way to reach Mr. Sidfern, to persuade him. As his Grandmother had so often said: The best defense against prejudice is to be offensive about it. Mr. Peepers pondered the thought for a moment. There were times when his Grandmother's homilies got slightly mixed up in his memory.

He had to wait for Mr. Sidfern quite a long while. The superintendent sent word through his receptionist that some pressing business had detained him. Mr. Peepers was ushered into a conservatively decorated office with several leather chairs, a desk, a couch and an enormous globe of

Mr. Peepers

the world. Mr. Peepers passed the time by examining the beautifully painted globe. The world is a very large place, he thought. It occurred to him that perhaps many people were facing the same sort of problem he was in many different countries. Far worse ones, too. The thought comforted him somehow. He spun the globe gently and smiled.

At that moment he heard Mr. Sidfern's voice. "Sorry I kept you waiting, Peepers," it said.

"That's quite all right, sir."

Mr. Sidfern seated himself behind his desk and beckoned Mr. Peepers to sit down before him. "Now then, what's on your mind?"

"Well, sir," Mr. Peepers said, controlling his anxiety as much as possible, "it's about that article in the school paper. The one about sitting on the lawn."

"Oh, yes," Mr. Sidfern said. "The one you deleted."

Mr. Peepers cleared his throat. The time for valor was upon him. "That's why I'm here, Mr. Sidfern," he said. "We didn't delete it."

Mr. Sidfern nodded proudly. "Good!" he said. "I'm . . ." Suddenly the full import of Mr. Peepers' remark seemed to have struck him. Abruptly his jowls began to quiver and redden. "You didn't delete it?"

"Well, no, sir, I didn't," Mr. Peepers said. "I feel, right or wrong, that the students have a right to express themselves."

Mr. Sidfern's expression hardened. Mr. Peepers had visions of his teaching career winging into the distance like last month's *Thecla titus*.

"Peepers," Mr. Sidfern said, "I won't have students criticizing my administration. That rule was made for a specific purpose."

Freedom of the Press

"I'm sure it was," Mr. Peepers said. He tried desperately to think of some eloquent way to present his case for the students. For a moment nothing occurred to him. Then he remembered his conversation with Wes. "Er . . . Mr. Sidfern, do you know Thomas Jefferson?"

Mr. Sidfern frowned. "Only by reputation."

Mr. Peepers decided to bull his tactic through. "Well," he said quietly, "Thomas Jefferson said something like this: 'No Government ought to be——' "

"I know what he said, Peepers," Mr. Sidfern interrupted, with some choler. Then he softened slightly. "A great man, Peepers. I'm a great admirer of Jefferson, but——"

"He said a lot of things about freedom of the press," Mr. Peepers interjected.

"I know, I know!" Mr. Sidfern said. "I feel the same way. But, Peepers, this is nothing but the scribblings of children——"

Mr. Peepers interrupted, with a new sense of confidence. "Mr. Sidfern," he said carefully, "you will excuse me, but, when you were their age did you consider your own critical writing 'just the scribblings of children'?"

Mr. Sidfern seemed to get the idea. "Well, no," he said, somewhat uncomfortably. "Quite the contrary. But there was a difference, Peepers. The school paper I helped put out presented the facts fairly—*all* the facts, not just one side! In this case, the editorial makes no mention of the fact that it costs the school department three times as much to maintain the lawns if we allow the students to go on the grass. I simply do not have that much money in the maintenance budget."

Mr. Peepers smiled at the superintendent. "The students don't know that, Mr. Sidfern."

Mr. Peepers

Mr. Sidfern had not quite heard him. "We simply cannot afford . . ." he continued vehemently. And then, "What?"

"The students don't know about that," Mr. Peepers said. "About not enough money."

Mr. Sidfern scraped thoughtfully at his jowls with his fingernails. "No," he said quietly, "I suppose they don't, at that."

Mr. Peepers decided to pursue his advantage. "If Tommy Sparks had understood your point of view, perhaps he wouldn't have written the editorial."

Mr. Sidfern thought the problem over for a moment. "Hmmmmm," he said.

"Or," Mr. Peepers added, "he would perhaps have written the editorial explaining to the students *why* they aren't allowed to sit on the lawns."

Mr. Sidfern looked at Mr. Peepers and nodded. "Well, Peepers," he said, "I confess I never looked at it that way."

Mr. Peepers continued earnestly. "Perhaps what the students need, sir, is a closer relationship with the administration."

Mr. Sidfern looked a little forlorn. "True!" he said. "But I can't spend all my time just running around to the schools."

"I realize that, sir," Mr. Peepers said, "so I have a small suggestion to make. Now, suppose once a week . . ."

The following afternoon a "Do Not Disturb" sign was hung on the outside of Mr. Sidfern's office for one hour. Inside, Mr. Peepers and Mr. Sidfern were conferring with Tommy Sparks, Homer Jansen and Arabella Simpkins. Tommy Sparks was taking notes in a small looseleaf notebook.

"Sir," he said respectfully to Mr. Sidfern, "I've got all

Freedom of the Press

the information I need now on the lawn ruling. I'll be glad to change my editorial, if the editor approves."

Homer Jansen nodded. "With you all the way, scoop."

"Now," Tommy added, "if it's all right, we'd like to ask about the monitor system, too."

"Yes," Arabella Simpkins said earnestly. "Why should all the monitors be Seniors? A lot of the Juniors are quite concerned about this."

Mr. Sidfern folded his hands together and leaned forward. "The reason is this: The Seniors are more mature, know the school better, and it gives the Juniors something to look forward to. That way, being a monitor becomes a privilege rather than a task."

Tommy Sparks looked up from the notes he was taking. "Is this for the record, sir?"

Mr. Sidfern nodded. "You may quote me," he said. "Well, any more questions from the press?"

The students shook their heads.

"In that case," he said, getting up from his desk, "suppose we adjourn until our press conference next week at the same time?"

The students stood up and smiled. "Thank you very much, sir," Homer Jansen said. His fellow pupils nodded approvingly.

As Mr. Peepers was making his way out of the office along with the students, Mr. Sidfern beckoned him aside. "Peepers," he said quietly, putting a hand on Mr. Peepers' shoulder, "I feel you handled this problem very adroitly. Very adroitly indeed. I thought I'd like to let you know."

Mr. Peepers could hardly conceal his pleasure. "Thank you, sir. I couldn't have done it without your wonderful co-operation."

Mr. Peepers

"Not at all," Mr. Sidfern said. He looked at Mr. Peepers strangely for a moment. There was a peculiar glint in his eye. "Peepers," he continued, "there's something I'd like to talk to you about sometime in the future. Perhaps at graduation. Would you be at all interested in changing your job for a good deal more money?"

Mr. Peepers swallowed nervously. He hadn't even thought that Mr. Sidfern liked him. To hear him offering a better job struck Mr. Peepers nearly dumb. "Well, sir," he said, "I . . . er . . . wouldn't want to leave the school or Jefferson City. I . . ."

Mr. Sidfern smiled. "Well," he said, "it's a bit premature anyway. I'll see you at graduation. Keep up the good work in the meantime. You have a fine relationship with your students."

"Thank you, Mr. Sidfern," Mr. Peepers said. "Thank you very much."

Outside, as Mr. Peepers and his three pupils boarded the return bus for Jefferson City, Mr. Peepers could not help smiling to himself. Homer Jansen nudged Arabella Simpkins. "Look, Arabella," he said. "Mr. Peepers must be telling himself stories."

Mr. Peepers overheard him but didn't let on. No, Homer, he said to himself happily, not just a story. Not a fantasy or a dream. The real thing.

For almost the first time in his life, Mr. Peepers felt as though he had won a victory.

CHAPTER IX

Mr. Peepers Speaks

HE WAS DUE to win another, but he didn't know it. On the day before graduation he was merely standing all alone in the school auditorium with a hammer in his hand. He'd been elected to build a lectern. Poor old Charley Meadow, the school janitor, had stuck his hand into the wrong part of the hot-water heater. He was, as the psychologists say, accident-prone. Mr. Peepers was the only other staff member conversant with carpentry.

He had finished the lectern in half a day, out of discarded flats of plywood. After putting the finishing touches on it, he set the hammer down and stepped back to take a look. It looked fine. Mr. Peepers smiled, took hold of both

Mr. Peepers

sides of the lectern, and stared out at the empty auditorium. For several seconds he cleared his throat. Then he looked to the left. "Mr. Mayor . . ." he said graciously.

He looked to the right. "Police Chief Harrison . . ." he said.

He looked to the left again. "Fire Chief Crump . . ." he said.

He looked back to the right. "Teachers . . ."

To the left: "Friends . . ."

And to the right again: "Students of Jefferson Junior High School, Class of Nineteen Fifty-Four . . ."

Mr. Peepers lifted one fist high into the air. "You must face the world," he cried, "with confidence!" He brought the fist down hard on top of the lectern. There was a loud, cracking noise. Mr. Peepers stepped back. The lectern was riven down the middle. Mr. Peepers watched silently as it fell into two clean halves.

Wes Weskit, who had entered the auditorium immediately after Mr. Peepers' delivery of the crushing blow, put a comforting arm around his shoulders. "Tough break, ace," he said, gazing at the scraps. "How'd it happen?"

Mr. Peepers sighed. "Just a powerful speaker, I guess," he murmured.

Wes Weskit stared at him. Then they both laughed. "We'll come in early tomorrow morning and fix it," Wes said.

"Thanks, Wes," Mr. Peepers said.

Standing there staring out into the empty auditorium, Wes was abruptly overcome with nostalgia. He shook his head wistfully. "Another year," he said, "another graduation."

Mr. Peepers' heartbeat slowed down gradually. He felt a

Mr. Peepers Speaks

little wistful, too. "Yes," he said, standing beside Wes, "another graduation."

Wes smiled. "Tomorrow night's the big night."

Mr. Peepers nodded. "That's the big night all right."

"Every time another class graduates," Wes continued, sighing, "I feel much older."

Mr. Peepers' shoulders slumped slightly. "So do I. Much, much older."

For a moment neither of them said anything. Then Wes broke the silence. "Very old," he said.

Mr. Peepers nodded. "Very old," he concurred in a rather feeble voice.

Wes Weskit shook his head. "Old," he said. "Not young."

Mr. Peepers' face was twisted into an expression of aged infirmity. "Do you feel a draft?"

Wes nodded sadly, "A little. I think I'll start wearing a sweater under my suit."

"Me too," Mr. Peepers said. "More dashing than a shawl."

They stared at each other. Wes Weskit began to laugh. So did Mr. Peepers. "I think we went a little far," he said with renewed vigor. "After all, you're only twenty-nine and I'm only twenty-seven."

Wes did some addition on his fingers. "That makes us fifty-six."

Mr. Peepers chuckled. "A very old fifty-six."

Wes folded his arms, remembering the past. "Can you remember when you graduated from junior high school, sport?"

Mr. Peepers smiled reminiscently. "Sure. Let's see—it's over fourteen years ago, but I'll never forget it. My mother bought me a brand-new brown suit."

Harvey Weskit stared at the brown suit that Mr. Peepers

was wearing. Mr. Peepers coughed. "Mom bought it big."

Wes smiled proudly. "I was the valedictorian of my junior high school graduating class."

"Really?"

"Uh-huh," Wes said. "What were you?"

"I was the one who moved when they took the graduation picture."

Wes made a sympathetic face. "Oh, that's a shame."

"Not really," Mr. Peepers said. "Nowadays, when I want to show that picture to someone, it's very easy to pick out the blur among all those smiling faces."

Wes nodded for several seconds. He couldn't quite see the advantage, but the point was hardly worth disputing. "You should've seen my graduation picture. Horrible. I was looking at it just the other night. Know something?"

"What?"

Wes smiled broadly. "I look different now."

Mr. Peepers was again overcome by a wave of sadness. "You're older," he said.

"In those days," Wes continued, "I had tons of dark brown hair that must've been piled four inches on top of my head. Disgusting! I looked as if I were wearing a hair turban! What'd you look like those days, Rob?"

Mr. Peepers shrugged. "I dunno."

Wes was astonished. "You don't know?"

"I moved."

"Oh, yeah," Wes said, "the blur. Incidentally, who'd you get for a guest speaker at graduation?"

Mr. Peepers cleared his throat. "Well, Mrs. Gurney and I decided on Caleb Hacker. He's chairman of the school board, you know."

Wes nodded seriously. "Good man."

Mr. Peepers Speaks

"Oh, yes," Mr. Peepers said. "A very powerful speaker. I remember his speech two years ago. It was just before I was recalled into the Army, remember? He spoke on 'Youth's Bright Horizon in Nineteen Fifty-Two.' "

Wes nodded gravely for several seconds. "Mmm-hm," he said, "What's he going to talk on this year?"

"Well," Mr. Peepers said, "he's decided to take it from a slightly different angle. He'll speak on 'Youth's Bright Horizon in Nineteen Fifty-Four.' "

The following morning, after Wes had helped him to repair the lectern, Mr. Peepers met with his students in the science room to conduct a farewell class. On the blackboard the children had written: HAVE A HAPPY VACATION, MR. PEEPERS. Mr. Peepers smiled as he entered the room. He picked up a piece of chalk and wrote beneath the students' sentiment: THANK YOU, CLASS. THE SAME TO YOU. The students applauded.

Mr. Peepers sat down behind his desk. He put away the last of his papers. Then he leaned forward and smiled at his pupils. "Well, class," he said, "vacationtime is just ahead. It might be fun, I think, if some of us tell the others what we plan to do with our summer vacations. Who would like to start?"

Elwood Hamper's assertive hand waved instantly in the air. Mr. Peepers smiled. For the first time, Elwood's hand seemed something other than a beacon of disaster.

"Very good, Elwood," Mr. Peepers said. "Will you come to the front of the room, please?"

Elwood took a proud position beside Mr. Peepers' desk and flashed his idiot's grin. Mr. Peepers grinned back. The two of them grinned at each other for several seconds. El-

Mr. Peepers

wood did not seem disposed to get on with his remarks. Mr. Peepers stopped grinning. Elwood had trapped him again. "Er . . . Elwood," he said, "go ahead."

Elwood turned his glowing face to the rest of the class. "This summer," he said loudly, "my gang and me are gonna build a tree house. We call ourselves the Tarzans. The members are: Walter Murdock, Leonard Gorf, Johnny Hanson, George Brown, Sidney Dorfman, Bruce Holbrook, Rusty Keeley, Red Levey, Frank Martinelli——"

Mr. Peepers tried to interrupt. "Er . . . Elwood."

Elwood, however, rolled merrily on. "Homer Patton, Carl Dagny, Roger Holbrook, the Susskind twins, Muggs MacNamara——"

"Elwood!" Mr. Peepers said with a little more volume.

Elwood halted abruptly. "Sir?"

"Well," Mr. Peepers said, "are there any boys in the class who are *not* in the Tarzan Club?"

Elwood grinned. "There's George Tarzan. His mother won't let him climb trees."

The students laughed. Mr. Peepers cleared his throat. Elwood saved him the necessity of making a comment by making one himself. It was, of course: "Yea, bo!" And further: "Would you like to hear our club yell, Mr. Peepers?"

Mr. Peepers would have preferred a moment to think about it, but Elwood gave the signal. Every boy but George Tarzan yodeled loudly for several seconds. When the yell was over Mr. Peepers found himself trembling slightly. "Splendid," he said softly. "You may take your seat, Elwood."

Emily Polson's hand flew up. "May I say something to the class, Mr. Peepers?"

Mr. Peepers Speaks

"Certainly, Emily," Mr. Peepers said. "Come right up here."

Emily made a determined way to the front of the classroom. She had a typewritten piece of paper in her hand. Mr. Peepers was a little surprised. Knowing Emily to be a retiring girl, he wondered what she had in mind. Emily straightened her dress daintily, adjusted her eyeglasses and held the piece of paper in front of her with a firm, two-handed grip.

"This," she said, "is a poem called 'The Banjo Player Next Door.'" She proceeded to read it.

> "There is a man on our block
> Who does the banjo play . . .
> Ta-ra, plunk, plunk,
> Ta-ra, plunk, plunk,
> You hear him every day.
> Now, when he plays ta-ra, plunk, plunk,
> Plunk, plunk, plunk, plunk, ta-roo,
> It makes my mother nervous . . .
> It'll make you nervous, too."

Emily finished with a contented sigh and handed the poem to Mr. Peepers. Mr. Peepers found it difficult to keep his fingers from quivering. The poem had made him a little nervous. "Emily," he said quietly, "the poem succeeds admirably, but I don't quite understand what it has to do with your vacation."

"Oh, nothing," Emily said. "It's just that I wrote this for Mrs. Gurney's poetry class, and she never let me read it."

"Why not?" Mr. Peepers asked.

Emily shrugged. "She said it made her too nervous."

Mr. Peepers

Mr. Peepers nodded. "I see. Well, it was very nice, Emily. You may take your seat." Mr. Peepers scanned the rest of the classroom. "Anyone else?" he asked, expecting the worst.

He was interrupted by Mrs. Gurney, who made a struggling way through the door. She was laden down with a large stack of yearbooks. Mr. Peepers hurried to her assistance. Between them they managed to get the pile of books to Mr. Peepers' desk. Mrs. Gurney breathed a sigh and straightened her hair. Then her expression turned bewildered as she looked at Mr. Peepers.

"Oh, Mr. Peepers!" she said. "Did you want to see me about something?"

Mr. Peepers was a little embarrassed. He hated to make Mrs. Gurney feel foolish. "Well, I . . . uh . . . this is *my* class."

Mrs. Gurney looked startled. She stared at the students. "Oh, my!" she cried. "So it is! Well, dear me . . ." She began to giggle. "Silly girl," she added cheerfully.

Mr. Peepers touched the stack of books. "So the yearbooks came in, eh?" He leaned over and lifted his glasses to get a better look. "My! Jefferson Junior High Trumpeteer!"

Mrs. Gurney clasped and unclasped her hands. She was as excited as a bride. "Aren't they lovely?"

Mr. Peepers nodded vigorously. "You and the journalism class did a wonderful job, Mrs. Gurney."

"Aren't you a dear boy," Mrs. Gurney said, simpering happily. "Bless you. We had quite a few difficulties putting it out this year. The printers wanted so much money. We only had so much. But still, they insisted on so much. Finally, we told them we could only afford so much. We got together and settled for so much."

"Er . . ." Mr. Peepers said, "how much?"

Mr. Peepers Speaks

Mrs. Gurney smiled beatifically at him. "The bill hasn't come in yet."

The school bell rang loudly, proclaiming the end of a purely token day. The students were to return home early and prepare for the graduation ceremonies.

"All right, class," Mr. Peepers said, grinning, "we're dismissed. You may pick up your yearbooks on the way out."

Elwood Hamper was the first in line. "Will you sign my yearbook, Mr. Peepers?" he said fiendishly.

Mr. Peepers tried to avoid the glare given off by Elwood's enthusiasm. "I'd love to, Elwood." He scribbled hurriedly on the flyleaf. "This is . . . er . . . a sort of humorous thing, Elwood," he said with some embarrassment. "I'm sure you'll get a kick out of it." He bravely determined to read it aloud. " 'Yours till the kitchen sinks—R. J. Peepers.' " He laughed softly, glancing at Elwood.

Elwood, true to his code, had no reaction. "Thank you, Mr. Peepers," he murmured.

When Walter Murdock appeared Mr. Peepers decided not to take any risks. He set his face into a serious, antijoke expression. "What would you suggest I say in your book, Walter?" he asked gravely.

Walter thought about it for a moment. "How about saying," he said blithely, " 'To Walter Murdock—my most brilliant student.' "

Mr. Peepers merely stared at him.

"Just say 'Good Luck,' " Walter said.

Mr. Peepers signed the book and handed it to him. When he had finished signing the rest of the yearbooks he opened his own and presented it to Mrs. Gurney. "Here's your picture, Mrs. Gurney," he said cheerfully. "Will you autograph it for me? It's standard practice, you know."

Mr. Peepers

Mrs. Gurney picked up a pen. "I'll write a little poem," she said. It took her two or three minutes. When she was through she giggled happily and returned the book to Mr. Peepers.

Mr. Peepers perused the inscription eagerly. It read: "Roses are Red, Violets are Blue, Your Friend Bernice Gurney in Room 202." Mr. Peepers looked at Mrs. Gurney. "Say," he said, with a fine show of heartiness, "that's nice! Did you just make that up?"

Mrs. Gurney leaned closer. "Some of it," she whispered.

"Very clever," Mr. Peepers said.

"I made up the . . . uh . . . 'Bernice Gurney in Room 202.'"

Mr. Peepers was delighted to see Mrs. Gurney so pleased with herself. "It's really lovely, Mrs. Gurney."

Mrs. Gurney pinched his cheek. "Eejabooo!" she cried.

Mr. Peepers tried to conceal his discomfort.

"Well," Mrs. Gurney said, "I'd better be running along. There are so many things to do before graduation. I have to call Mr. Hacker to see if his speech is ready. I have to run over the program notes. Oh, dear! I almost forgot the most important thing of all!"

"What's that?" Mr. Peepers asked.

"I have to try and locate my glasses."

Mr. Peepers pointed to the spectacles which were up-ended on Mrs. Gurney's head. "You're wearing them."

Mrs. Gurney felt the top of her head and smiled. Then she patted Mr. Peepers on the cheek. "Eejaboo encore," she said. "You're a dear boy for finding them. Well, I must go. I must. The geraniums won't water themselves."

On the way out the door she bumped into Wes Weskit. Wes stepped aside and bowed. "*Après vous*," he said grandly.

Mr. Peepers Speaks

"Oh, yes!" Mrs. Gurney caroled. "It *is* a lovely day!"

Wes stared after her for a moment. Then he plopped his yearbook onto Mr. Peepers' desk. "Well, ace," he said largely, "what do you say?"

"Hi, Wes," Mr. Peepers replied. "How about signing my yearbook, in the Faculty-at-Play section?"

"*Avec plaisir*," Wes said. He flipped Mr. Peepers' book until he came to a picture of himself with a tennis racket. "Here's a good one," he said. He began to write and chuckle at the same time. "This'll kill ya."

Mr. Peepers began to laugh, too. He always anticipated Wes's jokes with great enthusiasm. When Wes had finished writing he took the book and gazed eagerly at the inscription. Abruptly he stopped laughing and furrowed his brow.

"I don't understand it," he said with a vague sense of shame.

Wes was still chuckling. "It's a very old French joke. '*C'est vôtre à la cuisine tomber au fond!*'"

"What does it mean?" Mr. Peepers asked.

"Yours till the kitchen sinks!" Wes cried. He then proceeded to laugh until he was nearly blue in the face.

Mr. Peepers could not quite share his good spirits. "Are you sure that's a French joke, Wes?" he asked softly.

Wes spread his hands. "It's not only French, it's worldly!"

Mrs. Gurney suddenly re-entered Mr. Peepers' classroom. "Oh, dear," she was saying, "oh, dear, oh, dear, oh, dear, oh, dear!" She stopped at Mr. Peepers' desk and exhaled. "Oh!" she said.

"What's wrong, Mrs. Gurney?" Mr. Peepers asked.

"Mr. Hacker!" Mrs. Gurney said wildly. "Mr. Hacker won't be able to guest-speak at graduation. I mean . . . his grad-speaking . . . that is . . . I mean . . . Oh, dear!"

Mr. Peepers

"Oh, no," Mr. Peepers said.

"It's true," Mrs. Gurney said. "The principal of Westbury High is sick. They take precedence. I mean . . . they haven't got a president. Mr. Hacker, as chairman of the school board, has to speak there instead!"

"Gosh," Mr. Peeper said. "We'll have to get another speaker. But who?"

"Who?" Mrs. Gurney said. "Yes . . . Who, indeed?" She stared at Wes Weskit. "Who?" she demanded imperiously. "But who? What? I mean . . . Who?"

"Let's see," Wes said, thinking hard. "How about the mayor?"

Mr. Peepers shook his head. "The mayor," he said, "has a tendency to talk on subjects unrelated to the occasion. Remember his speech at the dedication of the bird-bath extension?"

"No," Wes said.

"The title of the speech," Mr. Peepers said, "was 'Texas Natural Gas—Hello!'"

"What about the fire chief?" Mrs. Gurney asked.

Wes Weskit shook his head. "Out of town."

Mrs. Gurney looked desperate. "Mrs. Fire Chief, too?"

"Uh-huh."

"Oh, yes," Mrs. Gurney said, her head trembling, "they went to the White Mountains on their vacation."

Mr. Peepers was a little puzzled. "The White Mountains? Don't they usually go to Willow Lake?"

Mrs. Gurney's eyes had a vacant look. "This is an election year," she murmured.

Mr. Peepers looked at Wes. Wes looked at Mr. Peepers. They both decided to ignore Mrs. Gurney's derangement.

"The kind of speaker we need," Mr. Peepers said

Mr. Peepers Speaks

thoughtfully, "is someone who can really give the graduating class some good sound advice."

Mrs. Gurney and Wes stared at him intently. Mr. Peepers was so absorbed in his thoughts he didn't notice them. "Someone," he continued, "who thinks ahead. A person who makes sense."

Mrs. Gurney and Wes exchanged nods. They bent even closer to Mr. Peepers. "Someone," he added, "to give them confidence, inspiration. A speaker for whom they have respect, admiration." He looked up and saw the two faces inches away from his own. The eager glint in all four eyes alarmed him considerably. "They . . . need . . . a person . . . who . . ." He decided it would be a good time to stop talking. He began moving his head slowly from side to side. "Oh, no," he said finally, "not me. . . ."

Wes smiled at him and nodded. "Yes, sport. You!"

It took Mr. Peepers a little more than an hour to write his speech. Wes then accompanied him to the auditorium for, as he put it, "a rhetoric lesson." After several false starts, Mr. Peepers put his speech down and looked at Wes pitifully. He felt very embarrassed and uncomfortable.

"I'm not a speaker, Wes," he said. "Let's get someone else."

Wes's expression became determined. "You . . . are . . . going . . . to . . . do . . . it!" he said emphatically. "I've read that speech and it's marvelous: simple, honest, unpretentious. All you have to do is learn how to deliver it in an effective way. Do you know what I mean by an effective way?"

Mr. Peepers sighed. "Yes," he said. "Complicated, dishonest and pretentious."

Mr. Peepers

"That's right!" Wes cried, "I mean—no! Now look, Robby—one of the most important things to remember in public speaking is to let the sounds come from wayyy dowwwnnn *here*!"

Wes slapped one hand firmly against his stomach and pushed hard. "Start the sounds down here," he said, pressing his hand against his diaphragm, "and then slowly . . . slowly, let them come up. . . ." Wes illustrated by moving his hand carefully higher and higher past his chest to his throat. "Up . . . up . . ." he said, getting louder with each word. "Up, and—" Wes rounded his mouth carefully and finished with a mighty roar—"OUT!" he cried.

Mr. Peepers jumped. Wes smiled modestly. "Sorry I frightened you."

"That's okay," Mr. Peepers said.

Wes pointed to the speech in Mr. Peepers' hands. "Try the introduction once."

Mr. Peepers stared wanly at the imaginary crowd in the auditorium. "Ladies and Gentlemen . . ." he whispered.

"No!" Wes said sharply, shaking his head. "No, no, no, no, no, no, no!" He stared remonstratively at poor Mr. Peepers. "Ace," he said quietly, "did that really come from down there?" He tapped gently at Mr. Peepers' stomach. "Did it? Now tell me honestly. Do you sincerely believe that came from down there? Do you?"

Mr. Peepers' face was crimson with embarrassment. "It came from someplace." Then it occurred to him that all such forensic practice was futile. "Oh, Wes," he said, feeling a little fatigued, "can't I just say it the way I'd say it?"

Wes Weskit demurred emphatically. "Sport, when you get in front of that audience, you're no longer Robinson J. Peepers, science teacher. You're an orator!" Wes had be-

Mr. Peepers Speaks

gun to shout a little. "You're powerful," he cried. "Strong, effective! Your voice must shake the walls! We want to hear your voice *ring* through the auditorium." Wes lifted one hand in the air for emphasis. "Ringgg!" he said, his voice ringing. "Now let's get with it. Lemme hear that voice ringgg!"

Mr. Peepers nodded. He cleared his throat and again faced the imaginary audience. "Ladies and Gentleman . . ." he whispered. He stopped and looked at Wes.

Wes nodded. "Now you're getting it."

Mr. Peepers smiled tentatively. "Did I ring a little that time?"

"Well," Wes replied, "the plaster didn't crack, but you're improving. Now another very important thing in public speaking—you've noticed the glass and pitcher of water they always have on speakers' stands?"

"Oh, sure," Mr. Peepers said, "I've seen them."

Wes folded his arms. His expression was very grave and intent. "Why do you suppose they're there?"

Mr. Peepers raised his eyebrows thoughtfully. "If the speaker gets thirsty?"

"Nope," Wes said.

"To wash his hands?"

Wes shook his head. "It's a public-speaking technique. A dramatic instrument in itself." Wes took Mr. Peepers' place at the lectern. "I'll demonstrate. He gripped the sides of the lectern. He pulled his mouth down into a combative, overpowering expression. "And . . . !" he began, in a deep, thick voice, "my worthy opponent asks: '*Why* should we take the Marines out of Northern Sumatra?' Why, indeed!" Wes Weskit paused, still staring grimly at his audience, and picked up an imaginary pitcher. He poured

Mr. Peepers

nonexistent water into a glass that stood on the lectern. Then, he picked up the glass, his head quivering with emotion, and sipped delicately at the mythical water. He glanced at Mr. Peepers and grinned. "They're sitting out there breathless," he whispered, "waiting for my answer. . . ."

Mr. Peepers looked out into the empty auditorium.

"Can you feel the tension?" Wes whispered.

"It gives me the shivers!" Mr. Peepers said.

Wes placed the glass carefully on the lectern. "Now," he whispered, "I hit 'em with the answer." He banged hard on top of the mended lectern. "I'll tell you why!" he shouted.

Mr. Peepers stared at him, taut with excitement. He waited a long time for the answer. Wes was still staring angrily at the audience. He seemed hypnotized by his own oratorical powers.

"Why?" Mr. Peepers asked finally.

Wes exhaled and relaxed. "Just a rhetorical question," he said. "Go ahead and try it."

Mr. Peepers resumed his place at the lectern. He cleared his throat for about twenty seconds. "Ladies and Gentlemen!" he began, with a startling show of spirit. "Parents . . . Teachers . . . Citizens . . . Laymen . . . Gentlemen of the press . . . and members of the graduating class!" He stopped for a moment and glanced at Wes Weskit.

Wes smiled and nodded eagerly. "You're doing fine!"

Mr. Peepers returned his attention to the auditorium. "On this auspicious occasion," he said loudly, "I . . ." He stopped and looked at Wes. "Water?" he whispered.

"Not yet," Wes said.

Mr. Peepers cleared his throat again. He tried to

Mr. Peepers Speaks

duplicate Wes's dominant, intense expression. It made his face feel uncomfortable, but he persevered. "On this occasion," he repeated, "I ask you—Should we take the Marines out of Northern Sumatra?" He turned to Wes again.

"Now!" Wes said.

Mr. Peepers picked up the imaginary pitcher, filled the glass and gulped greedily for several seconds.

"Hold it," Wes said.

Mr. Peepers stopped gulping. "What's wrong?"

"You're drinking too much," Wes said, taking the glass from his hand.

"How much should I drink?" Mr. Peepers asked.

Wes did some rapid calculations in his head. "Well—figure it this way," he said. "For a five-minute speech, drink about . . . oh, six ounces; ten-minute speech, nine ounces; fifteen minutes, twelve ounces."

"I'm supposed to speak about three minutes," Mr. Peepers said.

"Mmmm," Wes said. "Three minutes, three minutes . . ." He tried to estimate the solution on his fingers. "Three minutes . . ." he repeated. He had never been very adept at fractions. "Er . . . try it again."

Unbeknown to either Wes or Mr. Peepers, Mrs. Gurney came onto the stage at that moment. She stood silently behind them as Mr. Peepers cleared his throat again.

"And my worthy opponent asks," Mr. Peepers cried, "Should we take the Marines out of Northern Sumatra?"

"Never!" Mrs. Gurney shouted. "Never in a million years! Oh, never!"

Mr. Peepers and Wes Weskit turned and stared at her.

"I'm sorry," Mrs. Gurney said, feeling suddenly abashed. "I got carried away. I love the Marines so. Such dears."

Mr. Peepers

Mr. Peepers smiled at her. "Wes was just giving me a few pointers."

"Excellent idea," Mrs. Gurney said. "How is Mr. Peepers progressing, Mr. Weskit?"

Wes's expression became nearly transformed. "He . . . is . . . dynamite!" he said.

"Wonderful!" Mrs. Gurney said. "I'm so pleased. Er. . . I'd like to offer some advice, if I may. I know a little something about public speaking."

Wes suddenly stood erect. "An assist from such a gracious lady," he said passionately, "is always welcome." He leaned forward and made a low, sweeping bow. *"Noblesse oblige!"* he said.

"Ohhhh!" Mrs. Gurney cried. "You're so continental!" She cleared her throat busily and stared at Mr. Peepers. "Now then," she said, "it's very important that you prrrroooojecccttt!" She distorted her mouth with each subsequent word, enunciating with hair-raising clarity: "Shooold wee take the Marreeenss out of Northerrrnnn Soooomahtrah!" She looked at Mr. Peepers. "See what I mean? *Ee . . . nun . . . ceee . . . ate!* Rrrroouunndd firrmm tonnnesss! Open . . . theee . . . mouuttthhh . . . annnddd . . . shooowww yourrr teeetthh!"

Mr. Peepers tortured his mouth carefully to duplicate Mrs. Gurney's example.

"But don't forget," Wes cautioned, "let it come from you know where!"

Mr. Peepers held onto his diaphragm. "Ladeees and Gentlemmennn," he said. "Parrennnttts and Teachhherrrs . . ."

"Breathe!" Wes said.

"Enunciate!" Mrs. Gurney said.

"Enunciate!" Wes said.

Mr. Peepers Speaks

"Breathe!" Mrs. Gurney said.

"Try it again," Wes said.

"Ladieess and Gentlemmennn," Mr. Peepers began carefully. "Eeeenunnciate and Teachers . . . Oh, I'm all confused."

"You'll be all right," Mrs. Gurney said. "Keep practicing. Stiff upper lip. Loose lower lip . . . er . . . I must hurry and dress for the ceremonies. Good luck!"

"Bye, Mrs. Gurney," Mr. Peepers said softly as she left the auditorium. Then he looked ruefully at Wes Weskit. "I'm no speaker, Wes."

Wes put an arm around him. "You can do it, buddy."

"But gee," Mr. Peepers said, "I enunciate and I forget to breathe. I breathe and I forget to enunciate. I'll probably forget to drink the water. Maybe I'll forget the speech."

"Well," Wes said, "the most important thing is to make the audience hear you. Let 'em know you're up there. Boom your voice."

Mr. Peepers looked glum. "I might break the microphone," he said.

Wes looked horrified. "Microphone? Is there a microphone?"

Mr. Peepers nodded.

"Then forget the whole thing!" Wes said.

Mr. Peepers got a little frightened. "Everything?"

"Everything!" Wes repeated. "Except, of course, breathing, enunciation and the water."

At approximately nine o'clock that evening the graduation ceremonies began. After the diplomas had been given out by Mrs. Gurney, everyone stood up to sing the school song. As the final chorus, "Long may our banner wave . . . Chartreuse and Blue!" echoed through the auditorium,

Mr. Peepers

Mr. Peepers checked his coat pocket for the twelfth time in as many minutes. He was very anxious about having his notes in order.

"And now," Mrs. Gurney said gaily, "we are to be favored with a violin selection by Eileen Patton, grade Eight B. Her selection will be—" Mrs. Gurney stumbled slightly as she tried to read her notes—"Er . . . 'The Fly.'"

She sat down next to Mr. Peepers.

"You're next, Mr. Peepers," she whispered.

Mr. Peepers decided not to risk a reply. Instead, he nodded. He felt more than a trifle indisposed. As the final, elongated note from Eileen Patton's ill-tuned violin wafted sourly to the last row, the entire auditorium applauded furiously. Mr. Peepers wondered if they were merely happy to have it over with. Like any pain, Eileen's violin solos became sweet upon completion. Mr. Peepers couldn't help but liken his own speaking prowess to Eileen's musical ability. He hoped the audience would treat him as charitably as they had "The Fly."

"And now," Mrs. Gurney said proudly, "our speaker. A young man dear to all of us here at Jefferson Junior High. Our own Mr. Peepers."

The applause was very warm and friendly. Mr. Peepers, in confusion, stumbled slightly and blinked his eyes. Standing in front of the lectern he tried to keep his mind from dancing about in his head. He cleared his throat for several seconds, unable to think of anything but Wes's and Mrs. Gurney's advice: Enunciate. Breathe. Boom your voice. Drink the water. Mr. Peepers hoped he would remember everything.

"Ladies and Gentlemen," he began softly. "Parents . . . Teachers . . . And, most important, you graduates . . ."

Mr. Peepers Speaks

He noticed his fingers trembling. His heart was pounding furiously. He wondered if it might relax him to extemporize a few human touches into his rather stiffly written speech. The thought was worth a try.

"Well," Mr. Peepers said, "here we are—ready to graduate." He forced a smile onto his mouth. It froze painfully. His lips seemed to be adhering to his teeth. He gave up the idea of smiling.

"Ready to graduate," he repeated gravely. "Or, in the case of the parents, ready to watch your sons and daughters graduate. Or, in the case of the teachers, ready to—" Mr. Peepers cleared his throat—"Well," he said, "I think you see what I'm driving at."

He paused and leaned casually against the lectern. The lectern tipped quickly to one side. Mr. Peepers straightened himself and looked serious. He tried to remember Wes's advice about his voice.

"Now," he said loudly, "what do you think I'm going to tell you first? . . . Well, you'd be surprised!" He reached assertively for the water glass. Then he saw that there was no water pitcher on the lectern. He nearly fainted. He was holding an empty water glass, for no apparent reason. To fill the lapsing time, Mr. Peepers cleared his throat elaborately. He glanced offstage, his eyes searching desperately for Leonard Gorf. Leonard was in charge of chairs, tables and, Mr. Peepers presumed, water pitchers.

"The water pitcher," Mr. Peepers whispered. Leonard Gorf leaped to his feet. He looked very bewildered. Mr. Peepers, suddenly conscious of his obligations, returned his attention to the frightening sea of faces before him.

"Well, graduates," he cried, "I think I know how you feel today. You've cut your way through the dark jungle of

Mr. Peepers

junior high, overcoming seemingly insurmountable obstacles, which seemed insurmountable . . . to surmount. I mean . . . difficult. Er . . . and now you stand at the edge of the clearing. Out ahead, on the horizon, you see towering above you, like a menacing cliff, nothing other than . . . high school!"

The audience laughed. Mr. Peepers nearly jumped. He was terrified. He had tried to enunciate and breathe and boom his voice and everyone was laughing. He took advantage of the noise, however. He glanced again at Leonard Gorf and whispered fiercely: "The water pitcher, Leonard!"

Leonard, wild-eyed, stared at him. He didn't seem to know what Mr. Peepers was talking about.

Mr. Peepers sighed and looked back at the audience. Some of them were nudging each other and nodding. Everyone was smiling. Suddenly Mr. Peepers felt a nice, warm camaraderie welling up from them. Perhaps, he thought, it's all right that they laughed. Perhaps they like me anyway. He decided to forget about enunciating and breathing and water pitchers, too. He decided to speak as freely and simply as though he were talking to one of his classes. It wasn't the police chief or Mr. Sidfern or any of the notables he was talking to. It was the students. The same students he knew so well, who were now passing one of the milestones in their lives. Mr. Peepers at once felt calmer and happier. He glanced once more at his notes. Then he forgot them. Looking again at the audience, he returned their warm, friendly smile. It turned out to be remarkably easy.

"High school," he continued quietly. "Do you know something, class . . . I mean . . . everyone? There's nothing to be afraid of in high school. In fact, there's nothing

Mr. Peepers Speaks

to be afraid of in anything. You might say you have one really difficult job in high school: the job of choosing your life's occupation. A happy citizen is a good citizen. A person who likes his work is a happy person. It is difficult to be happy in a job for which you are not suited."

Mr. Peepers leaned both his elbows on the lectern. Miraculously, the lectern stayed in place. "Don't," he said earnestly, "make the mistake of doing what you think you *ought* to do. Do what you want to do. That's the only true test of a good job. People who do not like their work do not do good work. Therefore, to be a useful citizen, proper choice of vocation is your most important duty."

"Hear, hear!" someone shouted. Mr. Peepers couldn't tell who it was. It sounded suspiciously like Mr. Sidfern. The entire auditorium applauded warmly. Mr. Peepers suddenly remembered that his Grandmother had given him the very same advice when he was a young boy entering high school. Everyone but his Grandmother had wanted him to become a botanist. Mr. Peepers had wanted to go to Teachers' College. He had not fancied spending his life alone in a dark room staring endlessly through a microscope. He had wanted to work with people. Children, especially. And that was what he was doing. And he was happy doing it.

"That's what high school is for," he continued, "more than anything else. The discovery of your own interests and capacities. I feel that in a small way I can speak from experience. Because, although I haven't been here very long, I like my work. My work makes me very happy."

Mr. Peepers stepped back from the lectern, feeling a little abashed. He realized abruptly that he didn't have anything more to say. "I . . . I'm not much of a philosopher,"

Mr. Peepers

he added finally, "so I can't make my speech any longer. But if I can help you, or if any of the teachers can help you, in making that choice, please come back and discuss it with us. We'd be only too happy to help. Thank you."

Everyone stood up and applauded very loudly. Some of the children began stomping and yelling. Walter Murdock and Carl Dagny led a cheer: "Hooray for Mr. Peepers!" All the students joined them. Mr. Peepers blinked his eyes. He was very bewildered. He looked at Wes Weskit and Mrs. Gurney. They were smiling at him. Mr. Peepers smiled back. Leonard Gorf came running up to him with a pitcher of water.

"I'm sorry, Mr. Peepers," he said breathlessly. "I forgot about the water."

Mr. Peepers smiled at Leonard. "That's all right, Leonard. I don't think I needed it after all."

As he descended the podium, Mr. Sidfern emerged from the crowd and shook Mr. Peepers' hand vigorously. "Peepers," he said, "step over here for a minute. There's something I want to tell you."

Mr. Peepers complied, as the milling crowd broke up into small groups of three and four. He looked around for Nancy, but he couldn't see her anywhere.

"Peepers," Mr. Sidfern began heartily, "I'm convinced. That was a fine speech. I confess that I've had a few doubts about you. But when I hear a speech like that and see how much your students think of you, I must admit that you are a very exceptional young fellow."

"Thank you, Mr. Sidfern," Mr. Peepers said, gulping.

"Now," Mr. Sidfern said, "I'll tell you what I had in mind last month. Our state faculty adviser is leaving us and I must replace him by July. Since you did so well in a similar

Mr. Peepers Speaks

capacity here in Jefferson City, I wondered if you'd be interested in taking over the position. Of course, it would mean a certain amount of traveling, but since you are a single man I thought you might be available."

Mr. Peepers could hardly reply. "Well, sir," he said, "I . . . I'd have to think about it, sir."

Mr. Sidfern smiled at him. "You're under no duress, Peepers," he said. "I realize how much this school means to you. But think how important it is to all the students in this state to have someone to guide them and listen to their problems. State faculty adviser is a unique position. It requires an executive with a heart."

Mr. Peepers made a stunned way out of the auditorium. He didn't know what to make of Mr. Sidfern's offer. He decided it would be best to think about it later. He was too dizzy from the day's events to give himself advice.

Outside in front of the school Nancy Remington was waiting for him. She took his hand warmly. "It was a wonderful speech, Robinson," she said.

Mr. Peepers smiled at her. "Thank you, Nancy," he said. As they walked slowly down the street together into the moonlight, Mr. Peepers thought: I don't want to be an executive or conduct conferences. It's not my place. My place is in a classroom, talking directly to the students about rocks and insects and the way chemicals work. I don't want to sit behind a desk and tell other teachers how to teach. I just want to . . . I just want to . . .

He looked at Nancy. I just want to marry Nancy, he thought.

"What are you thinking about, Robinson?" Nancy asked.

Mr. Peepers swallowed. "Oh, nothing."

"Are you sure?"

Mr. Peepers

Mr. Peepers nodded. "Uh . . . let's sit down . . . for a moment," he said. They were in front of an elm tree. Beneath it there was a plaque, and in front of the plaque, a bench. The plaque commemorated the planting of the tree, which had taken place in 1821. It was the oldest tree in Jefferson City.

Mr. Peepers stared at Nancy. She would probably say no, he thought. Why should she want to marry me? I'm nobody . . . a cipher . . . a man who's just been asked to be faculty adviser for the entire state. Mr. Peepers felt something turn over inside him. A man, he thought, who just made a speech, and everyone jumped up and down . . . and cheered.

He inflated his chest and took Nancy's hands. Somehow he no longer felt inadequate. If he could make a speech to such an assemblage without fainting, he could do anything. "Nancy," he said carefully, "will you . . . marry me?"

Nancy Remington looked at him for a moment. Then something that was only part smile appeared on her lips. "Oh, Robinson," she said. "I've been waiting an awfully long time."

CHAPTER X

Mr. Peepers Takes a Vow

MR. PEEPERS heard a ringing sound. He shifted his position and stuck one finger in his ear. He wanted to hear Nancy's answer. The ringing persisted. Mr. Peepers rolled over onto his stomach and buried his face in the pillow. Nancy's mouth was forming a word, but he couldn't hear it because of the ringing. Then suddenly he heard her say something.

His eyes opened quickly. "She said yes!" he cried, bumping his head against the bedpost. He realized that his alarm clock was ringing. It read 7:30 A.M. Mr. Peepers rolled onto his back and let it ring. I am going to marry Nancy, he thought. And I am going to be an executive too, sort of. It occurred to him that his alarm clock might awaken the

Mr. Peepers

other residents. He pushed the button in and got up out of bed.

On the way to the bathroom he thought of Mr. Sidfern and his new job. Mr. Sidfern had said that Mr. Peepers owed something to the school system, something more than a mere teacher's duties. Mr. Peepers had disagreed, saying that the closest relationship he could have with his students was as a teacher, that his place was in a classroom and that to give it up for money or even honors did not seem to him worth while. Mr. Sidfern, however, had offered him the job on a pro-tem level, saying that Mr. Peepers would be relieved as soon as possible so long as he continued in an advisory capacity. Mr. Peepers couldn't refuse. Especially since the offer had given him the confidence to propose to Nancy. In fact, he felt very grateful to Mr. Sidfern. Tit for tat, he thought.

He smiled at himself in the mirror. I don't feel nervous at all, he thought. He held out his hand and observed it. My hand is as steady as stone.

He took his razor and shaving-cream dispenser from the cabinet, holding his hand out playfully to receive a squirt of lather. Suddenly his hand began to tremble. He squirted lather all over the mirror. He gave the dispenser another squeeze. It made a fizzing sound. "Empty," he murmured. He shrugged and scooped a palmful from the mirror. Perhaps I am a little nervous, he thought. Getting married and all.

After he had finished shaving he used a styptic pencil to patch up the cuts he had inflicted on himself. There were eight of them. Perfectly understandable, he thought. Excitement of the wedding and all.

He walked nervously into his bedroom. The clock read

Mr. Peepers Takes a Vow

seventeen minutes to eight. He wondered if Nancy was up yet. He assumed that she was. The wedding was to be at eleven o'clock, and Mr. Peepers and Wes were due at the Remington house at ten. Mr. Peepers gulped and picked up the phone. He kept one finger on the hook. What shall I say to her? he thought. Just hello? How are you? He decided a little practice session would help matters.

"Hello, Nancy," he whispered. "This is your husband. I mean—this is Robinson. Er . . . nice weather we're having, isn't it? Oh—it *is* raining . . . Well, I . . . I just called to say . . . uh . . . don't get nervous."

Unconsciously he released his finger from the hook. "I'm very calm," he continued, "and—always remember—I love you."

"Thank you so much," the operator said, "but what number, please?"

Mr. Peepers swallowed hurriedly. "Oh . . . uh . . . 4102, please."

"Right away, sir," the operator said.

A moment later Mr. Peepers heard Nancy's voice. "Hello?" it said sweetly.

Mr. Peepers started to speak and couldn't. He clutched at his throat with one hand.

"Hello?" Nancy was saying. "Is that you, Robinson?"

Mr. Peepers' hand began to tremble. He grabbed at the phone with his other hand. Both hands began to tremble. He set down the phone and hung up as quietly as possible. Perhaps I'm a little nervous, he thought. After all, I'm . . . getting married today.

At 10 A.M. on the dot Mr. Peepers and Wes, complete with top-hats, swallow-tail coats and striped trousers, were stand-

Mr. Peepers

ing on the front porch of the Remington house. Mr. Peepers had his finger poised in front of the doorbell. It stayed that way for some seconds.

"Do you want me to do that?" Wes asked quietly.

Mr. Peepers looked at him and nodded.

Wes cleared his throat and poised a finger. A moment later he looked at Mr. Peepers. "On second thought," he said, "it's only fitting that you do it. You're the groom, after all."

At that moment the front door opened. Mr. Remington stood before them looking a little distracted.

"What are you doing here?" he asked.

Mr. Peepers blushed. "You told me to pick up the keys to your car."

Mr. Remington nodded glumly. "So I did. Well, come in, boys. Come in. I was just going to the corner to get a cigar."

"We'll go with you," Mr. Peepers said quickly.

"No, no," Mr. Remington said. "No—I don't smoke cigars. It's just that I can't hold that doggone pipe between my teeth this morning."

He ushered them into the living room, and they all sat down.

"Well . . ." Mr. Remington said heavily. "This is it."

Wes nodded, his face ashen. "D-Day," he said.

Mr. Remington and Mr. Peepers stared at him.

"Just trying to cheer you up," Wes said.

"Thanks," Mr. Remington said. He looked at Mr. Peepers and pointed to a door. "They're all in there, you know. Every woman in this town. They threw me out just before you came."

Mr. Peepers was puzzled. "Why?"

Mr. Peepers Takes a Vow

Mr. Remington shrugged. "I started to cry," he said. Then he stared at Mr. Peepers again. "She's all I've got, you know. All I've got in this world. And once this wedding is over, she's not mine anymore—she's yours."

Mr. Peepers reddened and tried to smile.

"She'll be all *you've* got," Mr. Remington added.

Mr. Peepers felt very sorry for Mr. Remington. "I'll lend her to you now and then," he said, "for dinners."

Mr. Remington smiled gratefully at him. "I'd like that, son."

There was a pause. Mr. Remington brightened a little. "You know," he said, "I saw my little girl in her wedding dress. Not more than ten minutes ago."

Mr. Peepers smiled happily. "She looks beautiful, I'll bet."

Mr. Remington lifted his head and smiled. "Like nothing you've ever seen on this earth."

"All in white?" Wes asked.

Mr. Remington nodded. "All in white," he repeated. Then he began to cry again. "She's all I've got!" he wailed.

Mr. Peepers went to Mr. Remington and put one hand on his shoulder.

"Thank you, son," Mr. Remington said, patting his hand.

"After all," Mr. Peepers said, "you've still got Mrs. Remington."

Mr. Remington looked up at him and smiled. "You know, I never thought of that."

Mr. Peepers cleared his throat. "Uh . . . Mr. Remington," he said, "do you think *I* could see her for just a minute."

Mr. Remington looked puzzled. "Mrs. Remington?"

Mr. Peepers

"Oh, no," Mr. Peepers said. "I mean Nancy."

Mr. Remington shook his head slowly. "Bad luck," he said.

"No dice, Rob," Wes said. "I told you before."

"But why?" Mr. Peepers asked.

Mr. Remington shrugged. "It's a tradition. Nancy wanted to run over to see you an hour ago."

"She did?" Mr. Peepers said happily.

"Yup," Mr. Remington said. "Her mother caught her sneaking out of the kitchen."

Wes nodded at Mr. Peepers. "That's love, old-timer," he said.

Mr. Remington looked at his watch and sighed. "It won't be long now."

Mr. Peepers gulped. "Won't be long," he said hoarsely.

Wes Weskit stepped in front of him. "Steady, ace," he said. "Get a grip on yourself."

Mr. Peepers obeyed, clutching at his arm with one hand. Then he winced.

"What's the matter?" Wes asked.

Mr. Peepers stared at him. "It hurts," he said.

Wes nodded. "That's love, old-timer."

Mr. Peepers turned to Mr. Remington. "Would you mind if I get a drink of water?"

"Help yourself," Mr. Remington said. "You know where the kitchen is."

Mr. Peepers nodded and left. He had just reached the kitchen door when he saw Nancy in her wedding dress coming down the stairs.

"Ohhh!" he cried, covering his eyes.

"Oh, dear!" Nancy cried, running back up the staircase.

Mr. Peepers Takes a Vow

Mr. Peepers stumbled back into the living room. "What's the matter?" Wes asked.

"I don't think it will count!" Mr. Peepers said. "I crossed my fingers."

Mr. Remington, seeming puzzled, stared at him. "Did you get some water?"

Mr. Peepers shook his head. "I'm too thirsty to drink anything."

Mr. Remington shrugged and stood up. "Well," he said, stretching, "it won't be long now."

"Nope," Wes said, "it won't be long."

Mr. Peepers laughed hollowly. "Sure won't be."

There was a pause. Then Mr. Remington said: "Oh, I've got something for you," and opened a flower box on the mantel. "Your flowers," he said, presenting both with boutonnieres.

Wes Weskit grinned at him. "You know," he said, "it seems to me we're all pretty calm for a wedding party."

Mr. Remington nodded vigorously. "Doin' fine."

All three lifted the flowers to their buttonholes and began trembling. Mr. Peepers dropped his flower. Wes and Mr. Remington chuckled. They poised their flowers again and simultaneously turned pale. Two flowers fell to the floor. Mr. Peepers picked up his flower and inserted it in his buttonhole. "I think I'll get a drink of water," he said.

As he got to the kitchen door, it opened and Nancy stood there before him. They quickly turned their backs to each other. But neither of them moved.

After a suitable pause, Mr. Peepers whispered: "Is it all right to talk?"

Nancy nodded. "I think so."

Mr. Peepers

Mr. Peepers smiled at the sound of her voice. "Hi," he said.

"Hi," Nancy said.

"You look beautiful."

"Oh, dear—did you see me?"

Mr. Peepers shook his head. "Your father told me."

"I'll bet you look wonderful," Nancy said.

"I'm wearing striped pants," Mr. Peepers said. "They make my legs look tall."

Nancy laughed. "Are you nervous?"

Mr. Peepers nodded. "Uh-huh—are you?"

"Uh-huh."

Mr. Peepers looked at his wrist. He didn't have a watch on. "Er . . . won't be long now," he said.

"I know."

There was another pause. "You know," Mr. Peepers said finally, ". . . you're all your father's got."

"Oh, I don't know," Nancy said. "He's got mother."

Mr. Peepers smiled. "I never thought of that."

Nancy laughed. "I'd better go," she said. She turned quickly, with her eyes closed, and kissed her groom-to-be on the back of the neck. Mr. Peepers, too, had his eyes squeezed tight. When he opened them again he saw the last swirl of her dress going upstairs. He sighed and returned to the living room. He was in somewhat of a trance.

Wes Weskit watched him for a moment and laughed. "Hello, Robinson Peepers—wherever you are."

"I'm not thirsty," Mr. Peepers said.

It was three minutes to eleven. In the anteroom of the church, Mr. Peepers and Wes Weskit were seated on a

Mr. Peepers Takes a Vow

wooden bench. They had been sitting in silence for over five minutes.

"Feel okay, ace?" Wes said finally.

"Fine," Mr. Peepers said. "You?"

"Great."

Wes placed one hand on the stem of a potted palm. The palm began to shake violently. Mr. Peepers smiled at him. "There's nothing to be afraid of, Wes," he said, taking hold of another palm.

"That's right," Wes said.

Mr. Peepers' palm began to outshake Wes's.

"Looks like a storm's coming up," Wes said.

Mr. Peepers tried to laugh, but it froze in his throat.

"Now, look," Wes said emphatically, "let's relax now—what do you say? You're supposed to be happy. It's your wedding day."

Mr. Peepers managed a wan smile.

"It's a festive occasion," Wes continued. "Hahahahaha." He laughed woodenly. "Now—just try that."

"Hahahaha," Mr. Peepers said.

The first chord of organ music struck their ears, and Mr. Peepers nearly fainted. "Steady!" Wes said, pulling him to his feet. "The time for greatness is upon you."

Mr. Peepers pulled himself together when they reached the doorway. He smiled at Wes and shook hands with him. "Thanks for everything," he said.

Wes grinned at him. "A bagatelle," he said.

The music swelled through the chapel, and the two friends took their positions at the altar. Mr. Peepers could not resist glancing over his shoulder. His sister Agnes was leading the march, followed by Marge Weskit and Mr. Rem-

Mr. Peepers

ington and Nancy. Nancy looked so beautiful Mr. Peepers had to look away. Close by, he saw dear Mrs. Gurney weeping and next to her Mrs. Remington, whose face was hidden by a lace kerchief.

Then the Wedding March had ended, the organ was still, and Mr. Remington had delivered Nancy to his side.

"Dearly beloved," the minister began, "we are assembled here in the presence of God to join this man and this woman in holy marriage. . . ."

Mr. Peepers thought of all that had happened in so short a time. He thought of the Army and Mr. Monfrede and his first meeting with the Remingtons.

"He has instructed those who enter into this relation . . ."

He thought of Helen Fernley and the distant threat of Freddie Willis, which seemed so long ago; of Nancy's birthday party and trying to buy a car and eccentric Charley who ran the barbershop; of Mr. Sidfern and butterflies; of Rock Bellows and the cooking sherry and a lectern that split in half.

". . . in sickness, trouble, and sorrow; in honesty and industry to provide for each other . . ."

There were three things he had wanted: to do a good job at the school, to see Wes settled down, and to marry Nancy. And now he had them all.

"Robinson Peepers," he heard the minister saying, "wilt thou have this woman to be thy wedded wife . . ."

Mr. Peepers felt Nancy's presence next to him. So close, so warm and friendly. He was a lucky man. The luckiest he knew. And it was all so simple. Life itself was simple, if one thought of it that way—without fear or rancor or a mistrust of one's self.

Mr. Peepers Takes a Vow

"... according to the ordinance of God, in the holy bond of marriage?"

Mr. Peepers smiled at the minister. "I will," he said.

"Nancy Remington," the minister said, "wilt thou have this man ..."

Mr. Peepers looked at Nancy. Love was a new word to him. And he did not know what it meant. He knew that Nancy was someone he wanted to make happy. Someone he wanted with him in all times and places—to care for.

"I will," Nancy said.

"Who giveth this woman to be married to this man?"

Mr. Remington stepped forward and put Nancy's right hand in the hand of the minister. The minister put Nancy's hand in Mr. Peepers' right hand.

Nancy had told him that she'd loved him for a year. Ever since the night at her house when he had unraveled the rug. Mr. Peepers could hardly believe it.

"I, Robinson, take thee, Nancy, to be my wedded wife. ..."

So much shyness, he thought. Weeks and years are wasted because of not knowing; and never asking; and being lonely and afraid.

"And I do promise and covenant, before God and these witnesses ..."

It was as though life itself were a process of learning—about the job one did, about one's friends and loved ones, and about one's self. More that than anything. One's self. Mr. Peepers could feel a great burden lifting within him. As though, to that moment, he had never been fully alive.

"... as long as we both shall live."

He turned to Nancy as she repeated after the minister.

Mr. Peepers

Her voice was like the music birds made in the forest. A world Mr. Peepers felt so close to—it was here with him now in human form. The form was Nancy.

". . . as long as we both shall live."

They separated hands.

"This ring I give thee," the minister said, "in token and pledge of our constant faith and abiding love."

"This ring I give thee," Mr. Peepers said to Nancy, "in token and pledge of our constant faith and abiding love."

The minister's voice became musical, too. Mr. Peepers could not quite hear the words. There were only Nancy's eyes behind the veil, and the ring upon Nancy's sweet finger, and the beauty of Nancy's wedding gown, and a future that seemed forever.

"The Lord bless you and keep you; the Lord make His face to shine upon you and be gracious unto you. The Lord lift up His countenance upon you and give you peace; both now and in the life everlasting. Amen." The minister bent forward, saying softly: "You may kiss her."

Nancy lifted her veil and Mr. Peepers looked into her eyes. He kissed her delicately on the mouth.

And they were one.

ABOUT THE AUTHOR

WHEN THE *Army* interrupted *Wally Cox's* studies at the City College of New York, science lost a botanist—but gained a booster, for Mr. Cox went on to become the nation's favorite science teacher, TV's Mr. Peepers.

The transition was achieved in several steps. On his return to civilian life Mr. Cox studied handicrafts for a spell, then set up his own shop, where he designed cuff links, pins, and silver artifacts of various kinds. Meanwhile, he fell in with theatrical people, who were delighted by the monologues he delivered at parties and urged him to try them out professionally. After the third night of his first engagement, Greenwich Village lost a silversmith.

In the next three years he appeared with increasing success in a number of supper clubs, carried off critical honors in the Broadway revue *Dance Me a Song,* and enlivened some thirty-five radio and television shows. Finally, the NBC-TV network, in an inspired move, built a show around him and called it "Mr. Peepers."

Mr. Cox is married, lives in New York (he was born in Detroit, Michigan), and drives a motorcycle in the summertime.